The Last Wolf

*A thrilling Second World War saga
from a much-loved author*

In the summer of 1936, a teenage German boy, Reinhard Richter, is sailing in his father's yacht, *Sturmwind*, off Scotland. Moored in an island cove, he meets Stroma Mackay and is captivated by her. He persuades her to write to him in Hamburg, and their correspondence continues until war is declared. Reinhard joins the elite U-boat service, while Stroma serves as a plotter in the WRNS, helping fight the desperate battle against the marauding U-boats - the wolf packs. It seems impossible that they will ever meet again...

The Last Wolf

Margaret Mayhew

Severn House Large Print
London & New York

This first large print edition published 2012
in Great Britain and the USA by
SEVERN HOUSE PUBLISHERS LTD of
9-15 High Street, Sutton, Surrey, SM1 1DF.
First world regular print edition published 2011 by
Severn House Publishers Ltd., London and New York.

British Library Cataloguing in Publication Data

Mayhew, Margaret, 1936-
  The last wolf.
  1. Germans--Scotland--Fiction. 2. World War, 1939-1945--
  Fiction. 3. Germany. Kriegsmarine--Fiction. 4. World War,
  1939-1945--Naval operations--Submarine--Fiction.
  5. Submarine captains--Fiction. 6. Great Britain. Royal
  Navy. Women's Royal Naval Service--Fiction. 7. Large type
  books.
  I. Title
  823.9'14-dc23

ISBN-13: 978-0-7278-9837-1

Severn House Publishers support The Forest Stewardship Council
[FSC], the leading international forest certification organisation. All
our titles that are printed on Greenpeace-approved FSC-certified paper
carry the FSC logo.

MIX
Paper from
responsible sources
FSC FSC® C018575
www.fsc.org

Printed and bound in Great Britain by the
MPG Books Group, Bodmin, Cornwall.

For Tricia

ACKNOWLEDGEMENTS

I should like to thank Tricia Quitmann, Libby Hayward, and Rosemary and Paul Segrott for telling me all about their Islay and for kindly lending me books. Also, Sandy Mactaggart, who showed me the Green Cove where a German U-boat hid. Also, James McMaster, who always had patient answers to my questions on sailing, fishing and shooting. My husband, Philip Kaplan, gave noble help on our visit to Islay and I thank him for it.

1936

The loch water was dark and deep. It felt as cold as ice and yet as soft as silk.

When Stroma had been younger she had been afraid to swim in the loch because of the monster who lived at the bottom. He had once caught hold of her by the ankle and she had screamed her head off in terror. But she had stopped believing in him at about the same time that she had stopped believing in Father Christmas.

She sat in the stern of the dinghy while Hamish rowed to the windward end of the loch. When they had reached it, her brother shipped the oars and let the boat drift back gradually with the wind. She watched him prepare the split cane rod that Grandfather had given him, choose a fly from the box – also given by Grandfather – and attach it carefully to the hook. When he was ready, he stood athwart the boat to cast the line out into the water. He went on casting, twitching the line, pulling it in and casting again, and she went on sitting still and quiet until suddenly the line tightened and there was the swirl in the water which meant a take.

7

The fish would be diving downwards and Hamish would lift the rod to set the hook through its lip before he played it on the end of the line. This was the part that Stroma hated – the part where the fish tried to get away, where it struggled and pulled against the line till it was worn out and rolled, exhausted, on its side. She felt sorry for the fish – sorry, too, for the deer when they sank to their knees, and for the pheasants and the geese when they plummeted out of the air, and for the woodcock and the snipe, the teal and the widgeon, and for the hares and rabbits. But she was most sorry for the fish because they always fought so hard and because the fight took so long. Of course, she would never have admitted such a feeble thing to Hamish.

'Get the net, Stroma! Quick!'

She grabbed the net and lowered it over the side of the boat while Hamish towed the fish towards it.

'Now!'

She lifted the net out of the water, the fish trapped inside. It was a brown trout with a beautiful speckled back and a shining white front: a big one, at least a foot long. It lay gasping and helpless.

'Nearly two pounds, I reckon,' her brother said, pleased. 'Pass me the priest.'

She handed him the lump of wood; he held the trout in his left hand and bashed it quickly on the head between the eyes before he put it into the creel. At least Hamish never let a fish flop about suffering, as she'd seen other people do.

He caught three more big trout while the boat drifted gently back across the loch.

'You can have a go now, if you like.'

'Thanks.'

Grandfather had taught them both to fish – trout in the lochs, mackerel in the sea and salmon in the rivers and pools. Salmon fishing was still hard for her because she couldn't handle the big rod well enough; trout were easier because the rod was smaller, and mackerel easiest of all because it only needed a line with hooks on.

She chose another of Grandfather's flies – and it wasn't long before the line jerked and the water swirled, but she was too slow with the next bit and too clumsy.

Her brother shook his head despairingly. 'You let him get away, you idiot! Hopeless!'

Angus was standing on the loch shore, knobbled stick in hand. Even from a distance he looked like a giant. When they were small he had carried them both for miles across the island, one on each shoulder, striding over the moors and peat bogs, up and down the hills and across fast-flowing burns that might have swept them away. He had a thick red beard and whiskers and always wore the same clothes: ancient deerstalker, tweed jacket, waistcoat, plus-twos, woollen socks and heavy brogues. He lived with Grace, his wife, in the gamekeeper's cottage on the estate and his father and grandfather and great-grandfather had lived there before him. He had the Gaelic and a Scottish-English that was sometimes hard to understand.

Hamish rowed the dinghy in and Angus helped them haul it up on to the quartz beach. He peered at the trout in the creel.

'Guid enough to eat. Well done, laddie.'

He would have seen Stroma lose her fish, though he kindly didn't mention it. That was the nicest thing about Angus – he never said a harsh word or yelled at you if you got something wrong, and where praise was earned, he gave it. Lots of it. In a while, he'd start teaching her to shoot – same as he'd been teaching Hamish who had been allowed out last year with the guns when they had spent Christmas on the island. She was still practising with targets at the back of the barn and she'd have to get good enough to hit them properly every time. The kill must always be clean, that was the strict rule. Meanwhile, she made herself useful by beating on the shoots whenever they were at Craigmore in the pheasant season – scaring up the game with a stick and making loud bird noises. It was hard and rather miserable work, out all day in wind and rain squelching across the boggy land and watching out for the hidden peat hags that filled up with icy water. Some of the holes could be so deep that if you fell in you couldn't get out. Angus had rescued her many times – hauling her out with his huge hand so that she dangled in the air like a half-drowned puppy. One day, perhaps, she'd

10

go stalking, though the idea of killing such a big and noble beast as a stag seemed terrible to her.

Eating the fish made catching them more excusable – or so she reasoned to herself. At least they hadn't died for nothing. In fact, so long as you ate what you killed, it was all right. She and Hamish would often cook a fish on the loch shore or down on the beach by the sea. They would gut it, put a green stick through the mouth and prop it on two Y-shaped uprights, then they would light a wood fire underneath. When the fish was cooked they ate it with their fingers and it always tasted far better than any fish cooked indoors. This time, though, they were taking the trout back to the house for Ellen to cook for supper.

Angus went part of the way with them, striding out so that she had to hop and skip to keep up. He left them before they reached the house gates and went off with a wave of his stick towards the cottage where Grace would be waiting for him with a rich stew simmering over the peat fire and a large dram poured ready.

In the kitchen, Hamish presented the gutted trout to Ellen who inspected them with her sharp eyes before she passed them as good enough for the table. She was very particular. The plucking and the skinning and the gutting must be faultless and game had to be hung for just the right length of time. Anything not up to scratch was thrown to the gun dogs in the kennels. When Hamish had shot his very first rabbit Ellen had told him to get it ready for the pot: to take out the insides, hang it up in the outhouse for a day till it went stiff, then cut its head off and strip away the fur and skin in one piece. Even Hamish had been a bit squeamish that first time.

The kitchen maid, Sally, was frightened to death of Ellen, and so was Meg, the woman who came to clean the house every day. Logan, Grandfather's butler, was too old and deaf, and often too tiddly, to pay her any notice but there was a non-stop war between Ellen and Mack, the gardener, over the vegetables and fruit that he brought in from the kitchen garden. To Ellen, the vegetables were either too small or too big, the fruit under-ripe or over-ripe; to Mack, anything he grew and picked was perfect. Stroma had once come into the kitchen to find them fighting hand-to-hand, like wrestlers. Mack was trying to make Ellen take some runner beans and she was thrusting them back at him. They were too big and stringy, she'd said, and not fit for the table. Mack, who won prizes in shows for his beans, was purple in the face with fury and beans were flying all over the floor. In the end, of course, Ellen had won.

Almost all the food they ate at Craigmore came from the island. The milk came straight from the cows on the farm, carried over in a can and kept cool in the larder. They ate fish and game and venison and rabbits from the estate, fresh vegetables and fruit from the kitchen garden. The cooking was done by Ellen on a great iron range fuelled by peat dug from the

12

Craigmore moors.

Stroma's shorts were wet from the fishing so she went up to her bedroom to change them and to put on her sandals before supper. The grandparents didn't mind much what she and Hamish wore, except for going to the kirk on Sundays or if there were visitors, when they had to wear proper clothes and shoes. During the long summer holidays they were left to run wild on the island – to sail and row on the loch, to swim, to fish, to ride the half-wild ponies bareback across the moors among the gentle Highland cattle. They climbed the hills and tracked the red deer, watched the surf pounding against the western shores, the otters lolloping across the beaches, the grey seals lying on the rocks and followed the wild birds through Grandfather's old binoculars – sandpipers, geese, curlews, puffins, oystercatchers, choughs, cormorants, reed buntings, skylarks, countless gulls ... They slid down the sand dunes, collected fishy-tasting gulls' eggs, explored the rock pools at low tide – each one a limpid aquarium of scuttling crabs, flowery anemones, bootlace worms like liquorice, frondy seaweed and clinging limpets. They beachcombed for wreckage washed up from old sunken ships, hunted for the most beautiful shells and gathered driftwood to store in the barn for the winter fires.

Apart from the thousands of rabbits on the island, there were hundreds of adders – serpents, the islanders called them, which made them sound much worse than they really were.

They'd come across them basking in the sun and, once, they'd spotted the shed skin of one – left whole and perfect on the bank of a burn, the V-mark on its head, the dark zigzag pattern marking its back down to the tail. Hamish had picked it up carefully and taken it back to the house to keep on the mantelpiece in his bedroom. The weather never stayed the same for long; it changed, and changed, and then changed again, the clouds always on the move, the light and the shade coming and going, the gentle colours glowing and fading. When it rained, which was often, the rain was soft, like mist.

The island of Islay was shaped like a diamond – a precious jewel set in the southern Hebrides and studded with standing stones as old as time itself. Stroma's favourite place on earth.

In early September, when the summer holidays came to an end, they had to make the long trek back to London. The paddle steamer *Lochiel* took them over to Kennacraig on the mainland, and from there they went by bus and ferry and cart, in stages, across to Glasgow where the night train would bear them away clickety-clack, clickety-clack, down to London, and back to the house in Bayswater.

But not yet. Not yet.

She went over to the open window and looked out at the silver-grey sea. The wind carried the lovely smell of salt and seaweed to her, and the harsh mewing of the gulls. She shut her eyes, breathing in deeply.

* * *

Sturmwind had crossed the North Sea without
difficulty, the yacht helped along by the strong
south-westerlies, but sailing round the coast of
Scotland proved much trickier. After passing
south of the Orkneys and battling through the
rip tides of the Pentland Firth, they had rounded
the north-west corner of Scotland slap into a
fearsome head wind and an Atlantic swell that
had given them no sea room and done its best to
hurl them on to the shore. Once or twice Reinhard had thought *Sturmwind* was going to join
the other wrecks littering the coast.

At Skye, in the Inner Hebrides, they had re-
provisioned and sailed on to Mull and then by
the Strait of Corryvreckan between the north-
ernmost tip of Jura and Scarba. They had sailed
close to the notorious whirlpool – at flood tide
a swirling, roaring maelstrom that could suck a
ship down to its doom. According to Reinhard's
father, who knew those seas well, they were
among the most perilous in the world. Apart
from the Corryvreckan there were other whirlpools, treacherous currents, back-eddies, standing waves like solid walls, gale-force winds,
violent storms and jagged rocks.

None of this worried Reinhard – quite the
opposite. He relished the risk. His father had
taken him and his brother Bruno sailing since
they could walk and they were not afraid of
the sea, though they had plenty of respect for
it. Father had taught them that, too. A man foolish enough to disrespect the sea was likely to

15

die in it.

They sailed along the western coast of Jura, Father at the helm of *Sturmwind*, Bruno and himself a well-drilled crew following his commands. They sighted a minke whale, which swam around close to them before arching its back to dive deep. A group of dolphins escorted them for a while – show-offs somersaulting high in the air and vanishing beneath the ketch to reappear on the other side. As they passed the Rhuvaal lighthouse at the north-east point of Islay and entered the narrow sound between the two neighbouring islands, Jura and Islay, the wind moderated and the sea calmed. Colonies of seals slumbered on the rocks, wild goats leaped nimbly up the steep cliffs and deer and cattle and sheep roamed the beaches, grazing on the seaweed.

They passed a whisky distillery to starboard with a wooden pier jutting out into the sound and, to port, the misty mauve Paps of Jura sloped down to a narrow strand along the shore. There were a few stone cottages huddled round a slipway at the narrowest point of the sound where the ferry crossed between Feolin on Jura and Port Askaig on Islay.

Father had sailed here in the German navy during the Great War. He had served with the U-boat Force, commanded his own submarine and had been decorated with the Knight's Cross for his skill and bravery. Before the beginning of the war, he had told them, submarines had been thought a useless weapon against civilian shipping: they had no space to take prisoners on board and no spare crew to man a captured ship. But, once the war had started, it had been decided that it was not necessary to capture a merchant ship – merely to sink it. After that, the U-boats had prowled after enemy merchant ships and torpedoed them mercilessly. At the height of the war, one enemy ship in every four had gone to the bottom. Father himself had sunk no less than seventy-eight. England had been brought close to starvation and defeat by German U-boats until America had finally entered the fray and the convoys began to be escorted by Allied warships.

Father had talked about it all. He had told them what it had been like to go to war at sea for months on end with forty or more other men, to be sealed up in a metal tube less than a hundred metres long and six metres wide, and about the fetid air and the damp. He had told them about the all-pervading smell of diesel oil and the reek from the bilges, the stench of unwashed bodies, and the stink from the heads. He had described the green mould that had to be scraped off rotting food, the head-splitting pounding of the pistons, the non-stop rocking of the boat, sometimes pitching and corkscrewing and yawing so violently in heavy seas that men were catapulted out of their bunks. And he had talked of the lack of fresh air, exercise, privacy, comfort, of men driven mad by claustrophobia and the dread of a horrible death. But he had also talked about the comradeship, where every man shared the same hardship and fate and depended upon the rest for their lives.

He had described the thrill of the hunt for the enemy, the skill of closing in for the kill, the elation, tempered with any sailor's natural regret at the sinking of a good ship and the loss of a crew who would seldom be saved. Once, he had torpedoed a steamer carrying cavalry horses in wooden stalls on the decks. As he had watched through the periscope, the ship had gone down and the horses – beautiful, long-tailed beasts – had leaped in terror over the rails into the sea. He had turned his head away from the sight.

It had been during a patrol off Scotland, lying in wait for the British convoys approaching the Clyde, that Father had discovered the cove on the island of Islay. Urgent repairs had been needed to his boat and a safe, quiet place to carry them out. He had taken the submarine at periscope depth along the sound, hunting for such a place, and where it widened out to rejoin the sea he had spotted what had proved to be a perfect refuge – a hidden cove deep enough for the U-boat to enter submerged, even at low tide.

They had stayed in the cove until the repairs were done – spending the daylight hours concealed under water and surfacing at night. It had been a memorable time, he had said, smiling. Almost like a holiday. The cove was remote and well-hidden, their only observers sheep. After dark, the men were permitted on deck in turns and he had allowed them to go ashore in the moonlight, even to swim. During their stay they had killed and eaten one of the sheep – a rare feast of fresh meat for the crew.

The U-boat repaired and operational again, they had emerged at dawn, slipping quietly back into the sound. As they had moved down the coast, Father had noticed a grand old house up on a bluff, looking out over the water. He had admired it through the periscope – admired it so much so, in fact, that he had made a promise to himself to return one day, when the war had been won, and to buy it if possible.

But, of course, the war had been lost by Germany. Father had been forced to surrender his U-boat to the British and had spent months in a prisoner-of-war camp in Scotland before he had been released. His naval career over, he had joined the family ship-building business in Hamburg, which had managed to survive the war very well. He had married his fiancée, Katrin, and Reinhard had been born in 1919, Bruno three years later.

There had been several smaller boats while Father had been teaching them to sail. Then he had bought *Sturmwind* three years after Mother's death and they had sailed her every summer in the Baltic. This summer, however, he had decided to revisit his old wartime haunts off the Scottish isles, including the hidden cove – if he could find it again. To take a trip down Memory Lane he had said with a faint smile; and to have another look at the house.

Now, two hundred metres from the entrance, Reinhard and Bruno lowered the sails and Father used the engine to bring *Sturmwind* through the gap between the rocks and into the cove.

The water surface was like glass, the surrounding hillsides lush and green with long grass, tall ferns and trees that had soft, broadleafed trees, not the sharp, dark needles of the Scottish kind, or of Germany. After the open sound, everything was suddenly calm and quiet and peaceful. A magical sort of place, Reinhard thought: a place out of a story book.

Giant granite boulders had been used to make a jetty. They were thickly encrusted with orange and white lichen and set with rusty mooring rings. Traces of an old track led from the end of the jetty up into the woods on the hillside. Obviously, nobody had used the place for a very long time – except, perhaps, for his father.

As *Sturmwind* nosed alongside the jetty, Reinhard and Bruno jumped to fasten the bow and stern lines to the rings. When they'd finished, Father came ashore and stood, fists on hips, looking round.

'Twenty years since I was here. The woods have grown thicker but otherwise it's much the same. The house was on the next headland, if I remember correctly. We can't see it from here.'

Reinhard said, 'I could go up through the woods and take a look for you.'

'Yes, go and see, Reinhard. I should like to know if anyone is living in it. Take the binocu-

20

lars with you.'

He followed the track through the wood, making easy work of the steep incline. The trees were gnarled and bent like old women, the younger, straighter ones thrusting for living space. Oak and hazel, he thought, some apple trees too and other kinds he did not know. There were outcrops of granite poking up through the moss and ferns and wildflowers, and dozens of rabbit holes tunnelled into the hillside. Close to the hilltop, he paused and turned to look back. The cove was completely hidden from his view and so was *Sturmwind*. A wonderful hideout! He climbed on steadily and emerged from the woods on to an open stretch of rough grass and reeds and bracken where sheep were grazing.

And there was the house. It stood two hundred metres or so away, facing out to sea and partly concealed by a bank rising beyond a drystone wall. Reinhard focussed the binoculars to take a better look. The gabled roofs were slate, the stone walls whitewashed, the window shutters painted black. A massive old place with great chimney stacks and many chimney pots, and a large barn and outbuildings at the back. Not beautiful or elegant but certainly imposing. Designed to fit with the rugged Scottish landscape and built to withstand the Atlantic weather. He could see why his father had taken such a liking to it.

There was a high plateau of ground in front of the house on the seaward side and, from its edge, the land sloped down to a rocky inlet,

21

much shallower and more open than the neighbouring cove where *Sturmwind* was moored. He lowered the binoculars and walked on across the grass towards the house. As he drew nearer, he could hear voices coming from up on the plateau above him – young voices – and the loud thwack of a heavy ball being hit with some kind of bat. Cricket, perhaps, though he was not sure that the Scots played that dull and incomprehensible game. He found an iron five-barred gate in the stone wall and swung himself over and, as he started up the bank, a ball came rolling down towards him. It stopped near his feet and he picked it up; it was hard and heavy and made of wood, painted red.

The ball was followed by a child who appeared suddenly at the top of the bank and plunged down the slope. It was a boy dressed in grey shorts and a blue short-sleeved shirt. At first, the child didn't notice him, eyes down and intent on the search for the ball in the grass. After a moment, Reinhard called out in his best English.

'Is this what you are looking for?' He held out the ball.

The boy raised his head, startled. 'Gosh, yes.' He skipped over grassy tussocks to reach him. 'Thanks awfully.'

The child didn't sound Scottish – more like English – and, at closer quarters, he saw that it wasn't a boy, after all. The short hair and the clothes had had him fooled, but now that Reinhard could see the face better, he realized that it belonged to a girl – a small, thin girl of about ten years old with a pointed chin, wide mouth, dark eyebrows the shape of outstretched bird's wings and hair that stuck out in clumps round her face. Her skin was sunburned, her clothes dirty and torn, her feet bare. She looked like a gypsy child. He noticed, too, that there was blood seeping from a cut on her knee and trickling down her leg. He stepped forward and placed the ball in her hand.

He said, 'I am sorry. I should not perhaps be walking here. It is private?'

'No, it isn't,' she said. 'You can go wherever you like on the island. There's no law against trespassing.' She stared up at him; he saw that the eyes beneath the bird's wings were smoky grey. 'Where have you walked from?'

He turned to point at the woods behind him. 'From the cove down there. I am sailing with my father and brother and we have moored our boat there. I do not know the name of the place.'

'Glas Uig,' she said. 'That's the Gaelic. It means Green Cove. Hamish and I go there a lot.' She was frowning at him now. 'Actually, it's our special secret place.'

'I'm very sorry,' he said. 'We did not know that.'

'How did you find it?'

'My father sailed here many years ago. He remembered that it was there.'

'Oh.'

'Don't worry,' he said gravely. 'We won't tell

23

anybody else. It will still be your secret place. Who is Hamish, by the way?'

'My brother.' She nodded towards the plateau. 'He's up there. We're playing croquet on the lawn and I went and hit my ball over the top. I'm always doing that.'

'Croquet? I do not know this game.'

'Oh, it's good fun. Basically, you have to hit the ball through iron hoops stuck in the lawn.'

'Not so difficult, then?'

'Yes, it is, actually. It's really quite complicated. You have to keep thinking several turns ahead, sort of like chess, and the other players can knock your ball out of the way if they want. You can earn extra shots, you see, if you hit one of the other balls. Hamish always wins, but I'll beat him one day.'

'What happens when you hit your ball far away, like you did just now?'

'You can put it back three feet from the edge of the lawn and carry on. There's no penalty.'

She was very amusing, he thought. So serious about her peculiar game and its peculiar rules. And so worried about him finding her secret cove. The frown was still there, a small crease between the smoky eyes.

'What is your name?'

'Stroma.'

It was new to him. 'That is a Scottish name?'

'Yes. My full name is Stroma Rosabella Mackay but, basically, I'm only a quarter Scottish. My mother is English and the Rosabella is after my grandmother who's Canadian – that's my father's mother. She emigrated to Canada from Italy with her parents when she was a child and married my grandfather who's a Scot, so my father's half-Scottish and half-Canadian and I'm half-English, a quarter Scottish and a quarter Canadian.'

'This is very confusing.'

'Yes, it is, isn't it? What's your name?'

'Reinhard. Reinhard Max Richter.' He gave her a formal bow, as to a grown-up person. 'I am all German. And I come from Hamburg.'

She moved the ball over to her left hand and held out her right one. The frown had vanished.

'How do you do?'

He took her hand in his. It was filthy, he saw, the nails rimmed with black. So were her bare feet. He wondered if she ever took a bath.

'How do you do?'

She said, 'I thought you talked in a funny way.'

He rather prided himself on his English. They had been very well taught at his school and he was the best in his class. His father spoke it well, too. So had his mother. He said stiffly, 'I am sorry if my English is not so good.'

'Oh no, it's quite good,' she assured him. 'But you don't pronounce the words the same as we do. And I've never heard of a Christian name like yours. What did you say it was?'

'Reinhard,' he said.

She giggled. 'You sounded as though you were going to spit it out.'

He was not so amused. 'It's how we say our

25

Rs. It's normal to us.' He found the English Rs equally strange: scarcely pronounced, and in some words, not at all. It was a ridiculous language compared with the logic of German. Grammar, rules, spelling – all impossible.

'You can just say the R in the English way, if you want. It doesn't matter.' He looked up towards the big house again. 'You are living here?'

If so, he was very surprised that she should be so dirty and poorly dressed.

'Not all the time, worse luck. Basically, just in the summer. It belongs to my grandparents – my father's parents that I told you about. They have lived here for ages. My grandfather was born on Islay, in Bowmore, but he went off to Canada when he grew up and made lots of money in oil. Then he married my grandmother and came back and bought the house and all the estate.'

'What is the name of it?'

'Craigmore. It's my favourite place on earth. We come every summer for the school holidays. It's rotten when we have to go back to London – that's where we live with our parents.'

'They do not come here with you?'

'My father's too busy – he's a surgeon at a London hospital. And my mother hates it here, specially the weather. She used to come up with us but she stopped as soon as we were old enough to do the journey on our own. Sometimes we come at Christmas too but not every

26

year because the journey takes ages and we only have a month's holiday. Do you like living in Hamburg?'

'Very much. It is a very beautiful city. We have beautiful old buildings, museums, the largest harbour in Germany, a big river, lakes, canals, parks ... all kinds of good things.'

She seemed totally unimpressed. 'What's the weather like?'

'Nice in summer but it can be very cold in winter and we get many fogs from the sea. In summer we go sailing at the weekends and in the holidays.'

'Did you sail here all the way from Hamburg?'

'Not from Hamburg. We came from Schleswig where we keep our boat. Usually we sail in the Baltic Sea, but this year we came across the North Sea to sail around Scotland and to see the islands.' He could see that he had made a better impression now.

'What kind of boat?'

'A ketch. Two masts. About twelve metres long, you know.' He spaced his hands. 'Not so big and not so small. You have a boat too?'

'Just an old dinghy. Twelve feet.'

'That is how I learned to sail. In a small boat. I have sailed since I was very young. My father is a very good sailor. He has taught me and my brother.'

'Are you bird-watching?'

'Excuse me?'

'Looking at birds.' She pointed to the binocu-

27

lars hanging round his neck. 'Through those. There're hundreds of kinds here. The island's famous for its birds and people come here specially to see them. That's why I thought perhaps you had. Hamish and I sometimes borrow Grandfather's old binoculars but they're not as big as yours.'

He could hardly admit that the Zeiss binoculars had been used by his father from the bridge of his U-boat during the Great War, or that he had just been using them himself to spy on the house.

'No, I am just looking at the scenery. At anything interesting.'

'Did you see the whale's jawbone at Glas Uig?'

Whale? He was not sure he understood her. '*Walfisch*, you mean, perhaps? The big fish?'

She corrected him. 'It's not a fish. It's a mammal.'

'Yes, of course. I know that.' He swallowed his annoyance. 'No, I did not see this bone.'

'It's stuck in the rocks. My grandfather says the whale must have come into the cove by mistake and then got trapped there, poor thing.'

'Perhaps the whale was ill and came to die in peace. That is possible too.'

'It might have done. Anyway, it happened a long time ago.'

The blood had reached her bare foot and was creeping towards her toes.

'I think you have hurt yourself.' He had forgotten the English word for knee and pointed to his own. 'Here.'

'Have I?' She looked down. 'Oh yes, I did it earlier. It's nothing.'

'But you should wash it.'

'Whatever for?'

'To clean it. It might become...' He searched for another word. 'Poisoned.'

'Infected, you mean.'

'Yes, that is what I meant. Infected.'

'No, it won't. I get cuts all the time. They never go bad.'

Well, it was none of his business. He took a swipe at the cloud of insects that had been gathering round his head. 'What are these things?'

'Midges. They come up out of the grass in summer, but they're not too bad today.'

'Well, they are very...' He searched again for the right English word. 'Irritating. And they bite.' He swiped away some more.

'Yes, I know. But we're used to them and they don't bother us too much. You won't make them go away like that. Basically, it's better not to take any notice of them.'

'What does that word mean? I've never heard it before.'

'What word?'

'Basically.'

'Oh ... Well, it's like simply ... or actually ... or only ... That sort of thing.'

He was none the wiser.

There was a shout from above – a boy's voice up on the plateau. 'Come on, Stroma! What on earth are you doing down there?'

'That's Hamish. I'd better go. He's waiting.'

She turned and made off up the slope, pausing once to call back over her shoulder. 'Go wherever you want. Nobody will mind.'

She vanished over the top and he stood for a moment, staring after her. He had never met anyone like her. In Hamburg, little girls did not run wild in ragged boy's clothes without shoes. Instead, they wore pretty frocks, socks and polished shoes and ribbons in their well-brushed hair. They were clean and decorous and orderly. But perhaps not so interesting?

Presently, he walked down towards the open cove below the house and, on the way, came across a small dry-stone wall enclosure ringed by trees and shrubs and with an iron gate set in the wall. *Go wherever you want*, she'd said. *Nobody will mind.* So ... He opened the gate and found himself in a little garden.

In Germany, he lived in an apartment with his father and brother. It was a very large and pleasant apartment on the top floor of a tall building with wonderful views over the Alster lake, but there was no garden. He knew nothing about gardens but he could tell that this one had been created by somebody who did. No rough tussocks or reeds here but smoothly clipped grass, plants with leaves from palest to darkest green and beautiful flowers in bloom. The garden had been cleverly arranged to form sheltered nooks and, in one, he discovered a small waterfall running over rocks into a pool, and beside it, a wooden bench. He sat down for a moment, marvelling at the peace and stillness so close to the wildness of the Atlantic.

After a while, he made his way on down to the inlet, clambering over boulders to reach the rocks and the pebble shore. The tide was going out, brown seaweed and mud left behind, birds pecking about, gulls screaming and wheeling overhead. They had plenty of gulls in Hamburg and wild birds by the Baltic but some of these were strange to him.

He balanced on a rock and looked seawards through the binoculars. The sky was overcast, the water much more grey than blue. Scotland was all soft colours. Water colours, rather than oils. Nothing bright or gaudy. Some people, he supposed, would find that dull, but he didn't. He was used to northern skies and northern light. Hamburg, after all, where he had been born and lived all his life, was almost as far north as here. And he was well-accustomed to cold winds and rough seas. Today the wind was moderate, the temperature mild, the sea quite calm; in bad weather it would be very different. The wind would come roaring down the narrow sound between the two islands and the waves would rush into the wide and unprotected mouth of this cove and hurl themselves against the rocks in great clouds of spray and spume. But the other cove, where *Sturmwind* was tied-up, would make a safe, snug little harbour. What had the girl called it in Gaelic? Glas Uig, or something like that. It meant green cove, which was an apt description with its wooded slopes. He thought of his father bringing his U-boat stealthily down the deep channel of the sound and slipping silently into that hidden place under the very noses of the enemy. The cool nerve! The audacity! He smiled to himself.

'You were simply ages, Stroma. Why ever did you take so long?'

'I met somebody. I was talking to him.'

'Well, you might have been quicker about it. Who was it, anyway?'

'A German.'

'A German? What's a German doing here?'

'He's sailing with his father and brother and they've moored their boat in Glas Uig.'

Her brother frowned. 'Well, I wish they hadn't. We don't want anyone going there, especially not Germans. They might be spies, for all we know.'

Hamish loved reading spy stories. In the illustrations, spies were always short and dark and they spoke very bad English.

'He didn't look like one. And he found the ball for me.'

'That doesn't mean a thing. Spies always pretend to be nice. They have to fool everyone. Where's he gone?'

She shrugged. 'I don't know. I said he could walk anywhere he liked.'

Her brother strode to the edge of the lawn, wielding his croquet mallet like a weapon. 'I can see the blighter. He's standing on a rock and looking through binoculars. They're pretty

32

powerful ones, too. Zeiss, I'll bet. We'd better tell Grandfather.'

Grandfather was at his desk in the library, writing a letter. He seemed unconcerned by Hamish's news.

'We are not at war with Germany now, Hamish, and I hope we never will be again. The war finished long ago. But I tell you what we'll do. I'll send one of the men over to Glas Uig with an invitation to dinner this evening so we can take a good look at these spies of yours.'

Which meant that they would have to wash and change. Stroma would have to put on proper clothes and socks and shoes and brush her hair. The rule was that they had to look clean and tidy for visitors and it wasn't easy. Baths were only once a week. It meant un-hooking the zinc bath from the scullery wall and filling the copper kettle from the cold water tap over the sink. The bath took several kettles full heated on the kitchen range, which then had to be mixed with cold water.

And Ellen, busy stirring pots on the range, was in one of her cross moods. 'You'll have to make do with the basin upstairs. I'll no' have you gettin' in ma way. There's far too much work to be done.'

Stroma carried the heavy kettle along the corridor to her bedroom. She tipped the hot water into the dresser bowl, added cold from the jug and set to work, washing her face with soap and flannel and scrubbing her hands and nails. Her legs were not only dirty but covered in scratches, old and new, and the cut on her knee had started bleeding again. Her feet were the worst of all, dirt ingrained in the skin, and she had to put the bowl on the floor and stand in it to get them clean.

She put on her kilt and a clean jumper, stuffed her feet into socks and shoes and brushed her hair. Cutting it herself with the kitchen scissors had been a big mistake; she had cut too much off in some places and not enough in others so that it looked an awful mess. She brushed it hard and pulled a hideous face at herself in the wardrobe mirror.

The German boy had spoken English with a funny accent but he hadn't looked anything like the sinister spies in Hamish's stories. True, he had been staring through his binoculars, but he might just have been admiring the view and, anyway, there was nothing to spy on except the island ferry going to and fro between Port Askaig and Kennacraig, and the distillery boats and fishing boats passing by. Sometimes a Royal Navy ship went through the sound, but not very often. As Grandfather had pointed out, the war had finished ages ago, long before she'd been born. There was no need to spy any more.

Just the same, the Germans had known about Glas Uig, which was strange because the narrow entrance was hard to spot. It was easy to sail past without noticing it or realizing that there was a deep cove beyond. Once upon a time, years and years ago, the old jetty had been used for loading sheep and cattle on to boats to be taken across to Jura and to the mainland, but now they left from Port Askaig or Port Ellen and nobody went to Glas Uig any more. Nobody except her and Hamish.

The dinner invitation had been delivered by an estate worker and though the Richters had had difficulty in understanding his Scottish speech, the writing was clear enough.

Sir Archibald and Lady Mackay would be pleased if you would care to dine with them at Craigmore House this evening.
7.30 for 8.00 p.m.

They had no smart clothes on board, but Father insisted on them wearing the most respectable available.

'I do not wish us to be taken for pirates.'

The joke was that he could very easily have been taken for one in his U-boat days, and so could all his crew. There had been photos of Kapitänleutnant Richter returning from patrols in the war – bearded, long-haired, spotted scarf knotted round his neck, battered cap on his head. The U-boat men had always been welcomed back to their base by bands playing on the quayside, bouquets of flowers and smiling girls. They may have looked like pirates, but they were glorious heroes.

The lawn where the boy and girl had been playing their game of croquet lay on the seaward side of the house, a few feet below its level. As they walked up a gravel pathway to the front door, Reinhard could see iron hoops spaced out across the grass and a post painted with bands of colour in the centre. The girl had said that it was a complicated game but it looked simple enough to him.

The door was opened by a doddery old manservant who smelled of mothballs and whisky, and they followed him down a flagstone hallway lined with stuffed stag heads mounted on panelled walls. The manservant opened another door into a large room – a room with an elaborate plaster ceiling, fine old furniture and furnishings, rich velvet, Scottish tartan, a grand piano, silver-framed photographs, oil portraits and misty Scottish landscapes with shaggy, long-horned cattle, and a vast stone fireplace big enough to roast a sheep.

Their host rose to greet them. He was a tall, handsome gentleman with thick white hair. His wife was white-haired, too, and it was worn in an elegant coil at the back of her head. Reinhard could see that she must once have been very beautiful. This would be the Italian grandmother, Rosabella, who had emigrated as a child to Canada. He and Bruno followed Father's lead, clicked their heels together smartly and bowed.

The grandmother said to him, 'I believe you have already met my granddaughter, Stroma.'

He hadn't noticed the girl until she stepped forward and he scarcely recognized her from the little urchin he had met before. She was wearing a kilt and a dark green woollen jumper; there were white socks and shiny shoes on her feet, and her hair had been brushed. And she was clean. Clean face and hands and legs, the blood washed away, a sticking plaster stuck crookedly over the cut knee. Underneath the dirt, she was surprisingly presentable. He smiled at her. Bowed politely.

'Yes, indeed, we have met.'

She did not smile back.

'And this is my grandson, Hamish.'

The brother was taller and older than he had expected – about fourteen, the same age as Bruno. Dark-haired, like his sister. He did not smile either.

Drinks were served – Scottish whisky for the grown-ups, lemonade for the rest of them. They made stilted conversation for a while until the manservant returned to announce that dinner was ready and they moved into another room – wood-panelled, like the hall, and with a long table laid with silver cutlery and crystal glasses. There were more portraits and misty Scottish landscapes on the walls and more Scottish tartan draping the windows.

Reinhard was seated next to the grandmother. He had half-expected her to have an Italian accent but it was Canadian by the sound of it and she was quite easy to understand. Easier, in fact, than the English who swallowed their words. He answered her questions carefully, anxious to get his English correct. He was seventeen years old, he told her, and, yes, he was still at high school in Hamburg, but he would be leaving next year. When she asked what he would be doing after that, he hesitated. Father answered for him.

'We are a naval family, Lady Mackay. My late father and my grandfather were in the German Navy, and myself also, as my sons will be, in their turn. It is a matter of tradition, you understand.'

'How interesting.' The grandmother looked puzzled. 'But I didn't realize that there *was* a German Navy any more.'

'Oh yes. It was agreed at the Treaty of Versailles that we should keep a small one and, lately, we have been permitted to increase it, so long as we remain less than half the strength of the Royal Navy. We have an excellent Naval Academy of our own for training young officers, the Marineschule at Mürwik. Very strict entrance tests and very high standards.'

The grandfather leaned forward. 'Which branch of the German Navy were you in, Herr Richter?'

'The U-boat force.' His father smiled agreeably. 'But, of course, now I sail only small sailing boats.'

'You were a commander?'

'Yes, indeed.'

'There were a number of U-boats operating in this area during the war. Did you ever come our way, by any chance?'

Reinhard waited with interest for his father to

reply. He had not only come their way but hidden his submarine in their cove and stolen their sheep.

'Occasionally. The sound is deep enough in the centre for a submarine to be able to pass through.'

'Yes, we know that. However, I understand that the German Navy no longer has any submarines.'

'We have a few small coastal boats capable of submerging – so small that we call them canoes. They are of no significance.'

This was not the whole truth. Father knew all about the Ubootwaffe that was being built up in secret. The so-called canoes would soon be replaced by much larger under-sea boats; in the meantime, they made useful training vessels. U-boat crews were still considered special: an elite force, much admired and respected by everyone. Reinhard would have no hesitation in becoming one of them, assuming he passed the rigorous training.

The grandfather was speaking again. 'Your expansion into the Rhineland last March took us by surprise, you see. We are concerned, in this country, that Germany abides by the Treaty rules.'

Father said smoothly, 'We only reoccupied what was originally ours, Sir Archibald. To give us more living space, that is all. It was not so surprising.'

This was perfectly true. The Rhineland had belonged to Germany before the Allies had taken it away. The French had tried to make use of it and failed pathetically; it was only right that it should return to the Fatherland.

The girl, Stroma, was sitting on Reinhard's other side, and so far she had not uttered a word or even looked his way. Maybe it was shyness, but she had not seemed at all shy before.

He said to her, 'After I had met you, I found a very beautiful garden. A secret garden surrounded by a wall.'

'It's my grandmother's,' she answered, her eyes fixed on her plate. 'Mack made it for her.'

'Who is Mack?'

'The gardener. Grandmother wanted somewhere to sit out of the wind. She told him what to plant and where and he did it for her. And the men built the dry-stone wall. There's always a wind here.'

'Well, it's a very good place. I sat there for a little time myself. I hope that was permittable.'

'Permissible,' she said to her plate. 'You mean permissible.'

'Yes, of course. Permissible.' He flushed at his mistake. The English language tricked you all the time. Made a complete fool of you, if you weren't careful.

'Grandmother wouldn't mind you going there. Basically, you can go anywhere you like on the island. Nobody locks their houses, or anything like that.'

'The people must be very friendly.'

'Not really. If you weren't born on the island you're an incomer – that's what they call them.'

'You were born here?'

'No, I was born in London, where my parents live.'

'So you, too, are an incomer?'

'Yes. And Hamish. So's my grandmother. My father and grandfather are *ilich* though. That's Gaelic. It means they were born here.'

'I wonder what your islanders would think of real foreigners – like us?'

She muttered at her plate. 'They wouldn't trust you.'

He suspected that she didn't trust him either; nor did the brother. The grandparents were very polite and smiling on the surface but you could not tell what they were thinking underneath. The British were suspicious of Germans – his father had often said so. They wanted to keep them crushed under their heel so that they could never rise again. The Treaty at the end of the Great War had punished Germany very harshly and the Allies should not be surprised if Germans got tired of such humiliating and unfair treatment. Adolf Hitler, the Führer, had promised to undo the wrongs of the Treaty, to unite the German people and to give them space for living. He had taken back the Rhineland, which was of course theirs by right. But it was better not to speak about that. It would not be polite, as an invited guest. It was safer to speak of other things.

He said to the girl, 'I like this house very much. It has much character. Is it very old?'

'Yes. Very. There was a castle here before but

41

most of it fell down and the house was built with the old stones.'

He had looked in vain for lights. 'Is there no electricity?'

'Oh, no. Just oil lamps and candles. And there's only one tap with any running water in the house. In the scullery. It's cold water, of course. Very cold, actually. It comes straight from the burn,' she went on – rather gleefully, he thought. Perhaps she was trying to shock him? 'And the water comes out all brown because of the peat.'

'Peat? What is peat?'

'It comes from bogs on the island. You dig it up and dry it out for fuel. It doesn't smell much then, but when it burns it smells lovely. Like smoky flowers. They use it for making the whisky. Which is why it tastes so special.'

'But you only have one tap for water in such a big house? That is not very...' He struggled for the right word. 'Very convenient.'

'Oh, we don't mind. We have to tie an old sock over it to stop wriggly things getting through from the burn, but sometimes they do anyway. A serpent came out of the tap once.'

'A serpent?' *My God, what did she mean?*

'An adder. A snake.' She wriggled her hand along the table edge. 'It slithered around in the sink till Ellen, the cook, put it outside with a broom.'

'That must have been a big surprise.'

'Not really. There are lots of adders on the island but they're not really poisonous. Hamish got bitten once but it wasn't too bad.' She gave him a sideways look, probably still hoping to shock him. 'Craigmore's very old-fashioned. There aren't any bathrooms or proper lavatories, of course, and Grandfather won't have a telephone. He likes it that way. Ellen – that's our cook-housekeeper – does all the washing in the outhouse in a copper.'

'A copper?'

'It's a great big basin made of copper, with a tap on the side so you can drain it. You fill it with water and light a fire under it to heat the water up.'

He thought of the modern apartment in Hamburg – so well-appointed, so comfortably furnished, so civilized.

'Perhaps your grandmother would prefer to live somewhere else – somewhere more modern?'

'No, she loves it here. It was just the same where she was born in Canada. She's used to it.'

'So, your grandfather would never wish to sell the house?'

'Sell Craigmore?' She stared at him as though he had said something lunatic. Even insulting. 'Of course not. Why would he ever do such a thing?'

So if Father still had any hopes of buying the house, it seemed unlikely that it would be possible – at any price. Reinhard changed the subject. 'I have seen the bone of the whale you spoke of.' He had noticed it wedged in the rocks at the cove, just above the high-water mark. 'It must have been a very big whale. We have seen a minke whale near the sound from our boat but it was not so big. What kind was this one?'

She shrugged. 'I've no idea.'

'An orca, perhaps?'

Another shrug.

The grandfather was asking his father more questions. What route had they taken from Germany? What other islands had they visited? Where were they going after Islay? Father was answering the questions politely and he made it sound so simple. They had come directly across the North Sea, sailed round the northern coast of Scotland, between the Orkney Islands and the mainland, and then down through the Inner Hebrides. They had already visited Skye and Mull and now Islay and planned to explore some more islands before returning to Hamburg by the same way. They usually sailed in the Baltic but now that his sons were old enough, he had decided to widen their horizons. Give them some experience of other places and a bit of a challenge.

'Your wife's not a sailor as well?' the grandfather asked.

'She died some years ago.'

'I'm very sorry to hear that, Herr Richter.'

'Yes, it was a great loss to us.'

They progressed from the main course – a mutton stew, which reminded Reinhard of the stolen sheep – to a pudding made of cherries and sponge. It was good, though he didn't much care for the yellow sauce with the wrinkly skin that went with it.

Afterwards the grandmother suggested a game of croquet.

'Just you young ones while we sit and have coffee.'

Reinhard said, 'I regret that my brother and I do not know how to play this game.'

'Oh, that doesn't matter. Hamish and Stroma will show you.' She smiled at him. 'It's just for fun. There's no need to take it seriously.'

But he took all competitive sports seriously – athletics, tennis, swimming – and he didn't care to lose. His father had always stressed the importance of winning. Second best was not good enough, third was a humiliation, fourth a disgrace and anything else unthinkable. The girl's brother was watching him. *Hamish always wins*, she had told him.

The grandfather said, 'You can play doubles – you and your brother against Hamish and Stroma. Does that sound all right to you?'

Father would not expect him to refuse; it would be discourteous to their host. 'Yes, sir.'

'Excellent.'

Outside, there was still plenty of daylight left – a long Scottish summer evening. Even some sunlight. They went down mossy stone steps on to the lawn where the brother handed out the heavy sticks and told them the rules. There were six hoops and four balls – blue, black, red and yellow. One side would use the blue and black balls, the other the red and yellow. The point of the game, apparently, was to move your ball round the lawn by striking it with the stick (called a mallet), so that it went through all six hoops in the correct order and direction and then hit the peg stuck in the middle of the lawn. Both partners must achieve this in order to become the winners. Turns were to be taken in the sequence of the peg's four painted bands, starting with the blue. Passing through a hoop was known as 'running it' and earned an extra shot, and if you hit one of the other three balls this was called making a 'roquet' and you must then place your own ball in contact with the one you'd just hit and hit it again with your ball. This was called 'taking croquet' and could only be done once to that ball between hoops.

Hamish had spoken fast, running his words together in the way that the English did, but Reinhard had listened very closely and it all sounded quite easy. They tossed a coin for which side should start, and almost immediately he discovered that it wasn't easy at all. The brother was as good as he had feared, and Stroma, though she was wild with the mallet, was often lucky. Whenever the brother earned extra shots, which was frequently, he would use his own ball to whack one of theirs hard, sending it rolling across the lawn, far away from the hoop. Stroma did the same, if she got the chance, though she couldn't hit as hard.

'It's part of the game,' the brother told Reinhard when he protested. 'Tactics, you see. You have to plan ahead. A bit like chess.'

46

He played on grimly, convinced now that the match had been set up deliberately to humiliate them. Hamish and Stroma had both finished and won while he and Bruno were still trailing far behind.

'Bad luck!' the brother called out and they all shook hands in a very sporting English manner.

Luck had had nothing to do with it; they had never stood a chance. He swiped angrily at his ball and sent it cannoning over the lawn edge. When he went to find it, the girl came after him and helped him search in the long grass. This time it was she who found the ball and held it out. It was all he could do not to snatch it from her.

She looked up at him. 'You're jolly cross about losing, aren't you?'

'No,' he lied. 'Not at all.'

'Yes, you are. I can tell. You're scowling and looking awfully angry. Really furious, actually. You're not a very good sport, are you?'

He knew that the British set great store by good sportsmanship. If you lost you must look as happy as if you had won and be sure to congratulate your opponent as you shook hands, which he and Bruno had failed to do.

'I am sorry. I do not often lose. Winning is important to me.'

'But that's silly. It's only a game. It doesn't really matter whether you win or lose.'

'It matters to me,' he said.

When they climbed back up to the lawn, Bruno and the brother had disappeared. The

47

sun, he saw, was sinking down in a crimson blaze of glory.

'The skies here are very wonderful.' He tried to make up for his poor behaviour. 'I think they are even better than we have in Germany.'

She shrugged her shoulders. 'I wouldn't know. I've never been to Germany.'

From her cool tone he understood that she had not approved at all of his bad sportsmanship. 'Then you must come one day when you are older. It's not so far away to visit. You could come to Hamburg and stay at our home. When you are bigger. How old are you now?'

'Twelve.'

Older than he had thought; she was very small for her age. A little shrimp standing beside him. He could easily pick her up and carry her under one arm if he wanted – which would probably make her as angry as he had been about losing the game of croquet.

'I am seventeen.'

'Yes, I know. I heard you tell my grand-mother. And you're going to join the German Navy when you leave school. That's what your father said.' For some reason she didn't seem to approve of that either.

'If I am accepted into the Academy.'

'Will you be in a submarine, like your father?'

'I hope so. We call them U-boats.'

'I know. There are pictures of them in Ham-ish's war comics.'

'Comics?'

'Sort of magazines. Adventures about the war.

48

He's got stacks of them. They show German U-boats fighting with the Royal Navy and torpedoing our ships. Is that what your father did?'

'He sank some ships, yes.' Seventy-eight to be precise but, of course, he would not tell her that. It was on the tip of his tongue, though, to tell her about his father going in to Glas Uig and stealing the sheep, but he stopped himself in time.

She said, 'I think it's a sneaky sort of thing to do – hide under water to attack ships.'

He did not know the word she had used, but he guessed its meaning.

'Submarines are not always under water – they must often come to the surface. And the British Navy has submarines, too, you know.'

'They're not like U-boats.'

He couldn't see her expression because the wind was blowing her hair across her face, but he felt her deep disapproval.

She said, 'Hamish thought you were German spies.'

'Spies?' He was taken aback. 'But we are not at war now.'

'We might be again one day.'

'In Germany, we hope this could never happen.'

But he was not so sure that it was true. His country could not be kept subjugated forever. So, perhaps, there might have to be another war one day. Perhaps he might have to sink British merchant ships, like Father had done, and fight against the Royal Navy.

They went on watching the sky changing, the crimson spreading like spilled paint across the sky. He had certainly never seen such a sunset.

She said suddenly, and in a much softer tone, 'I'm very sorry about your mother dying. It must have been awful.'

'Yes. It was not nice.'

He remembered it very well: the visits to the hospital, his mother's efforts to keep on speaking and smiling as she grew paler and thinner, shrinking in her white bed. Towards the end, she had given up trying to speak and smile and lay still and silent with her eyes shut. He had been ten years old, Bruno seven.

'Who looked after you afterwards?'

'My father, and our servant, Greta, who we have had for many years. And we were going to school every day in Hamburg.'

She corrected him once more. 'We went to school – not we were going. You'd only say that if you were in the middle of going somewhere when something else happened.'

He said stiffly, 'We went to school.'

'What about during the holidays?'

'Father always takes us sailing and we always play much sport.' His English was probably wrong again but he went on quickly, before she could interrupt. 'We are always busy. But, of course, we are not so lucky to have a beautiful island like this.' He was trying to make more amends not only for being unsporting but also a suspected spy. 'When will you leave here?'

'In September. When we have to go back to

school.' She pulled a face. 'Ugh!'

'You do not like your school?'

'They're sending me to a new one next term – a boarding school miles away. I know I'll hate it.'

'Perhaps not.'

'Yes, I will.' She sounded very certain.

'Well, we leave tomorrow morning, so you must come and see our boat before we go. You and Hamish.' He gave her a winning smile – his most charming, which he knew was very charming indeed. 'Then we can show you that we are certainly not spies.'

They went indoors and, before the evening ended, the grandmother played the grand piano. He thought that the waltz was probably by Chopin and it was very pleasant to sit listening to it in the fine old room. He'd never learned any musical instrument himself, but his father had a big collection of records – the heavier-going works of Beethoven, Wagner, Bach, and so on. When the grandmother had finished and they had applauded politely, he asked the girl if she played too.

'A bit.'

'I am sure that you are very good.'

'Actually, I'm very bad.'

The grandmother said, 'Don't talk such nonsense, Stroma. Reinhard would like to hear you play, wouldn't you, Reinhard? I think the Nocturne would be very nice.'

She went unwillingly over to the piano and wriggled to the edge of the stool so that she

51

could reach the pedals. She was biting her lower lip in concentration as she started to play. So serious, so intent that he wanted to smile. She was not as good as her grandmother, of course, and her hands were too small to reach some of the chords properly, but she'd lied to him about being very bad. He listened intently, his eyes fixed on her.

Later that evening, once the visitors had gone, Stroma told her brother of Reinhard's invitation.

Surprisingly, Hamish agreed. 'I think we ought to go, so we can see if there's anything suspicious.'

'What sort of thing?'

'A radio transmitter ... secret code books ... cameras ... things like that. Keep your eyes peeled.'

'Reinhard wouldn't have asked us to go there if they were spies.'

'Yes, he would. To put us off the scent. Actually, I thought Bruno seemed quite decent – for a German. When I showed him my models, he thought they were brilliant.' Hamish's bedroom was full of model ships that he'd made. 'I asked him about their Navy and he said they don't have much of one at the moment. He's really more interested in planes and he'd sooner join their Air Force, though his father doesn't know it. They're only supposed to fly gliders at the moment, but I bet they don't stick to that. You can't trust them an inch.'

Stroma lay in bed that night, listening to the quiet splashing of the sea against the rocks, and thinking about the elder brother. He was sunburned, which made his eyes look very blue and his teeth very white, and the sun had bleached his hair blond. A spy would never look like that, whatever Hamish said. Spies were small and dark and ugly: nothing like Reinhard at all.

It was raining the next morning – misty curtains of drizzle drifting in from the sea and moving across the island. Reinhard waited on deck until he saw the brother and sister come out of the woods and clamber across the boulders on to the stone jetty. Unlike himself, they wore no waterproof clothing – only shorts and woollen jumpers – and their feet were bare. From the way they hopped aboard *Sturmwind* he could see that they were familiar with boats.

'You are very wet,' he said to the girl, who had ignored his outstretched, helping hand. 'I hope you will not take a cold.' Her hair was plastered flat to her head, raindrops running down her face and dripping off the end of her nose.

'Oh, no. We never do. We're used to it. It's *catch* a cold, not take, by the way. Just in case you wanted to know.'

He hadn't wanted to know at all. 'Well, I hope you will not catch one.'

His father, in a very good humour, took charge, conducting their visitors down the companion ladder and showing them the galley on the port side, the chart table on the starboard, the saloon which doubled as the main cabin, the forward cabin where he and Bruno slept. Everything was very clean and tidy and well polished; it always was.

Father clapped his hand on Hamish's shoulder.

'So, what do you think of our *Sturmwind*?'

'She's very nice indeed, sir.'

'Are you a good sailor?'

'I'm not too bad, sir.'

'And your sister?'

'She's pretty hopeless.'

His father laughed. 'But she will get better when she is older and stronger. If we come back to Islay one day, you must both come to sail with us.'

'Thank you, sir.'

Reinhard doubted that they would come back for years, if ever. By next summer he would have finished at high school and, with luck, he would be going to the Naval Academy as soon as he had done his National Labour Service. There would be no time for long sailing holidays; time only for study and hard work.

Back on deck, as they were leaving, he said to Stroma, 'I will write a letter to you from Hamburg, if you don't mind. Perhaps you will write also to give us your news?'

She blinked up at him through the rain. 'We don't really have any.'

'But you could still write,' he persisted. 'There is always something to say. And it would make my English more good.'

'Better. Not more good. It's good, better, best.'

Damn and blast the English language! It caught him out every time. And *besser* was so close.

'Of course, I remember this now. Good, better, best. Bad, worse, worst.'

'And I'd make it worse. I'm rotten at writing letters.'

'I do not believe this, Stroma. And you could correct my mistakes.'

He smiled down at her persuasively. He very much wanted her to like him, though there didn't seem any chance of it.

'It's Stroma. Not Shtroma,' she said.

'I am sorry. Strowmaaah.' He mocked her English pronunciation a little. 'Now, let us see if you can say my name properly. Or perhaps you have forgotten it?'

'No, I haven't.'

'So, what is it?'

'Reinhard.'

She pronounced the R in the flat English way, but at least she had remembered his name.

He persisted. 'Then you will write to me, please?'

She was looking down at the deck now, not up at him, drawing a circle on the deck with her big toe and leaving a muddy mark which would not please his father.

'Why?'

'Because I would like you to.'

He saw her cheeks flush. She was still busy drawing circles, still refusing to look up.

'Stroma? Will you?'

She shrugged. 'I suppose so – if you really want me to.'

'But I do not know your address in London, to send a letter.'

'You can write to Craigmore. They'll forward it.'

'Very well. And I will put my address in Hamburg for you to answer.'

The brother had already jumped ashore and was striding off, calling over his shoulder. 'Come on, Stroma.'

She lifted her head then and he looked down at her, wondering how he could somehow keep her a little longer.

'I must go,' she said. 'I'm sorry.'

He did what he had been longing to do and picked her up, cradling her against him. He carried her from the deck across to the jetty where he set her down gently.

Her cheeks were bright pink now but she hadn't protested or struggled. *She likes me after all*, he realized, amazed. *She has forgiven me for being unsporting and she doesn't really believe that I am a spy. She likes me ... as much as I like her. I'm sure of it.*

'So...' He took her small and dirty hand in his. '*Auf Wiedersehen*, Stroma.'

'What does that mean?'

'It means until we meet again.'

'I don't suppose we ever will, do you?'

'I hope so, very much. One day.'

When she tugged at her hand he had to let her go. He watched her running along the jetty and scrambling over the rocks. She turned to wave just once before she disappeared into the woods.

'Did you notice anything suspicious?' Hamish asked as they climbed the hillside.

'No.'

'Didn't you see that German camera on the table in the cabin? It was a jolly expensive one.'

'I expect they were taking pictures of scenery and things.'

'I say, whose side are you on, Stroma?'

'I'm not on anybody's side. I just don't think the Richters are spies. Anyway, Reinhard said he'd write to me. He wouldn't do that if he was a spy.'

'Write to you?' Hamish stared at her. 'What on earth for?'

The apartment in Hamburg had a fine view of the outer Alster. The leaves on the trees along the lake's edge were turning and some of them had already fallen to the ground. It would be the same in the woods above Glas Uig, Reinhard thought. The Green Cove would not be looking quite so green now.

Stroma and Hamish would have gone back to London and to their schools. He hoped that she liked her new school, after all.

It had been stupid of him not to ask for their

home address in London, but he would send a letter to Craigmore and the grandparents would surely forward it on. He could tell her all about their journey back, when *Sturmwind*'s rudder had broken halfway across the North Sea. They had managed to fix it up temporarily and had limped home, but it had not been at all easy. Even Father had been quite worried.

He would be sure to put his own address in Hamburg very clearly. Then, perhaps, she would write back.

1937

18 January 1937
Dear Stroma,

Thank you for your letter. I was believing that you would never answer. I am glad to hear that you and Hamish are well, also all your family.

I was sorry to hear that you do not like your new school and I hope that you will like it better this term. (You see, I have not forgotten good, better, best.) Thank you for giving me the address, so that I can write to you there.

The weather is very kald here in Hamburg and we have had much snow. At Christmas (we call it Weihnachten) when we have had two weeks holidays, we have gone to the haus of friends at Kitzbühel in the mountains where we ski. I ski since I was four years old. I like to go very fast, of course. So does Bruno. We race each other. Do you and Hamish ski also?

I am very busy with study at school. I must do examinations now in January and more in July. Some are very difficult and I have to learn many things. It is important that I succeed so that I will be accepted by the Naval Academy. What subjects do you study?

I think often of Scotland and, most of all, of Craigmore and of Glas Uig, and of you. It would be very nice if we could return there next sommer with *Sturmwind* but, unfortunately, I do not think this will be possible as I must work with our National Labour Service before I go to the Naval Academy. I must help to build new roads and I will also be working in the forests and mountains. This is necessary for all jung men in Germany.

I am sorry that this letter is not very interesting. Next time I will tell you more news. Also, I hope there are not a lot of mistakes in my English. Please correct them. Do you have a photographie of yourself to send me? I should like to have one very much.

From,
Reinhard

24th February, 1937
Dear Reinhard,

I'm sorry I've taken so long to answer your letter but we hardly have any spare time at school. I still hate it here, by the way.

We are learning Latin (ugh) and we do Mathematics, Physics, Chemistry and Biology, as well as English, French, History and Geography, Scripture, Art and Sewing, and I do the piano as an extra. I looked up Hamburg in my atlas, to see where you live. This term we play netball, hockey and lacrosse. My favourite is lacrosse.

Hamish and I have never been skiing. It sounds fun. Some winters there can be lots of snow up in the mountains in Scotland but I don't think there are any proper ski lifts like you have on the Continent. We don't have any skis, anyway.

If you really want me to tell you, there were five spelling mistakes in your letter. It's cold, not kald; house, not haus; summer, not sommer; young, not jung; and photograph, not photographie. And if you were English, you'd probably say 'I thought you'd never answer' and 'we've had a lot of snow', and 'at Christmas we went', not 'we have gone', and you'd say 'I've skied since I was four years old.' You got some other things a bit wrong, too, but I knew what you meant.

By the way, you have very nice handwriting. I wish I could write as well as that. Do they teach you at school?

I haven't got any photographs of me here, but I'll see if I can find one at home. We break up for the Easter holidays in three weeks, thank goodness. I wish we were going to Craigmore, but we will be stuck in London, worse luck.

From,
Stroma

12th March, 1937
Dear Stroma,

Thank you for your letter and for correcting my mistakes. Yes, I really do want you to tell me when I make them. And, yes, they teach us handwriting in school. We must always write very exactly.

I think you will soon be at home for the Easter holidays (we call this Ostern) and so I am sending this to your address in London. I also have a short holiday for Easter and I will finish at the High School in July, after I have done more exams.

The weather is warmer and we will be sailing *Sturmwind* again. First, we must clean her very well after the winter, and then we will go to sail out on the Baltic Sea. Bruno and I look forward to this. It will be very gud to be free from our studies.

What are you doing in London? There must be many things to see and I should like very much to visit there one day. We have interesting things in Hamburg, too. We have gud museums and historich buildings. There are some very old steamships in the harbour and also old barges on the canals. We have many canals and, of course, the River Elbe which is very important for the city. We can take a boot to England from the port. Perhaps one day I will do that.

Please do not forget to send a photograph of you (I spell it correctly this time).

Bruno and I give our best wishes to you and to Hamish.

From,

Reinhard

PS. When is your birthday?

17th April, 1937

Dear Reinhard,

Thank you for your letter. There isn't really any news to tell you at the moment. Hamish has gone away to stay with a friend from his school and I haven't done much except go to the zoo once in Regent's Park and read and practise the piano. I have to practise a lot because my piano teacher at school gave me a new piece to learn by heart in the holidays and she'll be furious if I haven't done it properly.

I went shopping with my mother, which was boring, and I've been to see friends in London, but we didn't do anything very interesting except go to the cinema and walk in the park.

Our cat, Delilah, had six kittens at the back of a kitchen cupboard. They're all black, like her, except one which is a ginger tom. We are going to keep him and find homes for the others. I wish we could keep them all because they're so sweet.

I go back to school for the summer term next week. We have to wear hideous brown and white frocks and a straw boater. We play tennis and rounders, and swim in the school pool (which is even colder than the lochs on Islay). Some of the girls play cricket. We have exams in July, like you.

You only had three spelling mistakes in your last letter. It's not 'gud', it's 'good'. Historic hasn't got an 'h' on the end, and it's 'boat', not

'boot'. A boot is what you wear on your foot.
From,
Stroma.
PS. I'm afraid I couldn't find a photograph to send you. My birthday is on 15th May and I'll be thirteen. When is yours?

3rd June, 1937
Dear Stroma,

I hope you received the card that I sent you for your birthday and that you had a very happy day. Have you grown very much, now that you are thirteen?

Thank you for correcting my bad spelling. Please always do this or I shall never learn.

I hope you are liking the summer term at your school. We also play tennis and it is a game that I enjoy very much. Perhaps one day we can all have a tennis game instead of croquet. Also, we schwim and have races and diving competitions from a high platform. Bruno and I have both won several times in these competitions but I remember that when we played the croquet game you told me that winning doesn't matter, so perhaps I should not say this?

What name you have called the ginger kitten?

Soon I will have more examinations so I must work very hard. When they are finished, I will write to you again and I will send the letter to Craigmore so that you will receive it when you and Hamish arrive.

After I leave the High School, I will do my work for the National Labour Service that I already told you about, and, when that is finished, I hope I will go to the Naval Academy at Mürwik if I have passed all the examinations.

Please write to me if you have any time.

I forgot to say that my birthday was on 16th February. I was eighteen.

From,
Reinhard

2nd July, 1937
Dear Reinhard,

Thank you for your letter and for the birthday card you sent me. I hope you had a happy birthday in February.

We are revising for our exams and so I haven't much time to write now. Good luck with yours.

By the way, it's swim, not schwim. And I don't mind you saying about winning competitions, so long as you don't go on about it, or get cross if you lose.

We've called the kitten Kipper.

From,
Stroma
PS. I've grown about three inches.

26th July, 1937

Dear Stroma,

I have now finished all my examinations and must wait for the results.

Soon I will have to start my National Labour Service and I am not looking forward to this very much.

The weather is very hot in Hamburg now but last week we went sailing in *Sturmwind* on the Baltic Sea and it was very pleasant to be away from the city. I am sorry that we will not be able to sail to Scotland again this year. Perhaps it will be possible next year. I hope this very much.

This week we went to a concert in Hamburg and listened to Beethoven's Fifth Symphony, as well as some other music. It was a very good evening, but I liked even better listening to you and your grandmother play the Chopin piano pieces at Craigmore. I always remember this. Did you finish learning your new holiday piece for your teacher? Was it also composed by Chopin?

Kipper is a very good name for a ginger cat. In German, we say *Raucherhering* for smoked herring, which would not be nearly so good.

Bruno sends you and Hamish his best wishes. We hope you have a happy holiday at Craigmore. Please write and tell me about it.

From,

Reinhard

10th August, 1937

Dear Reinhard,

As you can see, I am writing from Craigmore. The weather has been lovely today and Hamish and I went swimming in the sea. The water was very cold and rough and there was a terrific undertow so we had to be a bit careful. It can be quite dangerous sometimes.

There was a storm a few days ago and we collected a lot of driftwood from the beach and carried it up to the barn to dry out for the winter. We use it with the peat for the fires. Some of the wood came from old shipwrecks. There are lots of wrecks off the islands, as I expect you know from when you sailed here.

Yesterday, we took the dinghy out on the loch and fished for trout. Hamish caught six and I caught one and we ate them for supper. Hamish did all the gutting which was very decent of him as I hate doing it.

Tomorrow we are going out mackerel fishing on the sound with our grandfather. We use a line with hooks and trawl it along behind the boat to catch them, so it's easy, really. Hamish and I have been to Glas Uig several times, of course. Last time we fished off the jetty and caught some crabs. The whale's jaw-bone is still there, by the way. I should think it will be there for thousands of years.

Angus, Grandfather's gamekeeper, has been teaching me to shoot and I've been practicing with targets behind the barn. I'm to start with rabbits when I'm good enough – there are millions of them on the island because there are no foxes. Hamish shoots them quite often and then he has to gut and skin them ready for cooking, which is a horrible job.

I hope your exam results were all right.

I couldn't find any spelling mistakes at all in your last letter. You're getting awfully good.

Yes, I learned the piano piece all right. It's a Sonatina by Mozart and quite easy, really. Easier than the Chopin Nocturne.

We have a class called Musical Appreciation at school, we sit and listen to records. They played Beethoven's Fifth Symphony last term and I thought it was wonderful but it must be miles better to hear a live orchestra playing it.

From,
Stroma

24th August, 1937
Dear Stroma,

Thank you for your letter from Craigmore and all your news.

Bruno and I have also learned to shoot at targets, like you. They have teached us at school and we shoot with rifles.

I succeeded with my exams and so I am to go to the Naval Academy. My father is very pleased.

You have made a spelling mistake in your last letter! It should be practising not practicing. I know this only because we were told by our English teacher. He explained the difference to us. I think that English is a very difficult language to spell.

I do not yet know where I will be doing my National Labour Service, but if you will write to my home, the letter will be sent to me. If you find a photo, please send it to me.

From,
Reinhard

6th September, 1937
Dear Reinhard,

I'm glad you passed your exams and got into the Naval Academy. Congratulations.

By the way, it's 'taught', not 'teached'. And I don't mind your saying about 'practising'. I always get it wrong. English can be awfully tricky. Can you say these words right? Cough, bough, rough, plough, tough, dough? They all end in the same letters but every one is pronounced differently.

I shot a rabbit by the woods at Craigmore yesterday and I don't think I ever want to shoot anything again. It was running along happily and when I hit it, it fell down dead. I felt awful when I went to pick it up. It had such lovely soft brown fur and bright eyes. I've hung it up in the outhouse to go stiff and then I'll have to skin and gut it for Ellen our cook, which I know will make me feel even worse.

I hope your Labour Service goes all right. It sounds ghastly.

From,
Stroma

20th October, 1937

Dear Stroma,

Your letter took a very long time to come to me because I am far away from Hamburg. I am working to build a road between Rostock and Berlin. It's not exactly a new one. We are making the old one much wider so that there is room for more cars and lorries. It will be a hundred and fifty kilometres long when it is finished. We work for many hours in one day and at night we sleep in wooden huts or tents. It's not so bad but I have many aches with muskels and many cuts and bruises. They give us good food after we have finished work and we are always very hungry.

You should not be sorry about the rabbit. You killed it very quickly so that it will not have suffered at all. I think there must be too many of them on the island because you have no foxes, and they must eat a lot of grass and crops. The farmers will thank you.

I showed your list of words to someone here who has been in school in England and he told me how to pronounce them and their meaning. What a language you have! I should teach you German instead. It's much more easy.

I do not think I shall be able to return to Hamburg for Christmas but must continue to work with the Labour Service. But my father has written that he believes I will be permitted to start at the Naval Academy early which would be very good.

I am sending this to your school because, by now, you will be back there. Perhaps you are going to Craigmore for this Christmas? I remember you said that sometimes you go there.

From,

Reinhard

PS. Where is the photograph?

23rd November, 1937

Dear Reinhard,

Thank you for your letter. I hope you finish your road work soon.

You spelled muscles wrong, by the way, and it's 'easier' not 'more easy'. Easy, easier, easiest. English must seem difficult to a foreigner. But at least we don't have cases or genders and there's only one way to say 'you' since we stopped saying thee and thou. Not like it is in Latin or French. And I bet German is hard. I know you have tremendously long words.

We're not going to Craigmore for Christmas this year. My father is too busy at the hospital. I do wish we were, because Christmas is so lovely in Scotland. My grandmother decorates the house with greenery and we have big fires in all the rooms and candles everywhere. And we always have a huge Christmas tree. The men cut down one on the estate and carry it into the house on Christmas Eve. It always goes in the same place in the hall and we

71

always put the same decorations on it every year. New Year's Eve is fun too. My grandparents give a party and somebody plays the bagpipes and everybody dances Scottish reels. They all drink gallons of whisky, of course.

Kipper grew a lot while I was away at school. He's a beautiful cat and has big green eyes. I'm glad we kept him.

Hamish and I wish you and Bruno a Happy Christmas and a Happy New Year!

From,

Stroma

PS. I cut a bit out of our school photograph taken at the end of the summer term. I'm in the middle row, third from the right. Isn't the uniform hideous?

15th December, 1937

Dear Stroma,

I was very pleased to receive your letter and to have the photograph.

It is not very easy to see you, but thank you for sending it to me. I agree that the uniform is not very beautiful, but you are.

Yes, you are right, German does have some very long words – sometimes they are several words put together – but our grammar is very logical which makes it easier in other ways. (You see that I have now learned not to say more easy.)

The road that we are making wider will soon be finished – perhaps in January. Afterwards, we will be going to work in the forests to cut down trees and clear the land. I am very used to the hard labour now, and to the cold weather as well. There has already been snow. We are all very strong from the work. I could easily carry you for a long way now. Also, I have grown taller. You will never catch me up.

I am sorry that you will not be going to Craigmore for Christmas. I shall not be able to return to Hamburg either. Hamburg is very beautiful at Christmas, also. We have Christmas trees, like you, and everything is decorated and lit with many candles, and there is always a special Christmas market with very good things to eat and hot wine with spices to drink. I think you would like it.

I wish you and Hamish and all your family a very Happy Christmas. Frohe Weihnachten!

And I hope you have a very happy New Year.

From,

Reinhard

1938

In January, Reinhard was released early from his National Labour Service to begin his naval training. There was, apparently, an urgent need for young men to train as naval officers; the programme had even been drastically shortened to meet the demand.

During a week's leave at home, his father talked with him.

'Germany must be fully prepared for war, if necessary, Reinhard. Personally, I don't care much for our Führer and his party, but if they can end our twenty years of humiliation and suppression by the Allies, then I'm prepared to go along with them. Our country was treated shamefully at Versailles. They took away our land and all our resources and we have every good reason to rebel against those injustices.'

Reinhard said, 'The English don't seem very anxious for another war.'

His father agreed. 'The British lion is dozing peacefully at the moment, but if we poke him with a big enough stick he will wake up and roar. That is why our new U-boat force must be ready. Those pathetic little two hundred and fifty tonne submarines that we have been

74

allowed in our navy will be useless against the British Royal Navy. Fortunately, much larger and better U-boats are being built. They will be able to roam the oceans and you will be with them, Reinhard. Naturally, you are prepared to serve your country with unswerving loyalty?'

'Naturally, Father.'

'I expect nothing less. The Academy will instruct you in every aspect of seamanship, and the U-boat Force will make a submariner of you. It will be a hard road and a very tough and dangerous life – make no mistake – but it will be worth it. U-boat crews are men apart. The best of the best.' His father clapped him on his shoulder. 'You are already considerably taller than me, Reinhard. Don't grow any more. It's a nuisance for a U-boat commander to keep bumping his head.'

Bruno was envious. 'I'll be stuck at lousy school for three more years. If there's a war, it'll be over by then.'

'It may not even start.'

But Reinhard believed that it would. It was regrettable but inevitable. Germany would be forced into it if anything was to be achieved, and their fight would be against big odds. The German Navy would have to take on the whole might of the British Navy, as well as the ships of England's Allies. And for all their show of reluctance, the Americans might eventually join the battle, too.

The night before he left Hamburg Reinhard

went to the city's red-light district – no longer forbidden to him now that he was over eighteen. He swaggered boldly down the Reeperbahn and into the Herbertstrasse, the most expensive street where the girls were said to be the most beautiful. He chose one of them, sitting by her lighted window. He chose well. The girl was not only beautiful but a good teacher, and he was a star pupil, she told him, admiringly. It was a great pity, she said, that he was going away. Afterwards, he visited several bars and drank a lot of beer before ending up in a smoky dive in a narrow side street called Grosse Freiheit where he learned a good deal more from the explicit acts performed live on stage. It was five in the morning before he returned home.

The next day, he took the train north to Flensburg, nursing a thumping hangover. Checking through his pockets for his papers, he came across the cut-out photograph that Stroma had sent him. He held it up to examine it again, turning it towards the light from the window. She was half-hidden behind a tall girl standing in front of her. All he could see was a bit of her face, a bit of her hair and quite a lot of the hated uniform which, he had to agree, looked completely hideous. He had written to her in January and she had replied in early February – a few lines from her boarding school. She had found only one mistake in his letter, so his English must be improving. He had written another letter just before he left Hamburg.

The initial training for officers would take place on an island in the Baltic, and he had already heard from his father what lay in store and how tough it was. Physical fitness was essential – fortunately, he was very fit from his Labour Service. He could expect harsh conditions and brutal treatment from NCOs, endless drilling, saluting, parading, press-ups, inspections, long and gruelling route-marches laden with packs and rifles. One test of strength and character was to hold up a heavy iron bar while an electric current was passed through it. The considerable pain must be endured without dropping the bar.

Afterwards, he would be doing three months' training on a Navy sailing ship. He knew a good deal about smaller boats, but this would be rather different. The training ship had very tall masts, at least forty metres high, and cadets would be required to swarm up the rigging to the very top. Luckily, he had a good head for heights. If he didn't kill himself falling off the rigging, he would proceed to Mürwik for the officers' course at the Naval Academy. Another tough course, he had been warned. 'He who wishes to command must first obey' was a much-quoted slogan and one that must be learned quickly in order to progress. After that – with luck and his father's considerable influence – he would be assigned to the Ubootwaffe at Kiel.

He put the photograph away and watched the dull flat countryside go by, thinking about Stroma. She would write to him again, eventually, in her scrawly writing, the paper spattered with blots and smudges, giving him random scraps of news and correcting his English. He loved her – he knew that; he had done almost since he had first set eyes on her. But what chance or hope was there that anything could ever come of it? He wondered how much longer even their unlikely correspondence could continue. How long before a war between their two countries put an abrupt end to it?

'That German chap's not still writing to you, is he?' Hamish said. 'I thought he'd stopped long ago. What the hell's he up to now?'

'He's at their Naval Academy at somewhere called Mürwik.'

'Well, the Huns must be busy getting ready.'

'Ready for what?'

'For war, idiot. They've taken over Austria, in case you hadn't noticed. Goose-stepped into Vienna and been welcomed with open arms. And they've been giving General Franco in Spain a hand on the quiet, getting in plenty of target practice with their brand-new fighters and bombers. No more gliders for the Hun! Baggers says they're definitely brewing up to start another war.'

'Who on earth is Baggers?'

'Our history teacher at school. He says the Huns resent the way they were treated by everyone after we thrashed them in the last show. They want their own back on us now and Hitler's promised them he'll kindly arrange it.

Baggers says they'll be after the Sudetenland next. A lot of Huns live there so they've got a wonderful excuse to grab it, and probably the rest of Czechoslovakia while they're at it. Then they'll probably be after other countries as well, including us.' Hamish plucked the letter out of Stroma's hand, crumpled it in his fist and tossed it into the wastepaper basket. 'That's the place for that. And you shouldn't be writing to the enemy.'

'Reinhard's not the enemy.'

'He bloody soon will be.'

When her brother had gone, Stroma retrieved the letter and smoothed it out on her lap. It was longer than usual. In his last two letters, Reinhard had told her about his officers' initial training course, which had sounded unspeakably grim, and in the next letter he had written about training on a sailing ship at sea, which hadn't sounded much better. This letter was all about the Naval Academy at Mürwik and the lessons on naval history, navigation, naval tactics, marine engineering, weapons and oceanography. And about sailing, playing soccer, boxing, fencing, gymnastics, horse riding, and drilling out on the parade ground.

They make it very hard for us. We have only a few hours sleep each night and are very busy all day. Some cadets leave because it is too difficult for them, but I am still here. You will be happy to know that we are also given lessons to improve our English so perhaps you will not

have to make so many corrections to my letters.
I hope you will write soon.

He hadn't mentioned Austria at all. Or helping
General Franco in Spain.

In late July, Hamish and Stroma travelled up
from London to Islay. They took the night
sleeper to Glasgow, then a bus to Paisley and
another bus to Gourock. From Gourock they
hitched a lift in a fishing boat across to Dunoon
and picked up another lift in a farmer's cart.
The horse, head bowed, clip-clopped slowly up
the steep and windy glen between banks of
purple heather, craggy rocks, dry-stone walls
and tumbling burns. The farmer was going to
Kilfinan and, from there, the post bus took them
on to Portavadie where a ferry boat carried
them across to Tarbert. They stayed the night in
a small hotel at West Lock Tarbert and were up
early in the morning and on the bus to Kennacraig to catch the twice-weekly paddle steamer
for Islay. Sometimes, if the sea was too rough,
they had to wait for several days to make the
four-hour crossing, but this time they were
lucky.

Grandfather was waiting for them on the
quayside at Port Askaig and drove them the last
part of the journey in the old Humber. Since
there was no direct road along the east coast to
Craigmore, they had to go west across to Bridgend on the other side, then down to Bowmore
and Port Ellen and past the Laphroaig distillery

to Ardbeg. After that, the road petered out into a track and the off-shoot that led down to Craigmore was so rough and stony that the Humber dipped and rolled like an ocean liner on a stormy sea. Once past the peat moors, they descended into the woods and, when they emerged, there in front of them, beyond the fields and the grazing sheep and the dry-stone walls, stood the house and the rocky inlet and the sea.

One thing was not quite the same: Grandmother. Instead of being on the doorstep to greet them, she was lying upstairs in bed. She had caught a chill that had gone to her chest and Dr Mackenzie had recommended that she stay in bed for a few days.

'Nothing to worry about,' Grandfather said. 'She'll be up and about again soon.'

They went off fishing and sailing and swimming on the loch and they walked down through the woods to Glas Uig. When they were younger, they'd pretended to be smugglers or pirates but they didn't play childish games like that any more. Hamish kept talking about joining the Navy, and he kept on saying that there was going to be a war. Stroma maintained stubbornly that there wasn't going to be anything of the kind. They argued over it quite a lot.

'You won't believe it because of that bloody German chap,' Hamish said. 'Just because he writes nice letters to you, it doesn't mean a thing. He's joined their Navy, hasn't he? He'll probably end up in submarines, like his father, so he'll be busy torpedoing our ships. Maybe you won't think so much of him then.'

'I don't think much of him now.'

Actually, she thought of him quite a bit but she wasn't going to admit it.

'Well, I bet you still write to him, don't you?'

'Only when he writes to me.'

'So, don't answer his bloody letters. Simple.'

Colonel Crawford came over to dinner. He was an old friend of the grandparents, a widower who lived in Bowmore and had fought in the army in the Great War. Grandmother was feeling well enough to come down but Stroma thought that she looked awfully thin and pale, and she hardly ate a thing. Colonel Crawford didn't seem to notice; he was too busy talking about Adolf Hitler while swallowing a lot of Laphroaig whisky.

'All that nonsense he's been telling us about having to protect the Sudeten Germans in Czechoslovakia is just a red herring, you know. They're not being ill-treated by the Czechs at all. He just wants to get his hands on the Skoda munitions works so he can attack Russia. And Chamberlain's a fool if he believes a single word the fellow says. If we don't stand up to Herr Hitler now, we'll find ourselves facing another war with Germany. They're re-arming as fast as they can – riding roughshod over the Treaty rules – and as soon as they're ready, they'll make their move. Mark my words.'

Grandfather said mildly, 'A lot of people

might not agree with you, Robert. And they don't want to do anything to upset or provoke Hitler.'

'I know. I read it in the newspapers and I listen to the talk that goes on. Spineless appeasers! Don't tell me you're on their side, Archie?'

'No, I'm not, as it happens. And I think you may well be proved right about Hitler. But I don't think we should rush our fences. Negotiations should be given a chance. For one thing, we need time to build up our own forces.'

The colonel grunted. 'There's some truth in that. A chap who's in the know told me that the German Air Force has already got many more planes than the RAF – good ones, too. Heaven help us if that's the case. Well, at least we've got the Royal Navy to count on. Britannia still rules the waves, thank God.' He took another swig of whisky and looked across the table at Hamish. 'It'll be your war, this time, young man. You're going to have to do the fighting. What do you think about that as a prospect?'

'I can't wait, sir.'

'That's the spirit, my lad. That's the spirit.'

They went back to London in early September. There were rumours everywhere of the war that might have to be fought if Germany were to invade Czechoslovakia and, worse than rumours, there were clear signs. Trenches were being dug in the parks, cellars and basements turned into air-raid shelters, gas masks issued. Mr Chamberlain was said to be going to meet

Hitler in Germany to try to come to some agreement. France and Italy would go, too, but apparently the Czechs were not invited.

At school Stroma received another letter from Reinhard. He didn't refer to a war at all, or to any of the rumours, or say anything about Czechoslovakia. His officers' training would soon be completed, he wrote, and after a short leave in Hamburg he would be joining a submarine boat flotilla, though he didn't mention where. He enclosed a photograph of himself – a very formal one in his German naval officer's uniform. She didn't recognize the man that he had become: he was nothing like the boy she remembered on Islay. He looked so smart and so grown-up. Almost frighteningly so. On the back of the photo he had written: *For little Stroma, from Reinhard.* There were no spelling mistakes in his letter. Not even one.

One of the other girls was peering nosily over her shoulder.

'I say, who's that dishy-looking chap?'

She stuffed the photo away in the envelope. 'Nobody.'

At the end of the officers' training course at the Naval Academy, an Admiral of the German Navy came to make a speech. The graduates assembled in the square to listen to him. He was a big man and his voice boomed out across the square like a cannon firing.

'The time has come for you to show what you have learned – to prove yourselves for the sake of your country. Our Navy has ancient and honourable traditions. Germany will expect each and every one of you to do your duty.'

His own father's sentiments exactly, Reinhard thought drily. And, as it happened, also those of the famous Admiral Nelson, except that he had been referring to Englishmen, and to England.

The train to Kiel was packed with brand-new naval officers like himself, squashed into grubby compartments that were probably hopping with fleas. Outside it was raining hard.

Reinhard dozed, leaning his head back against the seat and risking the fleas. The brief leave in Hamburg had left him tired and hungover. Too much drink and too many visits to the Reeperbahn. Served him right that he was in such poor shape for what lay ahead.

He had no doubt that it was going to be tough. Tough and uncomfortable and dangerous, as his father had always warned. U-boats were risky things to go to sea in, even without a war. When the war came – and most of his fellow cadets at the Naval Academy firmly believed that it would – things would get a whole lot tougher, much more uncomfortable and much more dangerous. He had not thought about it during the past months; there had been little time to think of anything but learning and training and pushing himself daily to the limit, but the sobering fact was that the life he was enjoying so much could very soon be over. He might end it entombed in an iron hull at the bottom of the sea, or with his corpse floating around on the waves, the flesh being stripped from his bones by hungry fish. Not a happy thought.

In truth, he was not ready to make such a sacrifice. Not yet. Germany might expect him to do his duty, as the old admiral had bellowed at them, and he would do it, but he was damned well going to do his best to stay alive for as long as possible. Life was too pleasant. Good food, good drink, good comradeship, warm and willing women ... There was too much to live for.

He wondered if Stroma had received his last letter with the photograph. What would she would think of it? Had she been impressed? Probably not. She was not easy to impress. The photo made him look very serious – which, of course, it was meant to do. It was intended to show what a fine, upstanding young officer of the German Navy he was: a product of the famous Academy. Easy to play the part for the camera, but he had done absolutely nothing yet. One day, maybe, he would have another photo taken with a medal on a ribbon round his neck – the Knight's Cross, like his father. If he earned it.

Kleine Stroma. He smiled, remembering his first sight of the dirty, barefoot child scrambling down the hill towards him – her terrible hair, her torn clothes and her cut knee. Not so little now. He would very much like to know her when she had grown up into a woman but, by that time, unfortunately, he would probably be dead.

He looked round the compartment through half-closed eyes. His closest classmates, Max, Hans, Rolf, Werner, Klaus, Gunther, Harald and Paul, were dozing away like himself, the others in the next-door compartment were probably doing the same. The majority from the Academy had been sent to serve on destroyers, minesweepers and capital ships, but they had been singled out for submarine duty and had undergone weeks of special training which had included practice in simulators and attack runs on model convoys. They had finally been ordered to report to the 5th U-boat Flotilla at Kiel on the Baltic coast where they were to practise their new skills under the tutelage of an experienced commander. A special band of brothers, he thought drily: especially fearless and especially foolhardy.

It was still raining when the train arrived in Kiel. They stumbled on to the platform with their baggage and waited outside the station for a tram to take them out to the naval base at the northern end of the city. The base was surrounded by a high brick wall, its iron gates guarded by a sentry who took his time, inspecting their papers slowly and minutely while they were kept standing in the rain.

Klaus, always short-fused, cursed beneath his breath. 'Stupid arsehole! What the hell does he take us for? British agents?'

Once through the gates, they marched past barrack blocks to the waterfront where German warships rode at anchor out on the Bay of Kiel.

The tide was low and the strong smell of rotting seaweed mingled with the smells of salt, tar, oil and paint. The Tirpitz Pier stretched far out into the bay and as they walked along it, footsteps echoing, they passed a dozen U-boats moored in a double row. Type VIICs – the best. Very fast to dive (in twenty seconds from the given order), very mobile, with a maximum speed of 17.3 knots on the surface, 7.6 submerged, and a range of around 7000 nautical miles. Four torpedo tubes in the bows, one in the stern, and fourteen torpedoes to fire from them. Reinhard paused to admire them. His father had referred to them as grey wolves roaming the ocean. It was a good likeness. They had some weaknesses, of course, such as having to surface to recharge their batteries. They attacked with lethal torpedoes but their defences were limited to three guns mounted on the decks, seldom used when the better alternative was to dive out of sight. On the surface, the range of vision from the bridge was far less than a warship; under water, they were one-eyed, and any deeper than fourteen metres – the length of the periscope – they were completely blind. Only sound-locating hydrophones could tell them where the enemy might be. But, in his opinion, two strengths outweighed the drawbacks. The U-boats could hide and they could surprise the enemy.

The command ship of the flotilla was tied up at the end of the pier and they presented their papers again to board her. The Commandant's adjutant arrived with the news that the Commandant would not be available for an hour at least and they were free to leave the ship and to wander down the pier to take a closer look at the U-boats.

Outward appearances could be very misleading, Reinhard thought. Lying quietly at their moorings, the U-boats looked innocent enough, but he knew what lay out of sight beneath their sleek grey hulls. He knew all about the steel outer casing, the inner pressure hull, the watertight control room amidships. He knew about the Zeiss attack periscope, the bridge master sight and the fire interval calculator. And he knew about the fourteen torpedoes that could be launched through tubes in the bows and stern and with a deadly accuracy. The sleeping wolves were hiding their fangs from view.

They were given lunch in the officers' mess hall – roasted pork, cabbage and potatoes – and halfway through the meal, the Commandant joined them. At the end, he stood to make a short speech, along similar lines to the Admiral at the Academy, but without the bellowing. He spoke in a normal voice that carried easily in the mess hall. Much would be expected of them from their countrymen and from the German Navy. The U-boat Force that they were joining was an elite company, formed to play a vital role in Germany's future. A force capable not only of defending the nation, but of advancing her cause whenever and wherever it became expedient. Their training had equipped them to become part of the force; now it was time to put that training into practice and embrace their destiny.

'Kameraden, you must realize that you are serving in the finest and most effective service of our dear Fatherland. The destiny of our fellow countrymen lies in your hands. Prove yourselves worthy of their trust. We know no fear. Our motto is: "Go in and sink".'

They listened intently to every word.

After lunch, they gathered on deck to wait for orders. The adjutant arrived carrying lists and they gathered round him while he snapped out names in alphabetical order – first the name of the man, then the number of the U-boat and its port.

The lucky ones – Max, Gunther and Rolf among them – were assigned to the boats moored close by at the pier, but others were ordered to different ports. Hans, Werner and Klaus were to go to Bremerhaven; Harald and Paul to Wilhemshaven. Reinhard alone was ordered to report to faraway Koenigsberg on the other side of the Baltic.

He said goodbye to his classmates. They clapped each other on the back, wished each other good fortune, made ribald jokes. They were good fellows and he'd miss them.

The express train to Berlin arrived at Stettin Station soon after eight that same evening. He threaded his way through the crowds and out on to the street, carrying his two suitcases. It was still raining, the cobbles gleaming under the gas lamps. He had never visited the capital city before but he knew its heady reputation for music and arts – and for vice.

There was no train to Koenigsberg until early the next morning so he had to find somewhere to stay the night. But first he needed a drink, or several drinks, and then something to eat. There was a café a short way down the street – nothing special about it but the cases were heavy, so he went in and ordered a beer. The bar stools were all taken and when he looked round, he saw that all the tables were, too. There was a girl sitting alone at one of them – nothing special about her, either, but she had rather good legs. She was drinking coffee and reading a book and there were two empty chairs beside her. He went over.

'Do you mind if I join you, fräulein? You see, there is nowhere else to sit.'

He smiled as he spoke, but not too much in case he alarmed her. She was considerably older than himself. Perhaps twenty-seven, or twenty-eight. No wedding or engagement ring. He'd noticed that, too, as well as the legs.

She smiled back timidly. 'Yes, it's quite all right.'

The naval uniform, even a lowly midshipman's, was always a great help, he thought, as he fetched his beer and the suitcases. People trusted you. He could have warned her that, in his case, it might prove to be a mistake.

He raised his beer to her. 'Prost!'

91

She nodded and bent her head over her book again. He studied her over the rim of his glass. She was very different from the girls of the Reeperbahn or others he had since come across elsewhere. Natural hair, almost no make-up and the clothes were plain and modest. He had hoped for something more sophisticated in Berlin, but on second thoughts, she could make an interesting change.

He leaned forward. 'I am rather curious. May I ask what you are reading so intently?'

She raised her head, blushing a little. 'It's a book on English. I'm studying the language at a class in the evenings.'

'Do you enjoy it?'

'Not much. English is not at all logical and the spelling is confusing. But it's a good thing to know it for my work.'

'What is your work?'

'I am secretary to the managing director of an export company. So, you see, foreign languages are important. I already speak and understand French and Italian and some English, but I need to know it better. Just now, I find I can hardly understand a word of this passage.'

'Perhaps I can help. Let me see.'

She handed him the book: *Further Steps In English*. The passage in question was taken from *Great Expectations* by Charles Dickens. He translated it for her, pointing out the words as he did so.

'You make it seem very easy,' she said as he gave her back the book.

'It's not so difficult. But you are right; it is not at all logical and the spelling is very confusing. I have a friend in England and when I write letters to her she always corrects my spelling mistakes so that I learn.'

He ordered another beer and a coffee for her, offered a cigarette which she refused. He lit his own and found out some more about her. Her name was Katrin Paulssen. She came from Wegendorf, a small town some way from Berlin, and she lived in an apartment a few streets away.

'Only one room with a small bathroom and a cupboard for a kitchen. It's not very nice but it's the best I can afford.'

The beers had revived him but now he was very hungry and the café only provided snacks. The girl told him that there was a good restaurant in the next street.

'I hope you will join me, please,' he said. 'As my guest, of course. I hate to eat alone and I don't know anyone in Berlin. This is my first visit here.'

'I couldn't do that.'

'Perhaps you have already eaten?'

'No ... but I will have something at my apartment.'

He could imagine it. She would assemble some scraps in the cupboard kitchen. Cold sausage, bread, something out of a tin. Very poor fare.

'If you have not already eaten, then there are no excuses. Show me where this good restaurant is.'

She had been right to recommend it: the food and the beer were excellent. During the meal he learned more about her. She was an only child and her parents, safely at home in Wegendorf, were very strict.

They had not approved of her going to Berlin and insisted that she went home every week-end. Apparently there was no steady boyfriend, which was surprising, he thought. She was attractive, in her quiet way, and the shyness was rather appealing too.

'Do you like living in Berlin?' he asked.

'At first, I did. But now I am afraid to be here.'

'Oh? Why is that?'

'Because of what has happened ... since the Kristallnacht.'

'Kistallnacht?'

'When the Nazi soldiers attacked the syna-gogues, and the Jewish shops and homes. They burned buildings and smashed windows so that in the morning the streets were full of broken glass. It happened all over Germany and Aus-tria. Many Jews were murdered and thousands were arrested and taken away to prison camps. Surely, you must know about it?'

He had heard some stories. People talking at the Academy, accounts in the newspapers. But he had been too preoccupied with his training and study to give it much attention. If he re-membered rightly, it had all happened because some Polish-Jew had assassinated a German official. Well, that had been a crazy thing to do. The fellow must have been raving mad. The Führer had never made any secret of his hatred of Jews and blamed them for everything, which was totally unfair, of course.

'But there is no need for you to worry.'

'Yes, there is. You see, I am Jewish. My father is German, but my mother is a Jew, which makes me one, too. And no Jew is safe now.'

Now that he looked at her more closely, he could see the Jewish features – the skin tone, the dark hair, the nose and the unusual coloured eyes. He had known very few Jews – the family doctor in Hamburg, a professor acquaintance of his father's, one of the teachers at school, the elderly tailor who had made his naval uniform, a shopkeeper or two, but never any Jewish girls. It was not a question of prejudice; he had simply never come across them.

He said again, 'I'm sure you don't need to worry.'

'I am not so sure.'

'Then perhaps you should go home to Wegendorf.'

'That's what my parents have wanted me to do ever since the Kristallnacht. But even though I am very afraid, I still don't want to leave Berlin.'

He didn't blame her for not wanting to go back to some small, dull little place to live with her strict parents, and he admired her spirit. What was it about Jews that made them so hated and reviled? Their cleverness? Their talent for money-making? Their money-lending? Their weird rituals that set them apart from others? Their belief in being God's Chosen People? At school, in English class, he had studied Shakespeare's *Merchant of Venice*. He had found the archaic language difficult, but some of it had stayed in his mind. A remnant of Shylock's speech. 'For sufferance is the badge of all our tribe. You call me misbeliever, cut-throat dog, and spet upon my Jewish gaberdine ... and foot me as you spurn a stranger cur over your threshold.' He knew people who might do just that and he had probably given Katrin good advice when he had advised her to go home to Wegendorf.

Afterwards, she took him back to the small flat where he spent the night in her narrow and virginal bed. She seemed to have had no experience at all with men and he was careful to avoid doing anything that might shock her.

In the morning, they had breakfast in a café round the corner – strong coffee, ham, rye bread, cheese, eggs. For the poor and unemployed of Germany he knew that it would have been a wonderful feast. It was true that things were getting better under the Nazis. Now, at least, there were jobs to be had in munitions factories, aircraft factories, building tanks and ships and, of course, U-boats.

Katrin hardly ate a thing.

'Will you come back soon?' she asked. 'Perhaps on leave?'

'Impossible to say. I don't know where the

Navy will be sending me, or for how long.'

This was perfectly true. Also, he did not want any commitment, nice as she was. With so many girls available, it was stupid to get too involved with one of them. The fact that she was a Jewess had nothing whatsoever to do with it.

She fiddled with her coffee spoon. 'Your friend in England. The one who corrects the spelling mistakes in your letters. Is she special to you?'

The answer was yes, very special, but not quite in the way that Katrin imagined.

'She's only fourteen years old,' he said with a smile. 'Just a kid.'

She went to the station with him and he saw her wiping away tears as the train moved off. He was sorry about that; he hadn't intended to hurt her.

The train took him over the Pomeranian Plains, miles of heather giving way to endless pine forests. It stopped at the two borders, first leaving West Prussia to enter the Danzig corridor and, a few hours later, crossing into East Prussia. Danzig and the valuable corridor to the sea had once belonged to Germany but had been handed over to Poland at the end of his father's war. The Polish guards boarding the train were sullen and rude. It might pay them to be more friendly, he thought, if they didn't want their country to be carved up like Czechoslovakia. At the big international meeting in Munich last September it had been agreed that the German army was to occupy the Sudetenland and that all Czechs would be evacuated from it. There had been official photographs of the occasion with Adolf Hitler, Mussolini and the British and French prime ministers. No Czechs had been present, which was ironic. It had also been reported that the British prime minister had persuaded the Führer to sign some other piece of paper, a declaration that he would keep to his word about not taking over anywhere else. Mr Chamberlain had looked rather comical with his drooping walrus moustache and old-fashioned clothes, and he must be exceedingly naïve.

Reinhard arrived at Koenigsberg at dusk and followed directions to the naval yard. Several U-boats were tethered alongside a granite jetty – black silhouettes in the gathering darkness. One of them would be his boat.

The flotilla headquarters were on board an old liner. He carried his baggage across the gangway, reported to the officer on watch and was directed to a cabin. Later, he found the bar and the dining room for a drink and some dinner. The other officers present were older hands already with experience of sea trials. One of them, by the name of Friedrich Merten, turned out to be the First Officer of his boat and warned him that the commander, Kapitänleutnant Grindorff, would be unhappy to be landed with another beginner.

'He's very tough on new boys, but he's a good captain; that's the main thing.'

They had a few drinks together while Merten told him more.

'We've been doing a shakedown cruise in the Baltic so the boat's not looking her best, but she's reliable. No gremlins so far. Crew of forty-two – officers, petty officers, seamen, machinists and technicians. You'll know all that, of course. Our commander's licked us into shape, I can tell you. He's an old sea dog and his bite's worse than his bark. But I'd sooner be with him than with anyone else. In a submarine, we depend on everyone else to stay alive, and, most of all, we depend on our commander, and Grindorff is just about the best around.'

Reinhard went back to his cabin and to bed. He had drunk too much, which he would certainly regret in the morning.

There was a bitter wind blowing across the harbour. The U-boat was a type VIIC, like the ones at Kiel, and she lay in the oily water, hatches open. Streaks of rust showed beneath her grey paint and there was green algae along the flat wooden planking on the steel hull and some more rust round the barrel of the anti-aircraft gun on the foredeck. It gave her a seasoned look, an air of being on familiar terms with the ocean and its depths, which was reassuring.

He went aboard and presented his transfer orders.

'Herr Kapitänleutnant, I beg to report aboard.'

The old sea dog bared his teeth in a snarl.

'God in heaven! How many more of you are

they going to dump on me to wet-nurse? Nancy-boys in smart new uniforms who think they know it all. You're a damned nuisance, the lot of you; useless wasters of air and good for nothing but ballast.'

This was the boat's commander, addressed by his crew as Herr Kaleun and known by them as the Old Man, whatever his age. He was a broad, short man – a good deal shorter than Reinhard – and it was hard to tell exactly how old he was, but he looked close to forty. His clothes had the same worn look as his boat. There was verdigris on the brass ornaments on his captain's white cap and the white was well-spotted with dirt. His knee-length grey leather jacket and leather trousers were oil-smeared, his sea boots scuffed and salt-encrusted. Reinhard was uncomfortably aware of his own immaculate dress uniform and shiny buttons.

Friedrich Merten was summoned to give him a tour of the boat. As Reinhard followed the lieutenant through the dimly-lit pressure hull, he had to stoop, step up, step down or squeeze sideways past obstacles and men in order to progress along its long and narrow length. He hit his head painfully against pipes and ducts and on the low hatchways separating one water-tight compartment from the next – so low that he had to bend almost double to crawl through them. He negotiated them clumsily, in contrast to the lieutenant who swung himself through like a monkey. Even in port and with the hatches open to the fresh air, the U-boat stank of diesel oil and bilge and men.

The diesel engines, electrical equipment, air compressor and one torpedo tube lay in the aft section. Between the diesel compartment and amidships there was a very small galley, the petty officers' quarters – merely a corridor between eight bunks with a fold-away table – and one head, which was also used as a food store. The control room, nerve centre of the U-boat, was crammed with gauges, wires, ducts, switches, meters, hand-wheels, pumps, compasses, rudder and hydroplanes gear and the chart closet. The radio room lay forward with four more torpedoes, then the officers' quarters which doubled as a wardroom, so cramped there was barely room to sit, another head and the captain's cubby-hole of a cabin behind a thick green curtain. The lower ranks slept in tiers of narrow cots and slung hammocks in the bow compartment and ate at a makeshift table, with spare torpedoes chained above their heads or stowed below the deck plates. Since there were not enough cots for every man, they had to sleep in rotation as they came off watch: three men to each one. Nobody, from the commander down to the lowest crew member, ever undressed except to change out of soaking wet clothes into still-damp ones, ever ready to jump to action stations. In the humid atmosphere, with moisture running down the bulkheads, nothing dried properly; everything went mouldy. Leather coats and sea boots turned green and white with a salt covering like hoar frost. The fresh water taps in the heads were strictly for brushing teeth and a quick flannel wipe, otherwise it was salt water which produced no lather. On patrols nobody shaved.

The conning tower above the control room housed the attack periscope, the torpedo computer, and the helm. Buoyancy tanks, trim cells, oil and freshwater tanks were located throughout the boat and in the outboard tanks.

Reinhard had studied the layout of a Type VII very carefully, but now he found himself completely confused by the boat's complexity. This was not going to be anything like as simple as he had expected. It could take months, if not years, to acquire enough knowledge and skill to command a boat of his own – his ambition, just as much as it was his father's.

He was sent back to the HQ to be kitted out from the supply room. Three sets of coveralls, a long grey leather jacket and trousers, oilskins, two blue sweaters, knitted underwear, rubber boots, leather boots, thick gloves and binoculars. Also, a lifejacket and a breathing tube and mask. He lugged them all back to the boat and to the narrow berth allotted to him in the officers' quarters. Almost immediately, the order came to prepare for sailing and less than two hours later the U-boat moved away silently from the pier, powered by the electric motors until she reached navigable waters where the diesel engines rumbled into life. From the railed winter garden enclosure behind the bridge Reinhard watched Koenigsberg fade into the distance. The boat took a westward course. Waves slapping hard on the starboard side showered the hull and their wake streamed out in a swirling path of white foam. He could taste the salt on his lips.

To his disappointment, he was ordered below – down the vertical steel ladder from the conning tower hatch and into the pressure hull where every man on watch was at his post and the only noise was the hammering of the diesels. He was to be the general dogsbody. To assist at the helm and hydroplanes, to help the navigator at his plotting table, to give a hand to the Second Officer decoding top-secret messages and to spend as much time with the Chief Engineer as possible, learning all he could from him about the boat's construction, machinery, equipment, tanks, valves, torpedoes and artillery armament, to find out the purpose of every pipe – where it came from and where it led. He was given filthy jobs to do, crawling round under the plating and cleaning out the bilges. His fine midshipman's uniform was soon abandoned. In such little time as he had off-duty, he was to study manuals lying in his cramped bunk in the petty officers' quarters. As a sop, he was allowed to eat in the officers' wardroom.

The boat had moved into rougher seas and began rocking wildly, making him stagger like a drunk and grab at handholds. Just as he was passing beneath the conning tower hatch in the control room, a heavy wave came crashing down and drenched him to the skin. He forced himself to join in the crowing laughter.

They practised diving. First an orderly, standard procedure meticulously carried out and, later, an emergency crash dive when the alarm shrieked throughout the boat and the bridge watch came tumbling down the ladder, the officer sealing the hatch after them within five seconds. Men hurled themselves through hatchways to wrench at levers, spin wheels, monitor gauges. Air roared out of the tanks, water rushed in. The U-boat pitched her nose steeply downwards and the seas closed over her, leaving only a trail of bubbles which would soon vanish. It took thirty seconds to reach a depth that might, with luck, evade depth charges and the deeper they went the more difficult it would be to locate them.

Underwater, all surface noise ceased. No wind or waves, no thundering diesels, no humming ventilators; even the radio fell silent, cut off from radio waves as the aerial sank beneath the water. They went down to sixty metres and then still deeper to a hundred metres, testing the pressure hull's strength, the boat creaking and groaning loudly in protest. Some of the crew's faces grew tense but the Old Man showed no emotion whatever. Not a flicker of concern. They might have been out on a pleasure cruise, not chancing their lives near the bottom of the sea in a fragile tin can.

This is how a U-boat captain must always be, Reinhard thought. *Calm, confident, in complete control of himself and of the crew. Every man looked to him. To betray any fear, any doubt, any weakness could be fatal.* He, himself, had felt no fear or panic during the deep descent.

Finally, they surfaced. The control tower hatch was opened and fresh air poured into the boat, the ventilators began to hum again, the diesels resumed their thumping.

Later, lying off-duty in his bunk, he wrote a letter to Stroma. Of course, he told her nothing about the boat or where he was. Everything must be kept secret. Instead, he asked about her school and about the weather in England, and about when she would next be going to Craigmore.

Grandmother died at the end of December. The chill that she had caught in the summer had become something much worse. Hamish and Stroma travelled up to Craigmore with their parents before Christmas, as soon as the school terms were finished. The house was very quiet. There were no decorations, no dinners or parties or games or noisy bagpipes and reels, as there had been on other Christmases. Dr Mackenzie came and went, as well as a few visitors, and Grandfather spent most of his time sitting upstairs with Grandmother. Hamish and Stroma were allowed to visit her for short periods. She looked very small in the big bed, her arms thin as sticks and her voice weak. On one occasion, she asked to see Stroma alone.

'Bring me my jewellery box, Stroma. I want us to go through it.'

She fetched the black japanned box from the dressing table. The lid was decorated with oriental flowers and trees, a winding stream, a little wooden bridge and the figure of a Japanese woman in Japanese dress holding an open parasol over her shoulder. Inside, the box was lined with padded crimson silk and two brasshinged trays opened up to reveal more space beneath. Stroma had played with it many times when she was small, trying on the rings and necklaces and bracelets, fascinated by the way they caught the light and glittered and shone.

Grandmother opened the lid. 'Your mother is to have the amethyst set and Hamish will have the Mackay ring for his bride one day. I am giving Ellen the cameo brooch and Angus's wife, Grace, is to have the marquisites. My pearls are for you, Stroma, as well as all the other pieces. The rings, the bracelets, the necklace, the diamond watch ... everything left.'

'But I don't want them. They're yours.'

'And mine to give as I wish. So don't look so upset about it. Put the pearls on.'

'Must I?'

'Yes, you must. I want to see how they look on you now that you're getting so very grown-up.'

She put the beautiful pearl choker round her neck and fastened its heavy clasp at the front. 'Have I done it right?'

Her grandmother lay back against her pillows and smiled at her.

'Perfectly.'

* * *

The funeral took place on the last day of the year and Grandmother was buried in the graveyard of the ruined kirk a mile or so from the house where an ancient cross, hewn and carved from a single stone, had stood for eleven hundred years. Angus played a farewell lament on the bagpipes at the graveside.

Before they left Craigmore to start the return journey to London, Stroma went and sat in Grandmother's garden on the wooden seat beside the waterfall. The evergreen shrubs gave shelter from the cold wind sweeping down the sound and snowdrops were flowering beneath a tree.

1939

From her bedroom window, Stroma could see the silver barrage balloon rising majestically into the air above the park, dipping and bobbing at the end of its thick steel wires. The anti-aircraft balloons were tethered all over London, more and more trenches being dug, more and more air-raid shelters being built and more and more bags of sand being piled up against buildings.

Everyone talked about the prospect of war with Germany. Some people were in favour of fighting because they believed Adolf Hitler had to be stopped from becoming too powerful. Some were against it because the quarrel was about faraway countries and nothing to do with England. Hamish, of course, was all for it. He was going to join the Royal Navy and, in his words, give the Huns a good thrashing.

'You're only seventeen,' Stroma had pointed out. 'The Navy won't take you.'

'By the time things get going I'll be eighteen.'

'But you're supposed to be going up to Cambridge.'

'Cambridge can wait,' he'd said.

She watched the barrage balloon doing a sort

of stately dance – swinging slowly one way and then the other, graceful in spite of its huge size. Like an old dowager performing a gavotte.

There was a letter from Reinhard in her skirt pocket. He had said nothing at all about any war, only that he had been away at sea and had been given a few days' leave. He was spending it in the country, not at his home in Hamburg but with friends of his late mother's who bred horses and had taught him to ride as a small child. Now his leave was nearly finished and he would return to duty the next day. To a U-boat, presumably, although he didn't mention that.

It is a long time since I have received a letter from you. Please write to me with your news. You can address the letter to my home in Hamburg and it will be sent to me wherever I am. I would like very much to know how you are and what you are doing.

She had kept the photograph of him in his uniform, hidden away in her handkerchief sachet. Sometimes she brought it out to look at, but not very often because the other girls were so inquisitive. Rosanne, her best friend at school, had been rather shocked when Stroma had once secretly shown it to her.

'I must say, he's awfully handsome, Stroma, but he's a German.'

'It's not his fault. He can't help it.'

'No ... but all the same ... I mean ... *German*!'

The barrage balloon had stopped its stately gavotte and was floating quietly in the sky.

Now it looked like a great whale, which made her think of the jawbone in the rocks at Glas Uig.

There had been some horrible talk of them not going up to Scotland this summer because a war might break out. But then their parents had decided that if it did, she and Hamish would be safer there than in London. Hamish didn't care in the least about being safe – and nor did she – but not to go to Craigmore would be unbearable.

Blast Hitler! He was spoiling everything.

In March, the Germans marched into Prague, the capital of Czechoslovakia, and, by the end of the month, Mr Chamberlain had promised help to the Poles if they were attacked. More barrage balloons appeared, and even more trenches and shelters and sandbags.

Germany and Italy had signed some sort of agreement. It seemed as though a long, dark shadow had fallen over England.

Dear Reinhard,

Thank you for your letter. There were no mistakes at all in it.

I'm very sorry, but I don't think that there's much point in us writing to each other any more, is there? Nearly everybody here in England thinks that we will soon be at war with your country because of the way Hitler is behaving. So, I think this will have to be my last letter.

Whatever happens, I hope that you will be all right.

From,
Stroma

'I've sent for you over a very serious matter, Stroma.' Miss Calder, the headmistress, looked even grimmer than usual. 'Matron discovered this photograph concealed in your drawer. Perhaps you would explain it to me? Who is this man?'

'Somebody I met in Scotland three years ago.'

'I imagine you are aware that he is wearing the uniform of a German naval officer?'

'Yes, Miss Calder. He sent it to me when he graduated from their naval college.'

Miss Calder turned the photo over, holding it with the tips of her fingers as though it might contaminate her. 'Apparently, his name is Reinhard.'

'It's pronounced Reinhard.' She gave it a very guttural R, like he had done.

'Don't be impertinent, Stroma. It's of no importance whatsoever how it is pronounced. Are your parents acquainted with this person?'

'No. They've never met him.'

'Are they aware that you have been corresponding with him? Writing letters to him?'

'I don't write very often.'

'How often is not the point. It should not have been happening at all. It is the policy of this school not to allow girls to receive letters from males outside their immediate families. We discourage it unless the parents in question give their full permission – clearly not so in this case. Do you realize that our country is on the brink of a war with Germany?'

'Yes, I do, Miss Calder.'

'And yet you are carrying on a correspondence with one of their naval officers?'

'We're not actually at war yet.'

'Don't argue with me.' Miss Calder tore the photograph into four neat pieces and let them flutter into the wastepaper basket beside her desk. 'If any more letters arrive for you from this man, they will be destroyed immediately. You understand?'

At the beginning of July, they left Koenigsberg with several other U-boats on a fleet exercise ordered by the commander of the Ubootwaffe, Admiral Dönitz. The orders were to patrol the waters from the Shetland Islands off Scotland down to the Atlantic coast of France – to get a feel for what lay in store. From the Baltic they crossed the North Sea, taking a route along the eastern coast of England at a discreet distance from the land, doing trial dives, practice attacks, gun action stations, keeping a constant lookout. The commander was brutal about the slightest shortcoming.

Reinhard, on the bridge for the second watch, from four till eight, covered the port sector aft. Once the eyes were well-adjusted to the dark, it was amazing how much could be seen, even on the blackest night. The sky was lighter than the sea, the horizon visible, the U-boat's wake a glimmering phosphorescent trail. He steadied the heavy binoculars with the tips of his fingers, scanning the sea very slowly from one side of the ninety-degree sector to the other, and then he lowered the glasses to take in the whole sector at one glance before he raised the glasses to begin the slow and painstaking scanning process again. They were thirty kilometres off the east coast of Scotland.

As they ploughed on, the new day began to break. First, a faint strip lighter than the rest appeared above the horizon in the east. It widened, taking on a pinkish tone, until the top part of the sun suddenly showed itself. The boat emerged gradually from the dark.

The Old Man had come up quietly on to the bridge and lit a cigarette. Without turning his head, Reinhard knew he was there because he could smell the cigarette smoke. He kept the binoculars clamped to his eyes and continued the slow and steady sweep. In war, they would be searching for enemy shipping or enemy planes; this was only a rehearsal but must be taken as seriously as a real performance. Was that a seagull or a plane? At a distance, against a still-dark sky, it was ridiculously easy to mistake one for the other. He focussed hard on the small shape until he was satisfied that it was a seagull and not a member of the Royal Air Force out on a dawn patrol.

They continued northwards as far as the Shetland Islands, getting a feel of what the Admiral had called 'those stormy waters'. Even in midsummer the weather was vile, the wind savage, the seas violent. On the surface, the U-boat rocked and rolled, the crew staggering and stumbling and cursing, crockery smashing, tools and utensils flying about inside the pressure hull like lethal weapons. Diving below was a blessed relief – for as long as it lasted before they had to surface to recharge the batteries. While they were below the surface, it was amazingly peaceful: a soothing silence, broken only by the faint hum of the electric motors. The roar of the wind and sea had been abruptly cut off as they had sunk into the deep, and the incessant rolling and lurching stopped as the U-boat levelled out below. Under the electric light, there was no difference between night and day.

From the Shetlands they altered course south towards the Orkneys and Scapa Flow. The vast sheet of water, ringed by islands, provided a sheltered anchorage fifteen miles long and eight miles wide – big enough to take a whole British Navy fleet, if necessary.

In the officers' wardroom the Old Man moved salt and pepper pots about the table to demonstrate the layout.

'Seven entrances: Hoxa Sound between two islands here in the south is the big front door; Switha Sound next to it is narrower, and Hoy Sound over here is not much used at all. The

114

rest are small ones along the eastern side of the Flow but which are only big enough to admit fishing boats.' The Old Man paused before he added, 'Or naval ships ... the size of a sub-marine.' He looked around the table, from one face to the next. 'Two of our U-boats were sunk in the last war, trying to break in, and the British have since tried to plug the holes. It will be very interesting for us to observe these places as we pass by.'

The observing was done that night when the weather calmed down and the Northern Lights conveniently lit up the islands with a flickering and ghostly display – greenish swirls and waves of light, changing to blue, to red, to violet, to pink, to yellow and back again to green, dis-solving and re-forming, bright particles shoot-ing out in all directions. Reinhard, on watch on the bridge, had a grandstand view as the U-boat crept stealthily round the outside of the British base like a fox circling a coop full of plump chickens. Impossible not to feel the predator's excitement that his father had described so graphically. The thrill of stalking an unsuspect-ing quarry. Not so easy, though, in these waters. They had taken *Sturmwind* through the Pent-land Firth when they had sailed her around Scotland and he knew its treachery first-hand.

They left the Orkneys behind and continued south-west by the Hebrides, passing quite close to Islay as they headed for the Irish Sea and the Atlantic coast of France. Stroma's last letter had not surprised him; it had been almost inevitable. But it was a great pity. It was now even more unlikely that they would ever meet again. He had been very touched by her hope that he would be all right. He hoped so too, though that seemed equally unlikely.

He wondered if she and Hamish would be spending their school holidays at Craigmore, or whether, perhaps, they would stay in London instead this year because of the possibility of a war. As his father had said, if prodded with a big enough stick, the lion would wake up and roar and the Führer had been doing plenty of prodding. If it happened, he hoped that Stroma would be sent to Scotland where she would be much safer.

After three days, the Admiral recalled them from his headquarters on the Baltic coast and told them to hold themselves in readiness for war.

'Next time,' he signalled, 'it will be the real thing.'

Back at the U-boat base, Reinhard wrote one more letter to Stroma and sent it to the London address.

Dear Stroma,

Thank you for writing to me. I understand how you are feeling and I am sorry for this. But I shall miss your letters very much. If there is a war between our countries I hope that we will be able to meet again when it is finished. If I can, I will come to Craigmore and Glas Uig to

116

find you one day. Until then, I hope you will keep safe and well.

From,

Reinhard

In the end, Hamish and Stroma went up to Craigmore for the summer as usual. Hamish would far sooner have stayed in London in case he missed the war starting and he mooched around, spending most of the time in his bedroom making yet another model ship.

'What kind is it?' Stroma asked, watching him sanding a length of wood.

'The kind I want to serve in. A destroyer. Fast, lots of gun-power. It lives up to its name.'

'If there isn't a war, you won't need to join up.'

'Of course there's going to be a war. The Huns are getting ready to grab Poland and we've promised to help the Poles fight against them.'

'I don't see why we have to. It's got nothing to do with us.'

Hamish stopped sanding and stared at her crossly. 'You're hopeless, Stroma. Of course it has. If we don't stop the Germans soon, they'll be unstoppable. We've got to do something. You're an idiot if you can't see that.'

Angus took her out pigeon shooting and she found she could handle a twelve-bore easily now. It helped that pigeons were considered pests because they did so much damage to crops. 'Verrrmin', Angus called them, blowing them out of the sky. She plucked and drew the dead pigeons for Ellen to cook. Their plumage wasn't as beautiful as the pheasants', but they were still handsome with their soft grey and pink and white and she hated the job.

Grandfather gave her lessons in casting for salmon on the river. The rod was still heavy for her but she was getting the knack of it.

'Keep practising,' he told her, 'and you'll be ready when the season starts.'

Hamish went out stalking with Angus and she tagged along behind them, trudging for miles through the heather and the rain as they tracked a stag on the move on the hillside. The trick was to keep out of his sight, smell and hearing. Sometimes, she caught glimpses of the animal and his magnificent antlers turning as he paused and looked around. 'A puir old one', Angus called him, 'only fit to be culled'. The stag didn't look anything of the kind, but she knew better than to argue. Angus had once explained to her that the old and weak ones had to be killed for their own good and for the good of the herd. Only the strongest and best should be kept. She prayed that the stag would see or smell or hear them and make off, but he didn't. Instead, he wandered along, stopping now and again to look round, while they lay flat and motionless on the ground. Then Hamish fired. The rifle cracked, the bullet whined and the stag's front legs buckled as he sank to the ground. They walked across the heather to where he lay, his eyes sightless, his neck stretched out, his antlers twisted.

'What on earth are you crying for, Stroma?' Hamish said impatiently.

Angus laid a gentle hand on her shoulder. 'He didna suffer one bit, lassie. Twas a guid clean kill.'

On the first of September, Germany invaded Poland and on the third, Grandfather turned on the wireless in the drawing room so that they could hear Mr Chamberlain make his declaration of war. Ellen, Sally, the kitchen maid, Logan, Mack, Angus and Grace and the estate workers crowded into the room to listen. The Prime Minister's voice was quavery.

I am speaking to you from the Cabinet Room of 10 Downing Street ... This morning the British Ambassador in Berlin handed the German Government a final note ... I have to tell you now that no such undertaking was received and that consequently this country is at war with Germany.

At first, it was decided that Hamish and Stroma should remain on Islay. The Germans were expected to start bombing London at once – and air-raid sirens sounded on the very day that the war started – but it was a false alarm. No bombers appeared in the skies and no bombs were dropped, although a liner, the *Athenia*, was torpedoed while leaving England and sunk by a German U-boat. Many passengers drowned.

Of course, Hamish was furious about staying, but after a while they were sent back to London and to boarding school. Since both their schools were out in the country, they were considered safe.

At Stroma's school air-raid shelters had been dug big enough to take all the girls. Gas masks had to be carried everywhere and there were regular practices for putting them on and forming into lines and filing into the shelters. They sat for ages on wooden benches while names were called and heads were counted; it was all very boring and seemed rather unnecessary, as some people were saying that the war would be over by Christmas.

And then, in October, another German U-boat somehow sneaked into the Royal Navy base at Scapa Flow in the Orkneys and sank the battleship *Royal Oak* as she lay at anchor. And two days later, German planes bombed British cruisers in the Firth of Forth. So it had not been so safe up in Scotland, after all. Hamish was probably wishing that they had stayed there.

And where was Reinhard now, Stroma wondered. Was he serving in the U-boat that had sunk the defenceless passenger liner with all those lives lost, or in the one that had sunk the battleship lying at anchor and killed hundreds of British sailors?

Christmas in London was very grim this year. No brightly-lit shop windows, no winking neon advertisements or Christmas tree lights, only the faint glimmer of shelter signs and masked traffic lights, the shielded headlights of cars and the feeble beams of torches dimmed with paper. In the evenings, before darkness fell, every window had to be covered with blackout material so that not a chink of light showed outside. People who went out at night fell down steps, walked into lamp-posts and trees, tripped over kerbs, toppled off railway platforms, were knocked down by cars.

But still the German bombers did not come.

'It's the Bore War,' Hamish said. 'That's what everyone's calling it. I wish to heaven something would happen so we could have a crack at the blighters.'

Next March he would be eighteen – old enough to join up and 'have a crack at them', and Stroma would be sixteen in May. In two years' time, she'd be able to join up and have a crack at them too, although she imagined the war would be over long before then.

1940

It was so cold in January and February that the River Thames froze over for eight miles and snow cut off towns and villages all over England.

At Stroma's school, games had to be abandoned and they were sent out for long walks in crocodiles instead.

No German bombs had fallen anywhere in England. Nothing had happened, except for the Russians suddenly attacking Finland, which was too far away to worry about. It was still the Bore War.

Stroma and Rosanne walked side-by-side in the crocodile. Rosanne's brother, Jeremy, was in the army and had been posted to France in December.

'I had a letter from him this morning. He says the weather's awful there, too, but they're having a rather nice time. They've been billeted in some beautiful old chateau and the food's wonderful. Much better than over here. He doesn't think the Germans will try anything till the spring because of the bad weather. He says they'll soon send them packing, if they do.'

'I hope he's right. The Poles didn't manage to

do that.'

'That's different.'

They trudged on. There was a thin layer of ice on top of the snow and their walking shoes made satisfactory crunching noises.

Stroma said, 'Why should it be different for the Poles?'

'Well, their army wouldn't be nearly as well-trained as ours, or have the same sort of proper equipment. They still use horses, don't they? Not tanks. I read about it in the newspaper. Mind you, Jerry says he doesn't think much of the French army either. He says they don't seem very well organized.'

'I bet the Germans are.'

She remembered Reinhard's descriptions of life at the German naval academy – all work, no sleep, tough sports, marching up and down the parade ground.

Rosanne said, 'Anyway, our Royal Navy's the best in the world, isn't it? So they won't be able to beat us, no matter how hard they try. Has Hamish heard anything yet?'

'No, he's still waiting.'

'I'm sure they'll take him, being so good at sailing.'

Hamish had applied for direct entry to the Royal Navy Volunteer Reserve officers' training course. The parents had wanted him to wait until he had passed his Higher School Certificate in the summer term and there had been big rows during the Christmas holidays. But he had got his way in the end. And it wouldn't be a nice safe shore post either, but something at sea – probably on a destroyer or the like. Destroyers were built to destroy, as he had pointed out to her, which meant engaging enemy ships. It meant attacking them, and being attacked by them. Maybe even getting sunk.

'What sort of ship does your German sail in?'

'He's not my German. I don't write to him any more.'

'Well, you know what I mean.'

'He's on a U-boat, as far as I know.'

'A U-boat! Golly! They're the ones that sunk that passenger liner, aren't they? Hundreds of people drowned. Simply despicable! They hide under the water and fire torpedoes from miles away. What cowards they must be!'

Stroma said nothing. It was a sneaky way to fight, but she didn't believe for one moment that Reinhard was a coward. It must take a lot of courage to go to war in a submarine.

Easter was at the end of March. Hamish had already broken up when Stroma arrived home from school and he had finally received his call-up papers from the Navy. He was to report for basic training in two weeks. Afterwards, he would join *HMS King Alfred* at Hove on the Sussex coast. Not actually a ship at all, he explained loftily, but a college on shore for training new officers. The navy had requisitioned a marina being built for the public and taken over all the buildings as well as the swimming pool.

'As soon as I've finished my basic training,

there'll be three months of officer training in *HMS Alfred,* and then I'll join a real ship.'

'What about Craigmore?'

'What about it?'

'Will you be able to come up there this summer?'

'Of course not. Even if I happened to have a bit of leave, there wouldn't be time. Have you forgotten there's a war on?'

No, she hadn't forgotten. But the Germans seemed to have stopped doing anything, as though they were bored with it too.

But in April, everything happened very suddenly. The German army marched into Denmark and captured Copenhagen while other German forces landed in Norway. British ships and troops were sent to help drive them out. Next, the Germans invaded Belgium and Holland and the papers were full of frightening news from the Continent. Mr Chamberlain resigned and a new Prime Minister was chosen – Mr Winston Churchill.

The Second Officer said scornfully, 'I've heard he's a drunk and half-crazy.'

The Old Man glowered across the wardroom table. 'I wouldn't count on it, if I were you. Never underestimate the enemy. The British aren't stupid and neither is Herr Churchill.'

'Well, they are certainly making fools of themselves in Norway at the moment, sir. We're running rings round them, aren't we? And we already have the Danes safely in our pockets, which only took us a day. Before long we shall have the Dutch, and then, no doubt, the Belgians. All the British have been able to do is to lay a few sea mines while, on land, their army retreats in chaos.'

He was an arrogant little sod, Reinhard thought: the sort that gave Germany a bad name. Nobody liked him, least of all his present commander, but he seemed blissfully unaware of the fact. On the other side of the table, Merten caught his eye. The Chief Engineer muttered something inaudible into his soup and the Old Man drummed his fingers on the edge of the wardroom table – always a warning sign.

'The Royal Navy are doing rather more than laying a few mines, my friend. They are also very busy hunting our U-boats. You'll change your tune when you're sitting under their depth charges.'

Unwisely, the Second Officer stuck to his guns.

'If they can find us, sir. From all accounts, they're not much good at it.'

'I think you'll find they'll improve with practice. The British have been rather good on the sea for a hell of a lot of years.'

The Second Officer persisted. 'It's also well-known that the French and British army commanders in France are at odds with each other, and that the French will be quite likely to lay down their arms when the time comes to confront us. Which would leave the British forces struggling on alone, their backs to the

126

wall. Our way would be clear to invade England. The whole of Europe will eventually be ours. Nothing can stop us.'

The Old Man banged the table suddenly with the edge of his fist, so hard that cutlery jumped and the pea soup flew about. The table, screwed to the floor, stayed in place.

'I'll tell you what will stop us. Cocky talk like yours. You can't even do your miserable little job on this boat without fucking up, let alone conquer Europe!'

The Second Officer's pale face flushed scarlet and he was silent for the rest of the meal.

But he was partly right, Reinhard thought. The British *had* been making fools of themselves in Norway. Their attempt to send troops to Narvik to help the Finns fight the Russians had ended in a fiasco. And the Panzer tanks were steamrolling merrily across the Lowlands. Germany had come a long way since the modest reclamation of the Sudetenland and, despite the Old Man's explosion, a conquest of Europe was not, perhaps, all that far-fetched. If they could take France then they would control her ports and U-boats would no longer have to go the long way round to reach the North Atlantic. England, of course, was another question altogether. The British people wouldn't take kindly to any attempt to invade their islands. Not kindly at all.

So far as their own U-boat had been concerned, the last patrol had been totally unproductive. Their orders had been to remain unseen, which had meant diving the second any enemy plane or ship was sighted. They had returned in vile Atlantic weather and rounded the north-east corner of the British Isles with engines at half-speed. On the bridge watch, they had been up to their waists in icy water. He couldn't remember ever being so cold, even on the worst training exercises.

A damaged starboard fuel pump had slowed them still further and then a signal had been received to hunt for survivors from a Luftwaffe Ju88 downed in the sea. Not surprisingly, hours of patient searching had proved fruitless. The aircraft would have sunk almost at once and even if the crew had made it safely into the rubber dinghy, there had been almost no chance of finding them in bad visibility and very rough seas. All in all, the trip had been an unpleasant and frustrating experience. Back in port, the damage to the fuel pump had taken more than a week to repair but no leave was granted.

Now they had put to sea once more and the boat was nosing her way gingerly northwards through the waters of the Skagerrak – heavily mined by the Royal Navy so scorned by the Second Officer. They encountered the usual fishing vessels, always suspect in case they informed the enemy of their position. A British destroyer was sighted and they had to crash-dive to avoid being spotted – bells sounding, red lights flashing, the lookouts tumbling down the conning tower ladder, the hatch slammed and sealed above them.

The orders to wait around unseen meant staying submerged for hour after hour, only surfacing to recharge the batteries and ventilate the boat. From time to time they came up to periscope depth so that the Old Man could take a good squint round.

At last, fresh orders came to proceed to Narvik as fast as possible. The U-boat plunged northwards through heavy seas, waves breaking over the bows and crashing down in torrents on the fo'c's'le. On watch on the bridge, Reinhard had to keep wiping his binoculars over and over again in a monotonous ritual – glasses up to sweep the horizon, glasses down to clean them, glasses up again. The one consolation was that if they could not see clearly, then neither could they be seen.

By the following day, the sea had grown calmer and visibility improved. The Old Man's eyes stayed glued to the periscope and, as they approached the Norwegian coast, he spotted three large British transport ships, a cruiser and two freighters at anchor, busy landing men and equipment on to the rocky shore. Sitting ducks! The U-boat crept closer in the full moonlight.

'Damned moon.' The Old Man ground his teeth. 'We'll stick out like a tart's tits.' He waited for a dark cloud to come along. 'Stand by to attack. Bring all tubes to ready. Range two thousand metres.'

'All tubes clear, Herr Kaleun.'

'Los!'

The U-boat lurched as the torpedoes left their

tubes with a hiss of compressed air and the cox'n counted the seconds out by his stop-watch. Reinhard held his breath, waiting for the explosions. But nothing happened. No explosion, no flames, no terrible shriek of metal being torn apart. Silence.

Either they had miscalculated badly or the torpedoes were duds and had veered off on their own sweet course. It was known to happen quite frequently. The Old Man was swearing and barking questions, but it seemed that there had been no careless mistakes. The torpedoes were at fault, not the crew.

They surfaced to recharge the batteries and load the remaining torpedoes and by the time they returned to attack the same ships the day was dawning. The next torpedo veered wildly off its target and hit the rocks on the shore with an explosion that sent debris flying high into the air – clear and unmistakable evidence of their presence. They might as well have sent a signal to the British ships, Reinhard thought. 'We're over here. Come and get us.' As the U-boat turned to flee, it ran slap into a sandbank and stuck fast. Now *they* were the sitting duck.

'Stop both engines! Full astern together! All men not needed below, on deck at the double!'

The Old Man was rattling out orders at machine-gun speed. The ratings sent on to the decks began tramping to and fro, backwards and forwards, trying to rock the boat free while the Engineer let compressed air into the forward trimming tanks, expelling water in a hiss that might have been heard in Narvik. At the stern, the propeller blades churned the mirror-calm Norwegian coastal waters into a frantic white froth.

Well, this is it, Reinhard decided. *A quick end to my short and so far inglorious career in U-boats. In a moment, the enemy will be firing shells, or dropping bombs on us, and my corpse will be floating food for the fishes – just as I feared. Father and Bruno will be very upset, of course, and the Reeperbahn girls might be rather sorry, and Katrin in Berlin would certainly weep.* Stroma, though, would shed no tears – if she ever heard about his end. He was the enemy now.

The ratings went on tramping to and fro, the propellers thrashed away and, gradually, the boat began to rock until it heaved itself free of the sandbank.

'Half astern! All men below!'

The U-boat slid away into deep water and dived out of sight.

The homeward trip was uneventful except for the frequent sighting of enemy planes or destroyers forcing them to dive again and again.

They had been spared to fight another day. Either the British had been too busy landing their forces to notice their presence, or Lady Luck had been on their side. As for the dud torpedoes, full investigations were promised by the Flag Officer.

Only a handful of enemy ships had so far been sunk by U-boats since the war had begun, which was disappointing but, elsewhere, the news was good. The Panzers had broken through the Ardennes and crossed the Meuse into France, and the British forces were being systematically driven out of Norway.

Question 5. When Elizabeth Bennet first meets Mr Darcy she believes him to be proud and disagreeable. Why does she eventually change her opinion?

Outside, the sun was shining and in the examination room it was hot and stuffy. Heads were bent, pens scratching away. Miss Dunn, the invigilator, got up from her seat on the dais and walked slowly up and down the aisles between the rows of desks, making sure that nobody was cheating.

It wasn't a difficult question. English Literature was one of Stroma's best subjects and she knew *Pride and Prejudice* practically by heart, but her mind kept wandering. Whether she passed her School Certificate or not no longer seemed to matter – not after what had happened in France and what might happen now in England. Paris had fallen to the Germans. They had driven their tanks all the way across Europe and their soldiers had been goose-stepping down the Champs Elysees. Adolf Hitler himself had been to see the Eiffel Tower.

There didn't seem very much to stop them doing the same thing down the Mall. Just the English Channel, and it wasn't very wide. 'A moat', Shakespeare had called it. Everyone expected Hitler to try to invade very soon. And if he succeeded, it wouldn't matter a row of beans why Elizabeth changed her mind about Mr Darcy. Miss Dunn stopped beside her desk and frowned. Stroma bent her head again and began writing.

At the end of the summer term, she went home to London for the holidays. There was no question of her going to Craigmore; not with the invasion threat. Nor was there any question of her leaving school, as she had wanted. She was to stay on for two more years and take her Higher School Certificate, the parents said. She wasn't old enough to be called up and, as they had pointed out, she would be far safer at school in the country than in London. Not only German troops, but German *bombs* were expected. Hundreds of air-raid shelters had been built all over London and there was now one at the bottom of their garden – an ugly corrugated iron thing sunk into the mud and full of slugs. When the bombs started coming, they were supposed to go down there and, if it was night-time, sleep in the bunks. Shop windows had been boarded-up, statues taken away, anti-aircraft guns set up in the parks, yet more trenches dug, yet more sandbags piled high, miles of barbed wire unrolled.

In August, she went to stay with Rosanne's family near Reigate in Surrey. Rosanne's brother had been posted missing at Dunkirk and there was still no news of him. Rosanne was convinced he had been killed and Stroma did her best to cheer her up.

'He might have been captured and made a prisoner-of-war.'

'We'd have heard about it from the Red Cross by now.'

'Not necessarily. Our neighbours' son is missing, too, and they haven't heard anything either. Please, don't give up.'

The air in the house felt heavy with grief. Rosanne's mother tried hard to be cheerful but her eyes were red from crying and the father barely spoke. Mealtimes were sombre and silent – the clink of knives and forks loud against plates, the grandfather clock ticking away like a metronome. A framed photograph of Jeremy in his army uniform looked down on them from the mantelpiece. He looked very decent, Stroma noticed, which somehow made it all the worse.

One sunny afternoon they went for a long walk. From the back of the house, cornfields stretched away into the distance and, in the nearest field, a tractor towing a reaper was chugging round, the ripe corn going down in swathes before the knives. They leaned their arms on the five-barred gate and watched.

Stroma looked up into the blue and cloudless sky, shielding her eyes from the sun. Far above them, two shapes wheeled about like birds, the sun glinting off their wings. Only they weren't birds. They were planes. Fighters. One was chasing after the other, both of them twisting and turning. They had left vapour trails behind them – a pattern of white skeins like tangled wool against the blue. She caught hold of Rosanne's arm and pointed upwards.

Though they could see the two planes, they couldn't hear them – not until they came much lower and they heard the roar of their engines and the sharp stutter of gunfire. They flung themselves to the ground by the gate as the fighters streaked overhead. The leading fighter had RAF roundels on its fuselage and wings, the one that followed had sinister black crosses. The RAF plane banked sharply when it reached the trees at the edge of the field. One wing broke away suddenly in pieces and the rest of the plane hurtled on over the hedge and nose-dived into the next field, exploding with a bang that made the ground shake. Flames and black smoke rose up into the air and there were more explosions and a terrible stench of burning rubber and fuel. The German fighter shrieked past and circled the field triumphantly before it climbed away. Rosanne was screaming and screaming.

The tractor driver crawled out from under cover of his machine and ran towards the gate in the hedge where he stopped and stood staring into the next field. An inferno of flames was crackling away merrily, thick black smoke billowing upwards, Added to the stench of burning fuel and rubber was another horrible smell that might have been burning flesh.

The tractor driver was still staring over the gate. Rosanne had stopped screaming. There

135

was nothing any of them could do. They waited until a fire engine came bumping and swaying along the edge of the field, its bell ringing urgently and pointlessly.

Stroma went home at the end of the week. The newspapers were full of reports of the battle taking place between the RAF and the Luftwaffe. Streams of German bombers were coming over every day to bomb the aerodromes in the south of England and with them came German fighters, like the one she and Rosanne had seen. There were lists of casualties every day in *The Times* – RAF, Royal Navy and Army.

Towards the end of August, Hamish turned up on leave, looking very smart in his sub-lieutenant's uniform. He had finished his training at HMS King Alfred. Soon he would be off to war. He would be 'in the thick of it', he told Stroma enthusiastically.

'Where will they send you?'

'Don't know yet. It's on the cards that we'll be sent to stooge around the Channel – just in case the Germans are stupid enough to try and invade us.'

'Everyone seems to think they will.'

Hamish shook his head firmly. 'Well, I don't. They haven't yet succeeded in wiping out the RAF, and they'd have to do that before they have a hope. Anyway, they won't get past the Royal Navy, I promise you.'

'Will it be a destroyer, like you wanted?'

'Don't know that either. I hope so. They're

terrific attack ships and I can't wait to have a real crack at the U-boats. They'll be infesting the North Atlantic. They've got it far too easy now.'

'How do you mean?'

'Since France fell, you chump. The Germans have occupied all the French ports on the Atlantic so the U-boats will be camped right on the doorstep. Before that they had to go hundreds of miles to get anywhere near our convoys. Still, we've got a lot of new tricks up our sleeve, so they won't be having it all their own way, I can tell you.'

Hamish stayed for a few more days before he received orders to join his ship at Liverpool. To his disappointment it wasn't a destroyer in the end but a Flower class corvette, and, to his disgust, her name was HMS *Buttercup*.

The Germans bombed London on 7th September. It had been a beautiful sunny day and Stroma had spent it reading a book in a deckchair in the garden; she was still there when the air-raid siren suddenly started wailing. Her father was at the hospital, but her mother came running out of the house, carrying Delilah under one arm and a struggling Kipper under the other. They went and sat in the Anderson shelter with the slugs. Delilah settled quietly on one of the bunks, but Kipper, claws bared, escaped outside with an indignant yowl. Cats weren't stupid.

The bombers were evidently heading towards

the East End of London – hundreds of them, by the sound of it. The drone of their engines was like the rumble of thunder, and their bombs screamed as they fell and exploded with a dull crump. The raid went on until past four o'clock the next morning and when Stroma and her mother crawled out of the shelter at the All Clear they saw that the whole eastern sky was fiery red.

The bombers had gone for the docks. There were frightening photographs in the newspapers – pictures of blazing warehouses, terrace homes reduced to rubble, fire hoses snaking through dockland streets, exhausted firemen, wounded civilians and bodies.

And the bombing went on and on. Night after night, regular as clockwork, the German planes came over to bomb London – not just the East End now, but the rest of the city. The first ones would drop their incendiary bombs to set fire to buildings, then the ones following would aim for the fires. The anti-aircraft gunners did their best with ear-splitting barrages, so did the searchlight crews and the balloon operators, but they couldn't halt the Germans. Stroma's father was dealing with casualties at the hospital and hardly ever came home, and she and her mother spent the nights in the shelter where spiders had moved in to join the slugs. They took blankets and pillows but sleep was impossible with a raid going on overhead. How could you fall asleep when any moment you could be blown to smithereens? Stroma lay wide awake, listening to the bombers and the bombs and the guns while Delilah, oblivious to it all, slept curled up at the end of the bunk.

She went back to school by train for the start of the autumn term. Paddington Station had lost most of its glass roof and evacuees crowded the platforms – little children wearing luggage labels tied to their clothes and herded by large WVS women in green and maroon uniforms. Some of the children were crying but most of them were dazed and silent. Out in the country it was peaceful and although there were air-raid shelters at the school and everyone carried gas masks, they were never put to use.

The Germans went on bombing London and in November they started to attack other cities – Coventry, Birmingham, Liverpool and Bristol. Southampton, Portsmouth, Plymouth, Sheffield, Manchester. Coming back from school for the Christmas holidays, Stroma saw the damage as the train approached Paddington. Houses destroyed or blown wide open, floors collapsed, curtains left hanging at shattered windows, fireplaces still clinging to walls, a bath balanced crookedly on a beam.

The house opposite Stroma's home had taken a direct hit and the family who had lived there were all killed. Up and down the road, windows and doors had been blown out, roofs wrecked, broken glass and shrapnel swept into the gutters.

Hamish wrote a letter. Of course, he couldn't say where he was or anything about his ship.

Just that he was fine, that the food was OK and that he was learning a lot.

Christmas was quiet – not counting the air raids. The blackout and the bombs made going out to the cinema or theatre risky, so it was boring too, and most nights were spent in the shelter at the bottom of the garden. Condensation ran down the iron walls, the blankets felt ringing wet and there were pools of stagnant water on the floor.

On the last night of the year, Kipper went missing. As usual, he had refused to come near the shelter and he didn't turn up for his breakfast in the morning. Stroma hunted all over the house and garden, and walked up and down the neighbouring streets, calling his name, but there was no sign of him. He was never seen again.

1941

The U-boat left the port of Lorient in France on a bleak January morning. The off-duty watch were lined up smartly on the upper deck and an army brass band played on the quayside where a large crowd had gathered. Reinhard had a clear view of the scene from the winter garden behind the bridge: the musicians puffing and blowing, their jack-booted conductor chopping away with his baton, the crowd's faces all turned to watch the boat casting off – other U-boat men, soldiers, dockyard workers, nurses from the military hospital. It would have been much the same in his father's day, in a different war.

A small number of the watchers were French girls. Among them, he noticed, was Celeste, who had enlivened his shore leave. He could see her wearing a coquettish little red hat with black feathers, standing on tiptoe to wave and smile and blow kisses. He rather despised her and the other French girls for giving themselves so willingly to the enemy occupiers of their country, but perhaps he ought to despise himself instead? In any case, it was very likely that some of them were actually informers who would give away the time of a U-boat's departure to the enemy. Perhaps Celeste herself, who was still blowing kisses? And, if not the whores, then the dockyard workers. There were ears listening and eyes watching everywhere.

The massive bomb-proof concrete and steel-doored bunker that would provide a row of pens for the U-boat flotillas was beginning to rise up against the skyline. Before long, boats returning from a patrol would be able to enter a flooded pen directly and tie-up well out of sight and reach of the enemy. They would be repaired, refuelled, re-armed, re-stocked under safe cover and emerge again like wolves quitting their hidden lair. He liked the analogy: it was apt. A U-boat was very much like a wolf – a sleek, grey killer that hunted its victims by stealth and cunning, sometimes in packs, sometimes alone. And other captured French ports would provide similar lairs – Brest, St Nazaire, La Pallice, Bordeaux ... all within easy reach of the North Atlantic and the enemy.

Powered by electric motors, the boat glided on silently through the oily harbour water, past derricks and buoys, past a rusty old freighter lying at anchor. A patrol boat armed with anti-aircraft guns accompanied them like a vigilant nursemaid, and seagulls provided a winged escort, swooping around and over the boat, screeching a raucous salute, and flapping their wings in a – probably mocking – farewell.

The grating beneath Reinhard's booted feet and the iron railing under his gloved hands began to shiver and shake as the diesel engines started up. Their first uneven rumblings settled to a strong, regular beat and the sound of the jolly brass band music had faded away. The U-boat emerged from the port's outer basin and turned her bows in the direction of the Atlantic Ocean, leaving her patrol boat and her seagull escort behind.

As usual, they kept a sharp watch out for enemy aircraft. The Old Man, a squat, square figure in his thick grey leather coat, cleared the upper deck of men, preparing to crash dive if necessary, and ordered a zigzag course. He scanned the sky repeatedly through binoculars, head tilted back, the white crown fitted to his cap marking him out distinctly from the rest, plain for all to see. The boat's commander. The man who carried their fate in his hands.

'Thanks to our French friends ashore, the enemy will know exactly what time we cast off and they'll be waiting for us to walk into their parlour. We must make quite certain that we disappoint them.'

The remark was addressed to nobody in particular but those left on the bridge paid it very good attention.

The boat had provisions for a long patrol – every available space was crammed with supplies. Loaves of bread, sacks of potatoes, strings of sausages and hams hanging from hooks, boxes of apples and lemons, onions, eggs, jars of pickles, dried fruit and stacks of tinned food for when the fresh supplies ran out or turned too mouldy or rotten to be eaten.

The North Atlantic weather was abysmal. Howling winds, mountainous waves crashing over the conning tower, torrential rain, then driving sleet, visibility virtually nil. Impossible to see through the binoculars on a watch, no matter how assiduously one wiped them; impossible to keep a steady footing on a deck see-sawing wildly like a runaway rocking-horse; impossible to keep the lash of salt spray away from one's face and eyes or the icy sea-water from finding its way beneath the oilskins and into boots. At the end of his four-hour stint Reinhard staggered down from the bridge soaked, frozen and exhausted. His eyes were red, the skin on his face flayed raw, his arm muscles aching from the weight of the binoculars. He shed the oilskins and his sodden clothing and rolled naked into his bunk. Lay there inert while the boat corkscrewed violently around him. A slug of schnapps might have done some good but that was forbidden. Even a cigarette would have soothed, but smoking was only permitted out on the bridge.

At mealtimes, the boat's loudspeakers relayed German broadcasts of martial music, the sort that the farewell brass band had played on the quayside, or stirring passages of Wagner. Someimes, the radio man played his own favourite records instead, often producing groans of protest.

There were regular news bulletins from Berlin informing them that the Luftwaffe were still bombing London and other English cities to rubble while the British cowered cravenly in their shelters. Mr Churchill's vainglorious speech-making was fuelled by brandy and fooled nobody. An attack on Bremen by the Royal Air Force had been an abject failure and another attempt to bomb Emden had been equally unsuccessful. There was nothing to fear from the RAF incompetents. A National Socialist talk followed on the stupidity and evils of the enemy, the superiority of the German peoples and of their proud Fatherland. The Second Officer kept nodding his head in silent agreement, which earned him yet another furious blast from the Old Man who had plenty of respect for the enemy and very little for the Nazi Party.

'Only a cretin pays any attention to that propaganda crap.'

'But surely it's only the truth, sir.'

'If you believe that, then you're an even bigger fool than I thought.'

One thing was undoubtedly true in Reinhard's eyes: the Luftwaffe had been bombing London and several other British cities. A lot of damage had been done and many civilians killed. What had happened to Stroma? She could have been in London for the Christmas holidays but, by now, she should be back at her boarding school in the country and therefore safe. He could not picture her cowering in a shelter. She was more likely to be standing outside it, shaking her fist at the Luftwaffe bombers.

Cursing all Germans!

The U-boat headed west, its destination a secret from all but its commander. Signals and orders were sent to the Old Man in a code that only he could unlock. The rest of them were left to speculate.

Within a week officers and crew began to look less like an elite force of the German Navy and more like a gang of cut-throats. They were unshaven, unwashed, unkempt, their clothing a weird mix of official-issue uniform and personal preference, including enemy battle dress blouses abandoned by the Tommies when they had fled from France and woollen check shirts pilfered in large numbers from the defeated French.

The remaining fresh food was rapidly going bad, including the stock of lemons intended to be sucked daily against scurvy. The bread was riddled with pockets of green mould that had to be cut out like gangrenous flesh, the rancid butter smothered with jam to cover up its taste, the green on the sausages scraped away. Most meals now came cured or out of tins but wherever the food came from it tasted of U-boat – a particular taste of diesel oil and bilge water, strongly flavoured with mould.

The 4711 eau de cologne did little to sweeten the boat's foul atmosphere but was useful for cleaning off the sea salt encrusted on faces after a four-hour watch on the bridge. The boredom of an uneventful patrol was more difficult to remove: same routine, same faces, same irritating personal habits of other men. The rating who sometimes played the accordion in the bow compartment increasingly got on other men's nerves, even with 'Lili Marlene'.

Then, suddenly, the Old Man received orders to attack a convoy on its way across the Atlantic to England and they went to battle stations. Other U-boats in the area had been alerted and the grey wolves, let off their leash, gathered in a hungry pack astern the convoy. They closed in as darkness began to fall.

With the boat trimmed at periscope depth, the Old Man was crouched at the lens in the conning tower, a huge oil tanker in his sights. A big prize. Reinhard could see him licking his lips in just the way that a wolf might savour an especially juicy victim. The torpedoes were in place, the tubes flooded, the bow doors opened, the settings for speed, course and depth minutely adjusted. It was to be a salvo of three torpedoes at a range of five hundred metres.

'Achtung ... Los!'

'Torpedoes running,' the hydrophone operator reported.

They waited.

The explosions, when they came, were muffled booms that were followed later by an unearthly shrieking and cracking and tearing – the sound of the tanker breaking up. Their previous kills had been small beer compared with this one – a couple of freighters and an antiquated steamer – but the oil tanker was a prize indeed. Oil was vital to the enemy, as precious as liquid gold; without it, they could not wage a war. Reinhard could not see the sinking ship – only the Old Man could do that through the periscope – but he could picture its death-throes: dense smoke, gigantic flames, spilled oil surrounding the tanker with an impassable ring of fire, fanned to an inferno by the wind. Nothing could be done about the men who would be frantically lowering lifeboats or hurling themselves into the burning sea. An enemy escort destroyer was approaching fast and the Old Man had given the order to crash dive to eighty metres. The question, now, was not about saving the enemy but about saving themselves. They were no longer the hunter but the hunted.

The hydroplane operator was turning his wheel. 'Screws bearing zero-four-five, sir.'

'Steer zero-five-zero,' the Old Man said very quietly. 'Slow ahead both.'

The British destroyer's ASDIC pinged loudly and insistently against the U-boat's hull as it drew closer. The ship passed by overhead, propellers thrashing.

They went deeper to a hundred metres and began creeping away at a dead slow speed, trying to make an escape – whispered orders, no unnecessary noise or movement – but a second enemy escort had joined the first. Eight depth charge explosions rocked the U-boat violently, and they were thrown about the hull like dice in a shaker. Glass shattered and the lights went out, leaving them only with torch beams until the emergency lighting took over. There was other minor damage but no leaks. Not yet. They waited in silence, all machinery stopped so as not to betray their position, minimum movement and all talk in whispers. More eerie cracking and tearing sounds reached them as other ships in the convoy were sent on their way to the bottom. The rest of the wolf pack was busy.

Propellers churned back and forth overhead and depth charges went on exploding deafeningly above and around them. The boat shuddered and rattled and rocked, thrown this way and that, and Reinhard, grabbing at a metal pipe to keep his balance, could feel cold sea water dribbling down it beneath his hand. At any moment now the hull might cave in and that would be the end. A quick end, thankfully, and more merciful than it had been for the crew of the burning oil tanker. The depth charges were now so close and so violent that the submarine reared up on its stern like a frightened horse to fall back again.

It continued for several hours and it was impossible not to flinch at each explosion, though the Old Man, braced against the chart table, hadn't moved a muscle so far. Some of the men looked terrified – well, only a dolt would feel no fear – but the officers took their commander's lead. It was the Old Man's job to give confidence, as much as it was to give commands. Odd how almost everyone was looking up above their heads to where the noise was coming from, even though there was nothing to

149

see. The air was becoming so stale now that it was difficult to breathe.

But, at last, the enemy gave up and the churning of their propellers faded away. The Old Man gave orders to surface and the boat rose slowly, to emerge, water streaming from her hull, into a grey dawn. The conning tower was thrown open and clean, fresh air flowed down into the boat. Along with the men, Reinhard stood below the hatchway to fill his lungs.

Damage repaired, they continued westwards across the ocean. The weather was even worse. Much worse. In the officers' wardroom the steward had an impossible task as the boat pitched up and down and heeled over from port to starboard and back again like a thrill-ride at a funfair. What food reached the table soon left it, ending up in an inedible mess mixed with smashed crockery on the floor. The constant rolling and lurching was exhausting to the men and the U-boat could only make slow progress against waves like unscaleable walls.

At last, the Old Man gave the order to dive and they ran submerged for a while, untroubled by the weather. Though he was well used to it, Reinhard still found the silence of the deep eerie. A miraculous stillness and quiet reigned. No roar of wind or waves, no radio blasting away. Lights were dimmed, men off-watch lay on their bunks reading or sleeping and lowered their voices when they spoke. The loudest sound was the hum of the electric motors. Reinhard lay on his own bunk, hands clasped behind his head, listening to the peaceful snores of Fehler, the petty officer in the upper tier, a matter of centimetres above.

They'd been lucky that the damage had been moderate, but it had been a close brush with death – no doubt about it – and there would be plenty more like it. The Old Man didn't hang back when it came to engaging the enemy; he never chose the easy option. He hoped that, as and when his own turn came to command, he would exhibit the same conviction and inspire the same confidence in his men. If you couldn't do that, you'd no right to be a commander.

The cut-out photo of Stroma in her school uniform lived in a pocket of his leather writing case and he took it out to look at once again. The bunk light was dim, which made it even harder to see her. She had been fourteen then; now she would be almost seventeen. The grubby child would be almost grown-up. Almost a woman. He wished he could write a letter to her, but even if it were possible for it to reach her, what could he say? What good could it do?

Dear Stroma,

I hope you are safe and well in spite of being bombed for weeks by our Luftwaffe.

I am serving in a German Navy U-boat somewhere in the Atlantic Ocean and we are trying to sink as many British ships as possible, especially the ones bringing food and fuel to help you. As a matter of fact, we have just sunk a very big oil tanker belonging to the Merchant Navy and a lot of its crew were burned in the fire...

She would hate him.

They were ordered north to intercept a big convoy that had left the safety of Halifax harbour to begin its very unsafe journey across the Atlantic, bound for Glasgow or Liverpool, no doubt. There was no doubt either that it would be carrying all manner of very vital things for the enemy – food, armaments, rubber, oil, aircraft ... The Old Man was slavering already.

They found them in the mid-Atlantic and shadowed the convoy of forty ships until three other U-boats joined them. After dark, they all came to the surface for the attack.

Fifteen ships were sunk in that one night and on the next night another eleven. In the days that followed, as the wolf pack snarled and snapped at the heels of the scattered convoy, yet more ships were dispatched to the bottom – 290 gross tons in all. Their boat had scored ten ships and, as a nice bonus, they had also fished a dozen or so wooden crates out of the sea packed with tins of American Libby's fruit – peaches, pears, apricots, pumpkin, fruit cocktail – as well as tins of Carnation evaporated milk to go with them. The whole crew had a feast.

They returned to Lorient harbour at the end of the twelve-week patrol, their victory pennants fluttering aloft as they approached the quayside

– one for each ship sunk. They had put on their grey leather uniforms so that everything was grey – the men, their faces, the boat, the sea. The same band was playing the same music, and top brass officers were waiting to shake their hands. Girls in service uniform – some pretty, some not so pretty – presented bouquets of flowers and gave them kisses, and people crowded round to offer beer, wine, cigarettes and congratulations. Reinhard noticed that Celeste was not among them. Later, he found out that she had been arrested on suspicion of supplying information to the enemy.

The seamen fell on the letters waiting for them – letters from wives, parents, sweethearts who would have no idea whether they were alive or dead. The Naval HQ always waited for six months after a U-boat was overdue before posting them missing. There was a letter from his father and one from Bruno who had joined the Luftwaffe and was training to be a pilot. His father, naturally, was deeply disappointed, but it was no surprise to Reinhard. He had known for years that his brother's heart was set on flying.

Having shaved off his beard and scrubbed away the accumulated filth of the patrol in a hot shower, he joined up with Friedrich Merten and another first officer from a different boat to visit Paris. The three of them had a very good time indeed. They saw all the tourist sights, dined at the best restaurants and went to the most disreputable nightclubs. The French were only too anxious to encourage them to spend money, even if their welcoming smiles concealed their hatred.

On the third day, he met Mathilde in a café. It was debatable whether he had picked her up, or she him. She was a widow, she told him, and a countess. He didn't believe a word, any more than he believed that she was only thirty-seven years old. At least forty-seven, he reckoned – old enough to be his mother. But she had French chic and elegance and she supplemented his lessons from the girls in the Reeperbahn, teaching him more subtle, sophisticated ways. He was acquiring a French polish, he thought, amused.

For the last few days of his leave, he went home to Hamburg to see his father, who was still upset with Bruno.

'I tried to talk him out of it, to remind him of our strong family tradition, but you know how he is. He kept saying that we need pilots as much as we needed sailors.'

'He's right, Father. I've seen some of the damage the Royal Air Force have done to Hamburg on their recent visit.'

His father was dismissive. 'Nothing serious. I don't have a very high opinion of the British Bomber Command. It's all hit and miss with them – mostly miss. Even when they were dropping their ridiculous propaganda leaflets last year they fell in the wrong places.'

'But they'll learn from that, so we shall need Bruno to help keep them at bay.'

'Huh! I doubt they'll give you much trouble.'

He thought of the number of times they had been forced to crash-dive whenever an enemy plane was spotted and how close the bombs had always fallen, but he said nothing. Once his father had been in the thick of things and known all the secrets, but now it was impossible for them to discuss the subject.

The Reeperbahn girls had somewhat lost their appeal since France. Instead, Reinhard took a walk in the park, noting the early signs of spring – buds and fresh green shoots, grass growing, the weather improving. He now thought of it only in terms of U-boat operations. It would not be so vile out in the Atlantic, but not so vile for the British convoys either. The odds would probably remain about the same.

Back in Lorient at the end of his leave, he discovered that the Second Officer had been transferred elsewhere and that he was to take his place. He had been promoted to Leutnant zur See.

'Think you're up to it?' the Old Man, who had almost certainly engineered the move himself, asked caustically.

'Of course, sir.'

A grunt. 'Well, we'll soon see. I'm not putting up with another scheissekopf.'

Three ace U-boat commanders had been lost – Prien and Schepke had been killed in action, Kretschmer captured. Fresh tactics and tricks were required to outwit the enemy if they were to escape the same fate.

* * *

When the summer term finished, Stroma went up to Craigmore alone. Grandfather had asked to see her. He had asked for Hamish, too, but Hamish was away serving on his corvette somewhere at sea.

The train journey seemed to go on forever. King's Cross was crowded with service men loaded with kitbags and using them as battering rams. There were long queues everywhere – to buy a ticket, to get a cup of tea, to fight through the barrier on to the platform. Trains had been cancelled or delayed because of air raids and bomb damage.

There had been no question of getting a sleeper for the journey to Glasgow and she was lucky to find a spare seat in a compartment with seven soldiers. The blackout blinds were down and the blue bulb gave such miserably little light that she could hardly see the men sitting opposite. The corporal on her left moved up a bit so that she had more room. Where was she going, he wanted to know? When she told him, he said how lucky she was. She asked where they were going. He grinned and tapped the side of his nose. Careless talk cost lives.

They started to fall asleep and some of them snored. Eventually, she fell asleep herself.

The train click-clicked slowly over the points as it came into Glasgow. The corporal took down her suitcase from the rack and carried it along the platform for her as far as the barrier. When she thanked him, he gave her a smile and a salute.

'Look after yourself, sweetheart. And watch out for those wicked Jerries.'

She waved as he went back to join the others. His name was Denis – she'd learned that during the long journey – and he came from a place she'd never heard of in Kent. Just a village, he'd told her. A nowhere sort of place. She hoped he would watch out for the Jerries himself and get back home safely one day.

The rest of the journey went better. She caught the bus to Paisley and another to Gourock. Then she got a lift in the fishing boat to Dunoon and another one in the postman's bus which took her all the way up the glen and on to Portavadie. From there, she went by ferry-boat to Tarbert where she stayed the night at the small hotel in West Lock Tarbert, as she and Hamish had always done, and caught the first bus in the morning to Kennacraig and then the paddle steamer *Lochiel* over to Islay. For once, and it was rare, the sea was very calm and towards the last part of the four-hour crossing she went up on deck and leaned on the rail, watching for the first sight of her beloved island. The faint smudge on the horizon grew steadily larger until she could begin to see the soft contours of the green hills, the purple of the heather, the jumbled line of the rocky shore. Her heart beat faster because this was the place she loved best.

The paddle steamer entered the sound and continued up to Port Askaig – an important-sounding destination that was nothing of the

157

kind. Rather a grim and grimy little place, to be honest, with its weather-beaten cottages and shabby inn, but it was heaven in her eyes.

Normally, Grandfather would have been waiting for her with the old Humber, but this time it was Angus with a pony and trap. There was a deference when he climbed down to greet her that had not been evident before.

'Ye've grown, lassie. I dinna know ye.'

She understood that she was no longer a child in his eyes and that, from now on, he would treat her differently. It made her sad.

From Port Askaig they took the road across to Bridgend and turned south through Bowmore and Port Ellen, clip-clopping along at a good pace.

'How's Grandfather?'

'Nay so guid, but nay so bad,' was the enigmatic answer.

She said anxiously, 'He's not ill, is he?'

'I wouldna say that.'

'What would you say then?'

'That he's nay so guid.'

She knew that she'd get nothing more out of him.

As they passed the Laphroaig distillery it started to drizzle. Angus flicked the whip and the pony went faster, trotting along the long track that led from the road to Craigmore, the cart bumping and swaying over potholes and stones, past the peat bogs and down through the woods, until they came out above the house. When they drew up outside the front door

Angus handed her down. In the old days he would have swung her to the ground in his arms.

Logan opened the door, the worse for whisky, as usual, and more unsteady on his feet than ever. She found Grandfather sitting beside a peat fire in his study, and saw at once that he had lost weight and looked very thin in the face. But the hug he gave her was reassuringly strong and so was his smile.

She went to see Ellen, who was busy cooking supper on the range: a rabbit stew with a damson pudding to follow. There was no proper wartime rationing at Craigmore – they had plenty of fish and meat and eggs and milk and vegetables and fruit. But there had been changes, according to Ellen. Several men had been called up and left the island. Sally, the timid little kitchen maid, had gone to join the ATS – there was a disapproving sniff from Ellen about that. Meg still came daily to clean but – more sniffing – with her rheumatics she was getting as useless as Logan. Mack – the loudest sniff of all – was still as stubborn as an old mule, and ruder than ever. Even Angus wasn't the man he used to be.

'He's gettin' on, just like the master. It comes to us all in the end.'

She and Grandfather ate their supper on a small table in the library, beside the fire. Outside, it was still drizzling and drab – 'dreich', as the islanders called such weather. But inside the peat fire and the oil lamps gave a lovely warm glow to the room – to Grandfather's desk, topped with worn green leather, to the shelves of books lining the walls and to the giant map hanging on the wall, marking every detail of the estate, every loch and burn and wood and hollow, croft and dwelling, every bay and inlet. And Glas Uig.

After supper, Grandfather lit a cigar and sipped at his whisky.

'I've written a letter to Hamish to tell him what I'm going to tell you, Stroma. I wanted you both to know now, not later.'

'Know what, Grandfather?'

'I'm leaving Craigmore to you and Hamish in my will. Your grandmother and I talked it over before she died, and she agreed completely. When I'm gone, the two of you will own the whole estate together. What you do with it is for you and Hamish to decide. For one reason or another, you may think it best to sell, but I hope you will prefer to keep it and look after it, at least for some years. Your parents don't wish to be lumbered with Craigmore, and I don't blame them for that. It's a time-consuming responsibility far away from London, and your mother doesn't care for it here. But you and your brother are another matter. You both love the place and you're young with all the energy needed. What do you think about the prospect of owning it?'

She was trying not to cry.

'I don't know what to say.'

Her grandfather went on. 'You can't speak for

your brother, of course, Stroma, but you can speak for yourself. I'd like to know how you feel.'

'Craigmore belongs to you, Grandfather. I can't imagine anything different. That's what I feel.'

'Life always moves on, Stroma, as you'll discover. I can't be around forever, nor would I wish to be. Craigmore isn't the same without your grandmother, and I haven't the same strength or purpose to look after it. I'm rather depending on you and Hamish to take over my burden when the time comes. Do you think you could do that?'

She said unhappily, 'If that's what you really want.'

'It is. I'm very glad that's settled between us. Nothing more to be said.'

To her relief, he changed the subject and they talked for a while about the war. Her grandfather was unusually pessimistic.

'The Germans seem to be having most of the luck in Europe and Africa at the moment, and especially so in the North Atlantic. We may have sunk their *Bismarck* but their U-boats are sinking far too many of our convoy ships bringing us food and supplies; if we're not very careful we could be starved into submission.'

'That would never happen, Grandfather.'

'You sound very certain, my dear, but we have to find some way to stop the U-boats, and that won't be so easy – as I dare say Hamish would tell us if he were here. At the moment, the Germans seem to be holding all the cards. There have been sightings of U-boats off the island, you know. We're not far from one of their favourite gathering grounds where they lie in wait for the convoys to approach Glasgow. The RAF are bringing some of their Coastal Command flying boats to Bowmore to try and hunt them down, but the sea's a very big place. They're going to have a hard job finding them.'

She was silent for a while.

'Do you remember those Germans who sailed their yacht into Glas Uig years ago, before the war, Grandfather? You and Grandmother invited them to dinner.'

'I think so. A naval family – father and two sons.' Grandfather chuckled. 'Hamish was quite convinced they were spies, wasn't he? The father had been a U-boat commander in the Great War and had taken his boat through our sound. Some nerve!'

She said, 'The elder son, Reinhard, wrote to me afterwards.'

'I seem to remember forwarding a letter from him to you. You must have made a big impression. Did you answer?'

'Yes, we went on writing for quite a long time. After school, he went into the German Navy and was sent to serve on U-boats.'

'Keeping up the family tradition, I imagine,' Grandfather said drily.

'Then the war started, so we stopped writing to each other.'

'Well, there was no choice, was there? He was

162

very charming, though. Did you fall in love with him?'

'I was only twelve.'

'Your grandmother was just fourteen when we first met and I was eighteen. It only took two looks – one from me and one from her.'

'That's very romantic, Grandfather.'

'I've no doubt that this young man fell in love with you, which is why he wrote to you, and I don't blame him for that, but unfortunately we are at war with his country. He's the enemy now. So I'm afraid you'll have to forget him, Stroma. And he will have to forget you.'

'I'm sure he's already done that.'

Her grandfather smiled. 'Are you? You're not that easy to forget, my dear.'

Before Stroma went back to school for her final year, she went to see Rosanne and her family in the silent house near Reigate. Jeremy's body had been discovered in a wood near Dunkirk and Rosanne's mother had collapsed with grief, while her father had retreated into another world.

'I have to leave school,' Rosanne told her. 'So I can be here to look after them.'

'I'm awfully sorry.'

'Well, I never did like the place. We've always hated it, haven't we?'

'Yes.'

But lately, in the last year, Stroma had liked it better and she pitied Rosanne having to live in the silent house that was so heavy with grief.

'What will you do – besides looking after your parents?'

'I don't know. A boring secretarial course, probably. There's a place in Reigate. I could learn typing and shorthand.'

Poor Rosanne.

Before Stroma left, she took another look at the photograph on the dining-room mantelpiece: at the decent-looking Jeremy in his army uniform; a man who would never come home again. He was smiling at her, but it was a sad and wistful smile.

On the train back to London, she stared out of the window at the corn stubble fields and the dusty trees. *Please God*, she thought, *don't let it happen to Hamish.*

The forty-day patrol in October had been a triumph – six enemy ships sunk by their boat alone and eleven more claimed by other U-boats in the pack, all snapping at the flanks of the convoy. Enemy planes flying out of Canada had tried hard to drive them off but there was a fatal gap in the mid-Atlantic that was out of their range where convoys were left with only their seaborne escorts. With new and reckless daring, the U-boats had surfaced and gone down the lines between the ships, firing their torpedoes.

The wolf pack had pursued the remainder of the convoy across the ocean and as far as the west coast of Ireland, sinking three more freighters before British Sunderland flying boats had appeared in the sky like avenging furies, dropping their depth charges. The boat had had a narrow escape but, luckily, the damage wasn't too serious and they had slipped away and stopped later to carry out repairs in a sheltered bay on the south-west coast of Ireland.

'Charming people, the Irish,' the Old Man had observed blandly. 'Very sympathetic. No need to worry about any problems with them.'

Reinhard had been dispatched to take the rubber dinghy ashore with four of the crew, to see what could be foraged from the nearest village. As the Old Man had predicted, the natives were friendly and anxious to help. They had returned to the U-boat laden with bottles of Irish whiskey and Guinness, a side of bacon, eggs, butter, fresh bread and milk. Ashore, Reinhard had also seized the chance to leave a letter with the baker's wife and had paid her well to post it. The deutschmarks might come in useful to her one day, though she would probably simply throw the letter away.

Their welcome in Lorient was better than ever. A bigger band, even more high-ranking officers, a large crowd all cheering and waving, flowers, American cigarettes, French champagne flowing, smiling girls. One of the prettiest girls, a nurse, presented him blushingly with a single red rose which he slotted through a buttonhole before he kissed her.

He spent his leave in Paris again, living it up at The Ritz. Rather ironic, he thought, that the

French who had lost their war somewhat ignobly still dined like kings and the women still dressed superbly.

He could afford to splash out, after all. He had a very generous allowance from his father and an income from capital left to him by his mother, as well as his special U-boat service pay. And what was the point of economizing when the next patrol might be his last? Dead men didn't need any money. It was no trouble to find beautiful women to pass the time with; it never had been for him.

In December, Friedrich Merten was sent to do the commander's training course and Reinhard took his place as First Officer on the next patrol and, with it, promotion to Oberleutnant zur See.

'Your turn soon,' the Old Man said, 'if you keep your nose clean.'

Predictably, the Atlantic weather was vile. Hauling their fourteen torpedoes and 120 cannon shells, they charged through breakers whipped white by gale-force winds, looking for business. The U-boat's bow reared and fell in great spine-juddering jolts and below the deck, inside the pressure hull, a lunatic poltergeist was at work, hurling around anything that wasn't screwed or nailed down.

As it turned out, the new Second Officer wasn't up to his job and the Old Man turned as savage as a baited bear. Things went from bad to worse. A radio message came through with news of a convoy but it was too far away for them to reach. They battled on; and on. Still no enemy ships and still filthy weather. Several days later another message was received and the Old Man was suddenly all smiles – almost kind to the Second Officer. The Japanese had attacked the American fleet at anchor in Pearl Harbor in Hawaii and war had been declared between the United States and Japan and Germany. Restrictions on attacking American shipping no longer applied. The gloves were well and truly off.

It took another twelve days to cover the rest of the Atlantic and to reach the north-east coast of America where an astounding sight met their eyes. There was no blackout. At night, towns blazed with lights, ships were lit up, lighthouses and navigation buoys beamed at them brightly. They could fix their position with a hundred per cent accuracy from well-illuminated landmarks ashore. The Old Man could not believe his luck and kept rubbing his hands together.

At dawn, they sighted smoke on the horizon and closed in to attack a big American merchant ship. The polite old days at the war's beginning, when it had been customary to stop and search a vessel before sinking her, were long gone. Their opening torpedo struck her bow, the second, fired after her crew had taken to the lifeboats, finished her off. She was the first of a haul of more than twenty American ships sunk by five U-boats cruising up and down the eastern seaboard over the following days, and it was easy pickings. Their own special prize victim was another oil tanker. Two torpedoes got her. She exploded in a colossal mass of flames, two hundred metres or so high – the whole ship ablaze from bow to stern and all the water surrounding her was on fire. There was no hope for any of the crew. They could hear the agonized screams of men as they died; even the Old Man looked shaken.

One night, they slid into New York harbour waters and surfaced, like tourists, to admire the famous outline of the city – the Empire State Building, the Chrysler Building, the skyscrapers twinkling away and visible for miles. From the U-boat's bridge, Reinhard could see the car headlights moving along the roads, traffic lights changing colour, jolly Christmas decorations winking and blinking. All the ships in the harbour were clearly back-lit, presenting perfect targets.

What fools! What innocent fools!

In the wardroom on New Year's Eve, the Old Man raised his glass of beer, grinning from ear to ear.

'To our American allies – God bless them, every one!'

1942

The letter was lying on the hall mat. Stroma saw it when she came back from a shopping trip with her mother. They had been buying things for school – toothpaste, shampoo, soap, shoe polish, brown lisle stockings, that sort of thing.

It had come with the afternoon post and was lying on the mat with several others. She recognized the foreign writing on the envelope at once and hid it away in her coat pocket.

Upstairs in her room, with the door closed, she sat on her bed, holding the envelope. There was no name and address on the back, as he had always put before, but the writing was definitely his. The postmark was impossible to decipher and the stamp was a kind she had never seen before.

After a while, she tore the envelope open and unfolded the piece of paper inside. No address at the top and no date either.

Dear Stroma,

    I do not believe that you will ever receive this letter, but I write it in case I am able to send it to you somehow. I think of you often and I hope that you are safe and well.

It is now five years since I first saw you, but I still remember our meeting at Craigmore. You were twelve years old and you were wearing the clothes of a boy and your knee was bleeding. Also, I remember our game of croquet, and how I was so angry to lose. You thought I was a very bad sport, which was true. And I remember the beautiful sunset that we watched and how you played the piano afterwards. And I remember that you came with your brother to the Green Cove the next day to see our boat, *Sturmwind*, and that it was raining very hard. You had no coat or shoes and you were very wet. I was worried that you would catch a cold. When you left, I carried you over to the jetty.

You will soon be eighteen, I think, but I hope that you have not changed too much from the small girl I met on the island.

I will soon be twenty-three years old and I have changed very much. I am not sure that you would recognize me. I have a beard at the moment, so I am like a pirate and very dirty. It's better that you don't see me now.

My English is not so good because I do not have the chance to speak it for some time, or much time to think. Also, I do not have a dictionary with me. So, please excuse my mistakes. I have kept all the letters that you wrote to me, and I still have the photograph.

I am sorry that our countries are at war, and for everything bad that is happening. I hope that the war will soon be finished and that we will meet again. This is what I wish with all my heart.

From,
Reinhard

She'd forgotten about the knee but she could remember exactly how he'd looked and how tall he'd seemed to her. She remembered sitting next to him at dinner later and how she hadn't been very nice to him because Hamish had thought they were spies. In fact, she'd been rather rude.

Afterwards, they'd played the croquet match, which Reinhard and his brother had lost and which had made him angry. He'd been a very bad sport, and when she'd told him so, he'd apologized. They'd stood on the lawn, looking at the sunset, and talked about his dead mother, and about Hamburg where he lived and about her boarding school. When she'd told him that Hamish had thought they were spies he'd been shocked.

But we are not at war now. And they hadn't been – then.

She'd forgotten about the rain at Glas Uig the next day, because it was always raining, but she remembered that he'd picked her up and carried her to the jetty when they were leaving. She remembered that bit most of all.

Hamish came home for forty-eight hours' leave. In the evening, after dinner with the parents, he took her out to the pub round the corner where he drank several beers and smoked cigarette after cigarette.

The lounge bar was crowded and very noisy so it was difficult to hear what he was saying. Not that he could tell her much anyway – only the bare bones. Things were pretty bad, he said. The bloody Germans and their bloody U-boats were having it all their own bloody way, picking off the convoy ships like shooting game.

'We're chasing after them and getting nowhere. The trouble is finding the bastards, let alone destroying them. We can only do about twelve knots, which is useless, and they keep giving us the slip and getting away scot free. Our air cover's not good enough either. There's a gap in the mid-Atlantic which is out of range for the planes and, of course, the U-boats know it. That's exactly where the swine strike.'

Thank God he'd never find out about Reinhard's letter. Nobody would. She'd torn it up, thrown the pieces on to the drawing-room fire and watched them burn to ashes.

'You look dreadfully tired, Hamish.'

'I am. You've no idea what it's like at sea in a corvette in bad weather – we might as well go to sea in a bucket. The damn thing never stops pitching and rolling and everything's a shambles – on deck and below. You're soaked through and freezing cold. You can't get dry, or sleep, or ever stand up properly. And you get so tired sometimes you can't even think straight. The food's filthy – mostly corned beef and powdered potatoes – nothing else keeps. The only consolation is that it must be just as bad for the U-boat crews. Worse, in fact. I wouldn't be in one of those iron coffins for anything. We'll get them in the end, you know. We'll find out how to clobber them, and what a ghastly way to die! Caught like rats in a trap at the bottom of the ocean, suffocating slowly in the dark. No chance of escape. Just waiting for the end.'

She shuddered. 'How horrible...'

'Don't waste your sympathy on them, Stroma, for God's sake. They're ruthless killers and they deserve everything they get.'

He got up to fetch another pint from the bar. While he was gone an elderly woman sitting at the next table leaned over. 'Something wrong, dear? You seem a bit upset.'

She shook her head. 'I'm quite all right, thank you.'

When Hamish came back, they talked about Craigmore. He had got Grandfather's letter and the news had surprised him as much as it had her.

He lit another cigarette. 'I suppose I've always assumed that he'd leave it to the parents one day. They've never been that keen on the place, of course – Ma hates it up there, as we know – but I never thought he'd pass it straight on to us.'

'Nor did I. And I can't imagine Craigmore without Grandfather. How on earth would we manage to look after it properly?'

'Not too sure. I wouldn't want to spend all the time up there, would you? I mean, it's marvellous to visit, for the fishing and shooting and everything, but not for the whole year. We'd have to employ someone to run the estate for us, and keep on Angus and the men, and Ellen and Mack as well. Grandfather said he'd leave plenty of money for the upkeep, but personally I think we might be better off selling the place.'

'I'd hate that, Hamish. It would be a terrible thing to do. I love Craigmore. I thought you did too.'

'I do. But we're not kids any more, and when the war's over, things are going to be very different. We'll both have other lives to lead.'

'Supposing we don't win the war?'

'Of course we will. In the end.' He glanced at her. 'Don't look so tragic, Stroma. We don't have to decide anything about Craigmore right now. Grandfather's going to carry on for years.'

'I'm not so sure.'

'He was all right when you saw him last, wasn't he? He's not ill, or anything?'

'He didn't look very well, and he misses Grandmother.'

'Well, he would. But there's not much we can do about it. It'll be ages before I can get to see him and you're going back to school.'

'Worse luck.'

'Only two more terms and you'll be out of prison. What are you going to do then?'

'I want to join the WRNS – if they'll have me.'

'Lots of girls want to do that. The WRNS are pretty picky from what I hear, but I should think they'll take you.'

'There is a rumour that our Führer is opposed to us being kind to survivors. He would prefer us to shoot them.'

The Old Man's tone was conversational and his glance round the wardroom table invited comments. Nobody volunteered one.

He speared a tinned sardine on the prongs of his fork, waved it around. 'Well, Number One, what's your view?'

Reinhard said, 'That it wouldn't do us any favours in the long run, sir. The Allies would be less inclined to be kind to us, should we ever be in need of rescuing.'

'My own thoughts precisely.'

More than once, under the Old Man's order, they had provisioned lifeboats crammed with survivors and given them a course to steer for the nearest land. The Old Man had shouted out *Bon Voyage!* to them through the megaphone, and without a trace of irony. On one occasion a distress signal had even been sent off on behalf of the crew of a stricken freighter. Reinhard had drafted the message in English himself.

'And tell them to get a bloody move on,' the Old Man had urged him. 'Those poor sods won't last long in this weather.'

A war was being fought and ships sunk but there was no need for unnecessary savagery. Sailors had always gone to the aid of those in peril on the seas. It wasn't always possible, but where help could be given, it should be. Mostly, of course, it couldn't. Men went down with their ship or drowned in freezing seas unable to reach a lifeboat or raft. Or if they reached one, they soon died. There was also the inescapable fact that, unlike a surface vessel, there was no room in a submarine to take survivors on board. One or two, perhaps, but no more. The crew already took up all the hull and the only space left was out on the U-boat's open decks. What use was that, unless they happened to be very near land?

This time a patrol took them up the St Lawrence River, into Canada. Like a spider, they positioned themselves so that their victims came to them – merchant ships, laden with lumber and steel and crates of aeroplane parts, passed by in a slow parade as they set out for England. The corvette escorts swept the river from side to side, but their sonar beams were somehow distorted by the warmer, turbulent river water and the U-boats remained invisible, choosing their targets at leisure. It was almost too easy, Reinhard thought. Almost unfair.

Everything seemed to be in their favour now, even the weather and the long, black winter nights which gave them excellent cover. With such a low profile a surfaced U-boat was hard to see, even in daylight; in darkness it became virtually invisible unless there was a full moon shining or the Northern Lights happened to be putting on one of their spectacular shows.

More U-boats were being built and launched to join the battle. The wolves no longer attacked in ones and twos and threes but in packs of fifteen or more, prowling after the same convoy at the same time. And if the enemy escorts singled out one U-boat for attack, the rest of the pack pounced together on the neglected merchant ships. For the wolf packs this was a second 'Happy Time' – *'die Gluckliche Zeit'*. And the happiest fact of all was that the U-boats were sinking ships faster than the British could build them.

But how long could this state of affairs last, Reinhard wondered? Enemy planes were becoming an increasing threat. Fitted with radar, they could track a U-boat on the surface from miles away and attack as soon as it was in sight. As for the enemy ships, the convoy escorts were showing signs of having learned some useful new tricks. The Happy Time might soon not be quite so happy.

In May, they were lying in wait for a convoy in heavy seas and among drifting icebergs off the coast of Greenland, when a Canadian Air Force Catalina appeared without warning out of the clouds. It was too late to crash dive. The seaplane came in low, machine-gunning the decks and the bridge where Reinhard was standing. Four bombs fell along the boat's starboard side, sending great fountains of water high into the air. The aircraft circled and returned head-on towards them. The U-boats deck gun crew was ready but their single armament was a poor defence against enemy air attack and four more bombs dropped from the Catalina's racks. Again, they missed. It was very hard to hit such a narrow, moving target in rough seas.

They'd been lucky this time. No real damage to the boat and no casualties. The Catalina, all bombs spent, flew away, leaving them alone. Or perhaps not quite so alone ... ?

A second Catalina appeared, no doubt already tipped off by the first. Reinhard was last off the bridge, slamming the tower hatch shut and spinning the wheel to secure it as they dived.

A bomb exploded directly above them, tossing the boat about like a bath-time toy, and then another. He could hear the sea bubbling and roaring back into the vacuum. The Old Man gave orders to take the boat down further. They went to 100 metres and then deeper still, to 150 metres. More bombs exploded. There was nothing to do but sit there and take it.

They took it for four more hours. The second Catalina used up its bombs and went away but it was shortly replaced by another plane with a full load, and then a fourth plane after that one. And so on. A direct hit wasn't necessary to finish them off, as Reinhard well knew. All that was needed was for the detonation to be close enough to cause a rupture in the pressure hull – just as a hairline crack in an eggshell can destroy the whole egg. If that happened there was almost no chance of them being able to surface. They would sink to the very bottom of the ocean and if the hull wasn't crushed by water pressure they would go on sitting until their air supply finally gave out. Another possibility was sea water getting to the batteries, in which case they would all be choked to death by chlorine gas. Or the batteries that drove the electric motors under water, keeping the boat buoyant at a safe depth, might eventually run down. And since they could only be recharged on the surface, the boat would be forced to go up to face the waiting enemy. Of course, there was still the simple possibility of their air supply running out and the carbon monoxide level rising, which would be another urgent reason to surface.

No wonder there was terror in some of the men's faces. His own, he hoped, looked as inscrutable as the Old Man's who was leaning calmly against the periscope shaft, apparently engrossed in a book. Moving a bit closer, Reinhard saw that the book was upside-down. He smiled, but to himself.

Eventually the explosions stopped. Condensation from cold steel had run into the bilges and it dripped from pipes to soak their clothes. The air was thick with the reek of oil, urine, sweat and fear. They went on sitting, waiting to see if the enemy had really given up and left or was just fooling them.

The Old Man put aside his book. 'Stand by to surface.'

They rose slowly from the deep, up to periscope depth. The Old Man took a look round until he was satisfied that the coast was clear. He gave Reinhard a grim smile.

'Our enemy is improving, but he's still not quite good enough.'

The U-boat surfaced, shaking herself like a dog. They caught up with the convoy they had been waiting for and joined up with the rest of the pack. Three more enemy ships were sent to the bottom – well-laden merchantmen escorted by two destroyers, one frigate and four corvettes. The U-boats were attacking from every direction except ahead and the total pack tally was twelve ships sunk. But six U-boats were lost to the escorts. The enemy was certainly improving.

On their return to Lorient at the end of their patrol the U-boats and their men received the customary enthusiastic welcome. Reinhard was awarded the Iron Cross, First Class. Attached to a striped ribbon, it was presented by a jovial Korvettenkapitän with plump, white manicured hands. He had probably not been to sea for years, let alone out on patrol. Iron Crosses were two-a-penny, handed out like sweets to bolster morale and not to be compared with the well-deserved Knight's Cross won by his father and now presented ceremoniously to the Old Man who, it turned out, was only twenty-nine – not so old after all.

Even better than the Iron Cross, Reinhard was given the good news that he had been recommended for the commanders' training course. He was well and truly on the up.

In July, Stroma left school after taking her Higher School Certificate. A week later she posted her application to join the WRNS, together with two references – one from a titled godmother she hadn't seen for years and the other from Grandfather's old friend Colonel Crawford, who could be relied upon to say nice things about her.

She was interviewed at the WRNS headquarters at Admiralty Arch.

A Wren officer in a smart tricorne hat asked a lot of questions, including if she could type.

'I'm afraid not.'

'That's a pity. We need typists.'

'I can sail,' she said. 'I'd really like to be a Boat Wren.'

She'd heard about the Boat Wrens, who had a marvellous time swanning around harbours in cutters, ferrying naval personnel to and fro. They were allowed to wear bell bottoms and white lanyards and to do more or less as they liked.

The officer gave her a frigid stare. 'You can't pick and choose, you know. You have to do what you're told to do.'

She passed the medical easily and the WRNS seemed to have accepted her, so she signed on for the duration. The next step was basic training, which took place at a large house in west London where the bedrooms were called cabins, beds were bunks and the floor was the deck. The training consisted mainly of marching in ragged ranks, left, right, left, right, and then turning about to march back again, left, right, left, right. They also learned to salute – not the shielding-the-eyes-from-the-sun salute of the Royal Air Force and the Army, but the distinctive palm-outwards salute of the Royal Navy. She had been kitted out with uniform – rough navy serge skirt and jacket, white shirt with a stiff collar attached by fiendishly tricky studs, black tie, jaunty rating's hat – not the officer's elegant tricorne – unspeakable navy blue bloomers, black lisle stockings and heavy lace-up shoes. Her parents arranged for a studio portrait to be taken of her by a swanky photographer in Sloane Street and Grandfather was sent a framed copy to join the one of Hamish in his sub-lieutenant's uniform and the rest of the silver-framed family shots on the grand piano at Craigmore.

Reinhard was ordered to the U-boat commander's school in Neustadt on the Baltic coast, which involved a long and tedious railway journey. He joined a small group of prospective commanders and they practised on a simulator resembling the interior of a conning tower. The mock-up could be moved in all directions and they learned techniques, tricks and tactics, a good deal of which he had already gleaned from the Old Man. After two weeks he was sent to Danzig for active shooting. On the train journey he found a seat in a compartment crowded with Wehrmacht officers bound for the Russian front. Cigarettes were passed round. The soldiers seemed certain that they would easily overcome the Russians' stubborn resistance.

'We can afford to give them a few metres here and there,' one of them told Reinhard. 'Our lines will hold easily. They don't have our industrial capacity, you see, and their weapons are clumsy compared with ours.'

'All the same, I don't envy you the job.'

The man laughed. 'That's a good joke. I'd sooner be on the Russian steppes any day than in a U-boat.'

At Danzig, Reinhard's training started at dawn the following day when shooting practice began at sea with U-boats and surface vessels. The gruelling schedule was designed to train a commander to think and act fast in emergency conditions, to learn how to sense the enemy's next move, to know when to crash dive, when to stay on the surface and shoot, how to handle the U-boat under bombardment, how to deal with every imaginable problem that might occur. After four weeks, with very little time for sleep, he finished with the highest rating. He was assigned a brand new U-boat, still in the final stages of construction, and promoted to the rank of Kapitänleutnant.

He was given two weeks' leave and decided to spend the first one skiing in the Alps where the winter snows had already fallen. The train journey involved a change at Berlin. With a couple of hours to kill before his connection, he walked to Katrin Paulssen's apartment. As it was the weekend, he had reckoned there was a good chance of finding her at home, but there was no answer when he rang the bell. He rang several times and then stopped a middle-aged woman coming out of the building.

'I was hoping to see Fraulein Paulssen who lives here. Do you happen to have any news of her?'

'She doesn't live here any more.'

'Oh? Perhaps she has gone to her parents at Wegendorf.'

'I don't know where she is. They took her away several months ago.'

'Took her away? Who?'

'The Gestapo. They burst in here one night and arrested her.'

'*Arrested* her? What for?'

'Because she was Jewish. It has been happening all the time in Berlin. There was a lot of noise and she was crying. It was terrible. I don't know where they took her. Someone told me they send them to labour camps.' She was staring suspiciously at him, at his uniform, at the shiny new Iron Cross. 'Was Katrin a friend of yours?'

'I only met her once.'

'Well, I'm afraid you won't be meeting her again.' The woman turned and walked away.

He went back to the railway station and stopped at the café where he had seen Katrin sitting with her book *Further Steps in English*. He ordered a beer at the bar and then quickly asked for another. And then a third.

The Alpine resort was very peaceful. He had skied there with his father and Bruno a number of times before the war and nothing had changed. The chalet hotel still had its pine floors and its goose-feather beds, its overhanging balconies with wonderful views of the snow-covered mountains. The crisp, cold air was as invigorating as he remembered, the steep ski slopes as exhilarating. He skied from early morning until darkness fell, taking the most difficult pistes at top speed, taxing himself to the limit so that he had no time to think about the war, or about anything else. In the evenings, he drank and dined with other guests before he fell into bed to sleep soundly until dawn.

When he went home to Hamburg for the second week of his leave, Greta, their old servant, wept when she saw him and he gathered her up in his arms. His father had invited friends to the apartment to share in the reflected glory of his achievement – his Iron Cross and his promotion to commander of a U-boat. For his father's sake, he was polite and smiling at all the praise and compliments but he knew very well that the hard part was to come. He had yet to prove himself.

When the friends had all left, he talked to his father about Katrin Paulssen.

'It seems that she was arrested simply because she was Jewish – for no other reason. She wasn't a dissident or a trouble-maker; she did not belong to any political party, so far as I know. She was a blameless citizen, a nice girl doing an ordinary office job. What possible excuse can there be for such an injustice? How can such a thing happen?'

His father sighed. 'It would have been wiser for your friend to have left the country before, as many of the Jews have already done.'

'Why should she? Her home is in Germany.'

'I told you before, Reinhard, that I don't always approve of the Führer's methods, but without him we have no chance of prospering, and, worse, we risk Communist rule. Yes, he has certainly used the Jews as scapegoats, blaming them for many of our misfortunes, driving them out of Germany. And many people are only too pleased to see that happen. They resent the Jews for being so talented and successful and are thankful to be rid of them, often in order to step into their shoes. It's been very hard for those Jews that have chosen to remain. All these special laws about what type of work they may do, where they may live, where they may go, and so on ... Doubtless you are aware of them?'

'No, I am not aware of them, Father. It's not something we were taught at the Academy, or in any part of our training.'

'It will do you no good to get so angry, Reinhard. No good at all. Politics are not your concern. The Kriegsmarine has never been a political force, only a fighting one. Concentrate on what matters – winning this war for your country, preventing us from sliding back into that terrible mire again. That's what counts.'

186

Bruno turned up later in his Luftwaffe uniform, decorated with his pilot's wings, and more champagne was uncorked. Their father had got over the disappointment of his defection to the Air Force. He put his arms around their shoulders.

'I am so proud of my two sons. The whole of Germany will be proud of you and grateful for what you are doing.'

After their father had gone to bed, Reinhard and Bruno sat drinking brandy, smoking and talking. Like the soldiers in the Danzig train, his brother had complete faith in a German victory.

'The Royal Air Force have their good points, I admit – especially their fighters – but their bombers are useless. They're still dropping stupid leaflets and when they drop bombs they nearly always miss their target. Look what a mess they made of their last raid on Hamburg! Father says there was thick cloud cover and most of the bombs fell out in the countryside, miles away from the shipbuilding yards. And, thanks to you grey wolves, so busily sinking all their convoy ships, the British are in bad trouble. They have their backs to the wall and it shouldn't take much longer to finish them off completely.'

He rolled the brandy glass to and fro between his hands. 'The one small snag, Bruno, is that they're getting better at finding us. And the more they improve, the more of their ships will get through. The Atlantic battle's not over by a long chalk.'

'It's not like you to be pessimistic.'

'Not pessimistic. Realistic. Also, you've forgotten the Americans.'

'From what I hear, the Yanks aren't going to be any help. They didn't want to join the war in the first place and if it hadn't been for the Japs bombing their fleet they'd still be sitting on their backsides watching from the sidelines.'

'I didn't think they'd be much help either, but unfortunately they're fast coming to their senses. They've adopted the British convoy system and that's not good news for us. Not good news at all. And what about our former partners, the Russians?'

'They're more of a worry, I admit. Unlike the Yanks, they know very well how to fight and there are hordes of them. But our forces are far superior to theirs in every way.'

'We have to hope so.'

But the news from the Russian front was not good; the soldiers on the train had been very far from realistic.

They went on talking until late. It was a toss-up, Reinhard thought to himself later, which of them had the better chance of survival – Bruno in his Messerschmitt 109 or he in his U-boat. The odds were probably about even.

At the end of his leave he joined his First and Second Officers, Engelhardt and Mohr, and his Chief Engineer, Franz, at the shipyard where their U-boat was being completed. This was their chance to get to know her thoroughly and no demanding mistress ever received more assiduous or careful attention.

The rest of the crew arrived as the boat was being painted, its conning tower decorated with his chosen emblem – a flowing-locked Neptune rising from the deep, trident held aloft. Before they sailed he gave the customary commander's speech to his men assembled on the upper deck – part encouragement to do their best, part threat if they didn't, and the rest good humour. God knew they were all going to need it.

They went through two weeks of diving trials, silent running tests, dummy torpedo launches, reloading practices, testing the diesels and electric motors, the armament, the radar and sonar.

At a formal dinner on the evening before his U-boat's departure from Lorient, the Flotilla Commander rose to his feet to deliver a good-luck speech and to offer a toast in vintage champagne. They all drank a great deal as usual – and, as usual, Reinhard regretted it in the morning.

It was a good send-off. The brass band played a rousing march and the crowd waved and cheered as the boat backed slowly and silently away from the pier. Fifty metres out, Reinhard gave the order to start the diesels and the U-boat came to life, hull vibrating, screws churning the water at the stern into swirling white foam.

'Both engines half ahead together. Steer nine five.'

'*Jawohl*, Herr Kaleun.'

He was the Old Man now.

1943

Liverpool was a grim place. On the train journey from London, a Royal Navy rating, sitting with Stroma and six other Wrens in the compartment, had given them the gory details.

The Luftwaffe bombers had been going for the city ever since the war started, he'd said. Given it their full and undivided attention. The air-raid siren had never stopped wailing and the poor old place had copped it eighty times at least.

'Adolf's been after Merseyside and the docks, see. He wants to stop our ships landin' supplies there from across the Atlantic. We can't use our ports in the south no more – not since the Jerries nabbed France.

'The Luftwaffe came over Liverpool for eight nights in a row – hundreds of German bombers each night. Buildings blown to bits, corpses lyin' in the streets, people trapped in the ruins, old folks and little kids coppin' it with the rest of 'em, fires ragin' all over the city, thousands left homeless. Knocked the stuffin' out of the place for a while, I can tell you. Only Hitler didn't reckon with the Liverpudlians, did he? Didn't know about 'em. They're a tough lot.

Soon got back up on their feet. 'Course, it's all been kept out of the newspapers, so nobody else knows nothing about it, but you'll see for yourselves what's been happening.'

They saw indeed. Rubble, craters, shattered glass, boarded-up windows, blackened and burned-out buildings. It was raining hard and the cobbled streets were running with water that was choked and filthy with ashes and mud.

A truck took them from Lime Street station to Wren quarters in the Navy barracks. They'd been sent to become plotters at a secret Royal Navy and RAF Combined Services headquarters controlling the Western Approaches but, as Stroma had discovered from the other Wrens on the train, none of them knew exactly what plotting involved, nor did they know anything about the Western Approaches. A Wren Second Officer enlightened them with the aid of a wall map and a pointer.

'It's all to do with protecting our Atlantic supply convoys. Our convoys haven't been able to use our southern ports since the Germans occupied France and parked themselves on our doorstep.' The pointer tapped along the French coast. 'Brest, Lorient, Saint-Nazaire, La Pallice and Bordeaux have all become well-fortified German U-boat bases, very close to England and with direct access to the North Atlantic. So, the convoys have to head up round the north of Ireland and go into Glasgow and Liverpool instead.'

The pointer moved again.

'The Western Approaches is what we call this rectangular area of ocean off the western coast of Great Britain, where the enemy's U-boats are trying to blockade our supply ships. With some success, I'm afraid. Fortunately, we now have the eyes and ears to find out what they're up to and take action accordingly, and lately the U-boats have been suffering pretty substantial losses. All clear, so far?'

They nodded.

'Plotting is where you come in. You will be marking the position of the convoy ships and their escorts as they progress across the Atlantic so that the latest situation can be seen at a glance. You will also track any German U-boats that join the party. It's not difficult, but it requires absolute concentration for hours on end, so be prepared to get very tired. You'll be learning pretty much as you go along, I'm afraid. Basic instruction only – no time to spare for long training courses these days. You're going to have to jump in at the deep end and start swimming like mad straight away.'

Derby House on Merseyside looked innocent enough from the outside. There was nothing to show that it concealed the entrance to the secret headquarters. Down several flights of stairs lay a bomb-proof, gas-proof labyrinth of rooms under the streets of Liverpool, with ceilings and walls reinforced with concrete several feet thick, and where a desperate battle was being fought out in the Atlantic.

At the heart of the labyrinth lay the Naval Ops

Room – a vast room with a map of the North Atlantic Ocean spread out on a central table. The map, illuminated by overhanging lamps, was divided up into grids, while models and arrows marked the position and direction of the convoys and their Royal Navy escorts, of RAF planes and of reported enemy U-boats. Another map on a wall went as high as the ceiling, and had to be reached by tall ladders that could be moved along the length of the wall. There were other maps and charts on the same wall – a map of the British Isles and northern France, another of the east coast of America and Canada, and chalked-up blackboards listing the names of convoy escorts, the status of RAF aircraft, details of weather reports – all kept up to the minute. Service personnel sat at a long desk above the table map, banks of telephones in front of them and, on a higher level, the Commander-in-Chief of the Western Approaches and his senior officers observed everything that was happening from a glass-fronted cabin.

The noise never ceased: people talking, telephones ringing, teleprinters chattering, typewriters clattering. And the action never stopped. Map markers were constantly on the move, messages flooding in from all directions – from convoy escorts, from merchant ships, from Coastal Command aircraft. Notices were put up and taken down, charts chalked-up, rubbed out and re-chalked. Twenty-four hours a day. It was all Top Secret, and the most secret place of all was the decoding room, which was kept locked and guarded at all times.

They were given the basic instruction promised by the Wren officer and Stroma found it
simple enough to listen carefully to the information given through headphones and to
position the ships, planes and U-boats on the
table map with a wooden rake, or to climb the
tall ladder to alter the wall map.

But the Wren officer had been right about the
exhaustion. They worked in four-hour watches
over two days with a forty-eight-hour break
between. The four hours on and four hours off
made proper sleep impossible, and, while on
duty, there could be no lapse of concentration,
no question of letting the mind wander for fear
of a mistake that might cost men their lives. The
convoy ships and their escorts – sometimes as
many as sixty ships or more – zigzagged their
way steadily across the map of the Atlantic
Ocean while the U-boat packs shadowed them,
ready to pounce.

When things were going well, the Ops Room
was calm, almost quiet, but when they went
badly the tempo increased frantically, and so
did the noise. Stroma was on watch when a convoy from Halifax, Nova Scotia, was intercepted
by a pack of twelve U-boats in the mid-
Atlantic. More than half the merchant ships
were sunk, including one of the Royal Navy's
escort destroyers, and in icy winter seas that
gave almost no chance of survival.

The trick, she had soon discovered, was to try
to forget that the markers you raked to and fro

with such precision, and the sinking ships that you removed so deftly from the map, actually represented real ships and real men. You put it out of your mind and you kept your face as expressionless as a casino croupier. You tried not to think about a ship plunging to the bottom of the ocean, or about a tanker wreathed in raging flames, or about men dying in myriad horrible ways. A plotter had once burst into tears and had been sent off watch in disgrace.

Stroma was also careful to put the men in the U-boats out of her mind.

In spite of the grimness – or maybe because of it – there were always parties. A destroyer just returned from convoy escort celebrated a lucky crossing. Only one small merchant vessel had been lost, none of the escorts, and two U-boats had been sunk by the destroyer. A Wren on Stroma's watch had a cousin serving in the ship and took her along to the wardroom party. They wriggled their way through the mob to reach the lieutenant cousin and he introduced them to another lieutenant standing beside him. Both men were very smartly turned out – not a hair out of place, uniforms clean and pressed, buttons brightly polished. They looked as though they'd never been anywhere near a life-or-death struggle in the Atlantic. And yet she had been moving their ship through stormy seas and peril.

The other lieutenant said to her, 'I'm most awfully sorry, I didn't catch your name. There's such a racket in here.'

She told him. 'I didn't hear yours either.'

'Tom Lewis.'

'Congratulations on the two U-boats.'

'I don't deserve them personally, but thanks anyway. We've never even got one before, let alone two. It helps make up for all the others that got away.'

'Do they often get away?'

'Frequently. But I'm glad to say that we're getting a lot better at the game. All sorts of clever ideas thought up by the back-room boys. They won't be having it all their way for much longer. Actually, we fished some of our first U-boat crew out of the drink. Scrambling nets and all the rest of it. Ironic really, after all the trouble we'd gone to, trying to kill them.'

'What were they like?'

'Not so different from us. They weren't very grateful, actually, considering how nice and kind we'd been.' He smiled. 'Some of them didn't even say thank you.'

'How rude of them. What about the other U-boat? The second one?'

'They weren't quite so lucky, I'm afraid. Our depth charges got them. All we saw was wreckage.'

Serve them bloody well right, Hamish would say. This lieutenant might not use those words with her, but he was most likely thinking them.

She said, 'My brother's serving in a corvette. He says it's like going to sea in a bucket.'

'Corvettes do have that reputation.'

'I've heard U-boats can outrun them.'

'Another disadvantage.'

'But the U-boats can't outrun a destroyer, can they?'

'Fortunately not. Or we wouldn't be having this party. And I wouldn't have met you.'

It was a smooth remark but she could tell that he had meant it sincerely. At the end of the evening, he asked if he could see her again.

'It can't be for a while, more's the pity.'

The escort ships were never in port for long. There were too many convoys needing protection. Soon she would probably be moving his destroyer across the North Atlantic once more.

Reinhard had received orders to head westwards into AK 64, the square on the map where a British convoy had been sighted. They were to take up a position in a pack of thirty U-boats, remaining submerged except for brief periods. The enemy were getting a great deal better at using their radar and their planes had become damned pests, forcing them to crash-dive again and again. Worst of all, there was a new threat in the skies. The American B-24 bomber, dubbed the 'Liberator' by the British, had a long enough range to cover the gap in the mid-Atlantic that had previously been left unprotected. The old ruse of popping up to decimate a defenceless convoy halfway across was finished.

They had a few tricks up their sleeves themselves, of course: a new radar device that warned them of an enemy aircraft's approach; much improved torpedoes; new anti-aircraft weaponry, better radio reception to 30 metres depth. Some bright spark had thought up the idea of attaching strings of aluminium foil to balloons that were supposed to fool enemy tracking devices into mistaking them for a U-boat. But the British were seldom that foolish. Far from it. They were always hot on their trail. So much so that he sometimes wondered if they had somehow been able to understand the coded messages sent between U-boats and HQ. But that was surely impossible? The code was said to be unbreakable.

A U-boat ahead had made contact with their quarry and he received the signal to surface for the attack. They came up in time to catch the very last of the daylight. There was no moon; the sea was moderate for once, the wind blowing from the west. He went up on to the bridge and scanned the horizon to the north, leaning against the rail with the binoculars glued to his eyes. As yet, there was no sign of the convoy or of its escorts. Not a trace.

Beside him, Engelhardt said restlessly, 'They must be out there, sir. Unless it was a mistake.'

'It wasn't.'

He knew Nieman, the commander of the U-boat who had found the convoy – he had met him a number of times ashore, both drunk and sober. He was not the type to make mistakes.

'Don't be so impatient, Number One. Just keep looking.'

A moonless night-time attack on the surface

provided the best conditions for success. It was harder for them to spot their quarry, but once they had, they could get close enough to manoeuvre into the best position for attack without being seen. A submarine with her decks awash in a swell and only the conning tower above the surface was almost invisible. Reinhard sniffed the air, hoping to smell the convoy's smoke before it became visible, and ordered an increase in speed. The U-boat raced on, slicing through the waves. Their radar was picking up faint impulses from escort ships scanning the surface ahead.

Engelhardt said suddenly, 'Escort, starboard bow, three thousand metres.'

She was only a shadow and vanished again almost immediately, but not before Reinhard had identified her as a corvette. A tin box compared with a destroyer, but a tin box worthy of some respect: a corvette had almost succeeded in nailing them on the last trip. He knew all about His Majesty's Flower Class corvettes and their innocent names – Anemone, Primrose, Bluebell, Cowslip, Honeysuckle, Lavender – a fine example of English humour to name a ship of war after a pretty little flower.

He gave another command, calling for top speed, and the U-boat headed straight for the starboard side of the convoy, now visible.

The merchant ships always travelled in columns, with the escorts flanking them on each side, as well as ahead and behind. The most valuable cargoes, such as petroleum, generally travelled in the centre of the convoy – the safest place for them and the most dangerous for U-boats, though he had risked it often, penetrating the columns with the smaller escorts in hot pursuit. A tanker was well worth the risk.

He calculated the fine adjustments needed for speed, range and angle, picking three of the vessels as targets. Two torpedoes would be aimed at the largest and furthest ship, one each at the other two.

'Los!'

Four torpedoes left their tubes and he swung the boat round to run her parallel to the convoy and throw the escorts off the scent. In fifteen seconds the eels should hit.

A ball of fire erupted into the sky above the largest ship; he could feel the shock wave fan his cheek. The vessel had been hit on the bow and amidships and the flames engulfing her conveniently lit up her nearest neighbours. One of the other torpedoes had missed, but they scored a direct hit on the third ship – not as big as the first, but still a good size. Tonnage was what counted. Tonnage brought honour and glory and medals. U-boat commanders were judged and rewarded by the tonnage they'd sunk. He smiled grimly to himself as he prepared to increase his tally with a fourth cargo vessel, but the convoy had turned away on its zigzag course and the escorts came tearing after them.

He gave the order to dive and took the boat

down to 130 metres.

The escorts thrashed to and fro above them, criss-crossing the surface, their ASDIC ping-pinging loudly. Soon a series of depth charges exploded, then more, and still more, but at a distance. The sound of the convoy vessels' propellers and the pounding of their engines was making the escorts' job a tough one. Under cover of all the noise and fury, they slipped away.

He played the waiting game, letting three hours go by before they surfaced again to resume contact with the convoy. The sea was much heavier, the chase more difficult, the night even blacker. A white light showed suddenly on the port quarter. As they drew closer, he saw that it was the beam of a searchlight from a Royal Navy corvette directed on to a sinking merchantman – the victim of another member of the nine-strong wolf pack. The corvette was lying alongside the vessel, taking survivors on board. Reinhard observed the goings-on from the bridge with interest. The escort ship was only 700 metres away and broadside on to him. A helpless and stationary target. Her name was HMS *Buttercup*, he saw. *Butterblume*. The little yellow flower that grew in country meadows. He could remember holding one under a pretty girl's chin one summer many years ago to see if she liked butter. She did. And she'd liked him too.

The old-fashioned, chivalrous rules no longer applied. Those days were gone. It had become a savage fight to the death on both sides: dog eat dog. The corvette's captain would blow them to smithereens if he got the chance, but just now he was fully occupied in saving men's lives – not the lives of armed combatants but of ordinary merchant seamen. Stokers, cooks, deck hands – many of them older married men or lads not much more than children. He'd seen them huddled fearfully in lifeboats or clinging to wreckage. Their only hope lay in being picked up by one of their own escorts, which was in itself a very risky business for all concerned. As he was just about to demonstrate...

'Quite a gift, sir,' said Engelhardt. 'I almost feel sorry for them.'

He debated with himself for a moment, watching the hurried activity between the two ships through his binoculars. Finally he lowered the binoculars.

'We'll leave them to it, Number One. Just this once.'

He snapped out an order and they turned quietly away. He'd probably regret it one fine day.

In fact, he regretted it rather sooner than he'd expected. When they had caught up with the convoy once again and were readying to attack a heavily loaded freighter, a corvette burst out from behind another cargo vessel and rushed at them guns blazing. She was probably called something like *Sweet Pea*. They escaped but only because they could go faster. Soon after that, a destroyer sailing astern of the convoy chased them so recklessly that it was obviously intent on ramming them. Once again they escaped, but it took all his wits and cunning.

When dawn came, it brought with it every aircraft the enemy could muster. Everything from four-engined bombers to single-engined planes appeared in the skies, or dived out of cloud whenever the U-boat came near the surface. No sooner was the boat up than it had to plunge down again to avoid a hailstorm of bombs and bullets. A hit on the diesel tank would have left a long oil slick trail in their wake and finished them. Over and over again he had to save their skins while showing none of the strain. It was the commander's job to maintain morale. He had learned that lesson early on from Grindorff, his own Old Man. Forty-four men's lives were in his hands, each one depending on every decision and move he made.

During a brief time on the surface, they picked up a signal from one of the other U-boats: *attacked by aircraft; sinking* and then another signal: *aircraft bombs; sinking*. Nothing could be done for the crews. Either they would have gone down with their boat, or abandoned it, in which case they were at the mercy of the ocean and the enemy who might or might not stop to pick them up.

They carried on with the chase, pursuing the convoy doggedly across the ocean, surfacing to recharge their batteries whenever they had the chance. Another wolf in their pack, gnawing too close at the convoy's heels, was attacked by an escorting destroyer and was sunk too.

The dark night that followed gave Reinhard the chance to claim one more vessel, but she was only a pathetic old tub – a sad straggler unable to keep up with the convoy's pace. He took no pride in despatching her. Before the next day dawned, he had notched up a better kill, this time a large freighter that went down by the stern in a matter of minutes.

The fight went on for four more days – an endless succession of desperate crash dives and ear-splitting explosions that pulverized the body and exhausted the mind. At the end of it, the score made poor reading. The grey wolves had sunk only five convoy ships – three of them his work – but out of the nine U-boats, six had been destroyed by the enemy. One of them had been commanded by his good friend from Lorient, Hans Nieman. Finally, he must have made a mistake.

They were ordered to return to base. On the way, in order to cheer the crew's shaken spirits, he told the radio man to tune in to the American forces' broadcast. Swing and jazz blared from speakers in an irresistible beat that had his men clicking their fingers, nodding their heads and tapping their feet. The leaders in Berlin would not have approved, but who cared? The leaders did not have to endure such close and regular brushes with death.

The welcome home to Lorient was not quite as jolly as usual. The band played loudly, but there were some anxious faces in the crowd and not so many smiles. Word had already got around the base that *die Gluckliche Zeit* might be ending. It looked like it would not be such a 'Happy Time' for the U-boats from now on. He noted the empty pens in the concrete bunker and the empty chairs and places in the mess hall.

There was a letter from his father waiting for him, as well as the usual fan letters from people who had seen his photograph in the newspapers, usually returning from a successful patrol. They asked for signed photographs, for letters in reply – some of the women even wanted to marry him.

The Flotilla Commander sent for him and complimented him on his three kills. But the pack's performance, he said, had been very disappointing. A disaster, in fact. Only five enemy ships had been sunk against the loss of six U-boats. Could he offer any reason for such a lamentable result?

Reinhard endeavoured to describe the determination and ferocity of the enemy's attacks, which were becoming more determined and more ferocious by the month.

'They had a hard job to find us at the beginning, but now they're getting surprisingly good at it. They turn up wherever we go – always one jump ahead. It's uncanny.'

'Their ships and planes have all got radar now, as well as ASDIC. What else do you expect?'

He said slowly, 'I think it's more than that, sir. I think they may have found a way to decode our signals.'

The Flotilla Commander stared at him. 'Rubbish! The code is unbreakable. The Gross-admiral has complete confidence in it. If you're looking for excuses, that one won't wash.'

'I'm not looking for excuses, sir. You asked me for a reason for the patrol's inferior performance and I'm suggesting one.'

'Well, it's an absurd idea. I think the truth is that we've been resting on our laurels, enjoying our successes and all the admiration. That's got to stop. We have a war to fight and to win, and that means sinking as many British ships as possible.' The Commander laid an avuncular hand on his shoulder. 'Come now, Reinhard. You need a good drink, a good dinner and some rest.'

He went to a bar in town and got drunk. It was what most U-boat men did at the end of a gruelling patrol. A natural reaction to surviving a fearsome ordeal and the most effective antidote to the stress and strain. He drank champagne – the best and most expensive available – to celebrate the fact that he was not fish food out in the Atlantic, like poor Nieman.

First one French girl, then another, sidled up to him but he waved them away. What he most craved was sleep and when the bottle was finished he left the bar and walked through the blacked-out town to the Hotel Beau Séjour in the market place where he was billeted. The air-raid siren was wailing shrilly, but he ignored it, as well as the distant drone of approaching enemy bombers and the thunder of the flak guns. He fell asleep instantly in his bed, deaf to the falling bombs, and dreamed vividly.

He was standing on the croquet lawn of the big house in Scotland, and Stroma was standing beside him. He was a grown man in his Kapitänleutnant's uniform, but she was still a child – a little shrimp dressed in a kilt and jumper. He was apologizing humbly for being such a bad sport.

'Winning is important to me.'

'That's silly. It's only a game,' she reproved him. 'It doesn't matter if you win or lose.'

'It matters to me.'

Later in the dream, they were standing on the deck of *Sturmwind* and he picked her up and carried her across to the stone jetty. Only this time she was no longer a child, but grown-up. He held her in his arms but her face was turned against his chest so that he could not see it.

He thought about the dream when he woke up. There was almost no chance that they would ever meet again, so he would never know what she looked like as an adult. And winning would matter to her now, just as much as it did to him. Only this was not a game of croquet, but of war.

Grandfather died in April. Ellen had found him in his chair beside the fire and had thought, at first, that he was simply asleep. He must have died instantly, Dr Mackenzie said, which was a good way to go. Comfort could be taken from it. The funeral took place the following week and Stroma was given compassionate leave to attend. Her parents travelled up from London but Hamish was away on active service at sea.

It was raining when Grandfather was buried beside Grandmother in the graveyard of the ruined kirk. The islanders had gathered to pay their respects and Angus played a heart-rending tune on the pipes. Stroma wept.

Mr Pirbright, Grandfather's elderly solicitor, had come over from Glasgow with a younger partner, Mr Ross, and afterwards they sat in the study while he read the will. As Grandfather had told her, the house and the entire Craigmore estate had been left in two equal shares to Hamish and herself and a trust fund had been set up to be administered by Mr Ross for the next ten years. Apparently, there was plenty of money to run the estate and although some of the younger men had gone off to war, the older ones had stayed and there was still Angus to oversee things.

The house itself, however, was another matter. Logan had fallen down the cellar steps and broken his leg and was in hospital on the mainland; Meg's rheumatics were getting too bad to deal with the daily cleaning; Mack could no longer cope with the gardens and Ellen's sister in Boughrood was ill and needed her to help take care of her five children.

Ellen was very sorry about it, she said, but blood was thicker than water and she'd have to go. Besides, with the Master gone, there was nobody to cook for or look after.

There was nothing to be done but shut the house up for the duration. Get out the dust sheets, close up the storm shutters, and leave it to the cold and the damp, the spiders and the mice until the war had ended and she and Hamish could open it up again. Angus's Grace would come and take a look round every so often and there was no need to worry about burglars – not on the island.

Stroma took her raincoat off the hall peg, pulled the scarf from its pocket to tie over her hair and went out for a walk. The island rain had never bothered her. Unlike in other places it was soft and gentle – more mist than rain. She went down to the inlet below the house where the tide was coming in across the seaweed and surging over the rocks. The water was greenish-gray, the sky almost exactly the same colour, so that the two merged as one, mingled with the misty rain.

To the north, beyond the narrow sound between the two islands lay the open waters of the North Atlantic Ocean. Mountainous waves, shrieking winds, savage storms. Convoys struggling through. U-boats preying on them.

'We got one of the bastards at last,' Hamish said. 'It's taken enough time, but we finally did it.'

He looked haggard; much worse than when she'd last seen him. Chalk-white face, dark

209

shadows under red-rimmed eyes.

'Yes, I know,' Stroma said. 'Well done.'

'I suppose you would know.'

He was aware of where she worked, but not exactly what she did.

'Well, we were pretty pleased with ourselves, I can tell you. For once, we dished it out to them. Gave them a taste of their own bloody medicine. They're devious devils, too. They'll send up oil and stuff to fool you, to make it look like they've been hit, but this time there was a whole lot of wreckage and human remains. No doubt about it. We all cheered like anything.'

Hamish's ship had come into dock for urgent repairs and a message from him had reached her. It was the first of her two days off duty when, normally, she would have slept for hours to recover from her two days on shift. She had met him in the bar of a hotel – a gloomy place with a bomb-damaged ceiling, broken window panes and plaster dust.

He had been promoted to Lieutenant with two gold rings on his sleeve, and he was the First Officer on his ship. Not long, she thought, before he gets his own command.

He put down his gin. 'Mind you, it wasn't easy. They're clever, I'll say that for them – slippery as eels. Only this one made mistakes. He didn't dive fast enough or deep enough and we got him pinned down. Gave him everything we'd got. He hadn't a chance, really – not that that worried us. They never give their victims any chances.' He picked up his glass again, drank some more. 'It was a hell of a trip. Lousy weather with the bloody U-boats sticking like leeches to us all the way. Every time we stop to pick up survivors we're sitting ducks for them. So far we've been lucky, God knows how. Maybe the torpedoes have missed.'

'You mean they'd attack you when you're rescuing survivors?'

'Of course they bloody would. They're murdering bastards with no scruples whatsoever. For God's sake, Stroma, surely you've learned that by now. You've no idea what it's like out there. It's kill or be killed. We're finished if we don't finish them.'

She said quietly, 'It must be terrible.'

'You couldn't possibly know how terrible unless you'd been there yourself. Nobody could.' He signalled to the waiter. 'I need another drink.'

Craigmore was a safer subject. She told him about Grandfather's funeral, about Angus playing the lament, about old Mr Pirbright and young Mr Ross, about Logan's broken leg and Ellen's sick sister and Meg's rheumatics and the gardens finally getting too much for Mack.

'We had to shut up the house, you see. Let things go. There wasn't any choice.'

'It doesn't matter,' he said. 'Not at the moment. All that really matters is winning this war. Nothing else is important. How were the parents?'

'Very upset about Grandfather.'

'So am I. He was a very decent bloke. We'll

211

miss him.'

'Yes, I know. They're very worried about you.'

He shrugged. 'Can't help that.'

'Do take care of yourself, Hamish.'

He took another swig of gin. 'My job's not taking care of myself, it's taking care of the Huns.'

Tom Lewis took her out to dinner at a Chinese restaurant – a strange place in a small back street, walls painted with writhing dragons and lit by gaudy paper lanterns. It was the first time she had seen him since the wardroom party and he looked as tired as Hamish. On his last convoy from Newfoundland, a ravening pack of U-boats had managed to sink seven merchant ships, including an oil tanker. He didn't talk about that, of course, but she'd seen it all happen on the Ops Room map.

He picked up the menu. 'Ever eaten Chinese food before?'

'No, never.'

'Then you're in for a treat. They do the real stuff here.'

The soft-footed little Chinese waiter who appeared like magic wore embroidered silk robes and a pigtail. Tom showed her how to use chopsticks and she tried all kinds of exotic dishes that she had never tasted in her life before.

She learned more about Tom. He came from a naval family and had been at Osborne and

Dartmouth. The war had broken out soon after he had passed out of Dartmouth and he had joined the destroyer later. He had a brother also serving in the Navy in the Far East but his ship had been sunk in 1942 by the Japanese and he had been taken prisoner.

'As far as we know he's still alive, but the Japs don't tell you much. All we have is a six-month-old printed postcard that my brother signed, but which says virtually nothing. Still, I suppose it's better than hearing no news at all.'

She thought of Rosanne's brother and the no news that had turned out so badly.

'I'm sorry. It must be awful for you.'

'It's the same for thousands, isn't it? There's a war on. Nothing to be done except get on and win it.'

The war was the reason and the excuse for everything, she thought. For all the brutality, all the suffering and misery, the grimness and the greyness and sadness. 'Don't you know there's a war on?' people asked all the time. As though it were possible not to know, possible to forget, even for a moment.

She said, 'You must hate the U-boat crews, Tom.'

'Hate's not exactly the word. I just con-centrate on destroying as many of their boats as possible. It's not personal.'

'My brother says they're murdering bastards.'

'If killing in war counts as murder, then they're certainly very good at it. Actually, we're not too bad at it ourselves, when necessary.'

'How can the Germans fight for someone as evil as Hitler? For the Nazis? That's what I don't understand.'

'I suppose they believe they're fighting for the glory and honour of their Fatherland which got rather dented in the last war. *Deutschland über alles* and all that.' He smiled at her. 'I honestly wouldn't let it worry you too much. We'll beat them – in the end.'

'That's what my brother says, too.'

'He's right.'

It was still light when they left the restaurant – a mild June evening with a light breeze blowing from the Mersey. He insisted on taking the bus with her as far as the Navy barracks outside the city, walked with her up to the gates.

'Can I see you again, Stroma? Next time there's a chance.'

'If you like.'

'I would, very much.'

If it had been dark, he would probably have kissed her, but it was still light and the sentry on duty was watching them. She wasn't sure whether she had wanted it to happen or not.

'Take care of yourself, Tom.'

She had said the same to Hamish and it was just as meaningless. How on earth could they?

He answered with a wry smile. 'I'll do my best.'

The hydrophones had picked up propeller noises approaching. Through the periscope, Reinhard could see the outline of an enemy destroyer on the starboard bow. He watched as she came closer, travelling at twenty-five knots or more. For a moment, he had thought that they must have been spotted lying in calm water just below the surface, but the destroyer carried on, passing them within a few hundred metres. He waited until she was a safe distance away before he raised the periscope higher to make a slow sweep round the horizon. And then he stopped. A veritable forest of masts was approaching from the west, trailing giveaway smoke: the convoy that the destroyer had been guarding, bound for England. Thirty cargo ships at least, two cruisers, four more escort destroyers, and – a glittering prize and fortuitously at the tail-end of the procession – a large and once luxurious passenger liner pressed into war service.

In the early days, convoy ships had sometimes scattered in panic under attack, but not any more. They were hardened. They'd learned that their best chance lay in staying together.

He ordered full speed and headed towards the convoy at periscope depth – turning as he came closer to approach on a parallel course, like a wolf slithering on its belly alongside the fold. He waited for the procession to pass and for the liner at the end to come into his sights, calculating the firing angle carefully. A spread of four torpedoes set to run at a depth of seven metres and from a range of five hundred. All four would have a chance to hit. The U-boat's bows swung slowly towards the liner so that she crossed them at right angles. He waited a few more crucial seconds.

'*Los!*'

As soon as the torpedoes had left their tubes, he ordered the U-boat down in a steep dive and she was still diving when the four explosions were clearly heard as the torpedoes found their mark. Soon afterwards they heard the cracking and shrieking noises, the dying groans of a ship going down, followed by the unmistakable sound of her boilers blowing up under water.

He took the U-boat as deep as he dared, close to the crush depth. The enemy's ASDIC could already be heard and the first of the depth charges exploded. For more than five hours they stayed motionless at 300 metres, all auxiliary machinery stopped, bilge pumps idle, water spurting in through weak points of the hull, the boat creaking ominously. The atmosphere was stifling and foul, the men's faces shining with sweat, rigid with fear.

If he'd had a book to hand, Reinhard might have imitated his former Old Man's trick of casually reading a chapter or two while they waited – except that he'd have made sure he was reading it the right way up. He glanced at his Number One, Engelhardt – not a flicker of concern showing there – and Mohr, his stolid-faced Number Two might have been out on a routine training exercise. He was lucky with his officers, lucky with the whole crew. Fear was natural under bombardment, but they kept it under control. On his first boat, he'd seen a man suddenly go berserk and lay about him wildly with a spanner, smashing everything within reach. He'd been quickly overcome by the others and the Old Man, who kept a loaded gun locked up in his cabin, had put him under close guard. The man had been removed from service as soon as they had returned to port. Fear was contagious.

The depth charges were all wide of the mark and he realized that the escorts had no idea where they were. Not often, but sometimes the ocean turned guardian angel. Layers of sea water at different temperatures and density could confuse the ASDIC's ultrasonic sound waves and make a submarine undetectable.

Another hour passed without any more depth charges being dropped, and Reinhard took the U-boat to the surface. He sent a signal to headquarters about the liner: *Sinking noises clearly heard. Depth charged but no damage.*

By the time they returned to Lorient at the end of the patrol they had sent four more enemy cargo ships to the bottom, one of them a six-thousand tonner, and it was Grossadmiral Dönitz, no less, who greeted them, his stern, spare figure standing on the quay, flanked by high-ranking officers. The military band struck up a fanfare, as if for royalty.

Reinhard was congratulated on his tonnage of enemy shipping and awarded the Knight's Cross of the Iron Cross. The Grossadmiral placed the brilliantly coloured ribbon around his neck and said a few words. He was noted for the personal interest he took in his submariners.

'Your father lives in Hamburg, I believe, Kapitänleutnant?'

'That's correct, sir.'

'Have you received any news?'

'News, sir?'

'You didn't hear about Hamburg on the radio while you were at sea?'

'No, sir.'

There had been too much wearying propaganda. They had listened instead to records or to the American jazz on the radio.

'I'm sorry to have to tell you that the city has been badly bombed by the Allies. I regret that I can give no news about your father, though. The situation is very unclear. I hope you find that he is safe.'

'Thank you, sir.'

He saluted and, with a nod, the Grossadmiral moved on along the line of men. A smiling girl in uniform thrust a huge bouquet of flowers into Reinhard's arms – sweet-smelling, full-blown summer roses. He shook hands with more people, was offered more flowers, more smiles, more congratulations, a bottle of vintage champagne, which he waved aside. A staff officer gave him more details about the Hamburg raids.

'They've bombed it twice – the second time just two nights ago. Nearly eight hundred aircraft. There was a terrible firestorm – at least forty thousand people dead, they think ... Shocking business.'

He took the first available train to Paris,

another to Frankfurt and then another to Hamburg, which crawled along for the final part of the journey. From the train window he could see a gigantic grey cloud hovering over the city.

He walked from the railway station into devastation. The dense cloud had blotted out the sun and the air beneath it was oven hot and so thick with smoke and dust and soot that it was difficult to breathe. Before him lay street after street of burned-out ruins, fires still flickering and flaring. Corpses lay buried in the rubble. He saw a clenched claw poking out, the pathetic foot of a child, a woman's scorched head, hair frizzled, face blackened, mouth stretched wide in an agonized scream.

He found a way through to the lakeside and the apartment block where his father lived. The building stood at the edge of the area of devastation but it had not escaped. The roof and floors had collapsed and only a shell remained.

The police headquarters had been destroyed but a workman labouring in the ruins directed him to an emergency station that had been set up. He found it crowded with people coated in grey ash, dazed with shock, weeping hysterically, children screaming. He caught an official by the arm.

'Who is in charge here, please?' The man would have moved on, but Reinhard held on to him. 'I must have news of my father.'

A pause, a glance at his uniform, at his face. 'I doubt if there will be any, but you had better come with me, sir.'

He followed him into a room at the back where a senior police officer sat at a desk, studying a street map laid out in front of him. Another officer was standing beside him. They both looked up at him wearily.

'I am here to ask for information about my father, a resident of the city.'

The senior man said, 'I am very sorry, Herr Kapitänleutnant, but there is very little information that we can give you at the moment. There are thousands of people missing, you understand. Some may be safe, others still buried alive in the ruins, but most must be dead. We cannot know for sure who or how many until the survivors have registered with us, and in many cases it may be impossible to identify the bodies. It will all take time. If you will give us your father's full name and address, as well as your own, we will see what we can find out.'

When he had written it down, the police officer said, 'I know your father by repute, Herr Kapitänleutnant, and I sincerely hope that he has survived this terrible tragedy. The apartment building was not within the firestorm area and so there is a chance that he may have survived. I will inform you at once if there is any news of him. Did he live alone?'

'We had a servant, Greta Nord, but my father had sent her away to the country.'

'That was fortunate for her.'

'I've never seen such devastation. What happened?'

'The enemy has found a new way of making

war. First they bombed the city centre, then they dropped a ring of high explosives. And, after that, an outer ring of incendiaries. Unfortunately, we've had no rain for some time and the weather has been very warm. The result was a huge inferno as one fire joined up with another – so hot that buildings collapsed in the heat. People had no chance of escape. Nowhere safe to go. They were suffocated in the shelters, or blown along by the violent winds and sucked into the fires to be burned to cinders. It was the most dreadful thing that you can imagine. Even in your war at sea, I do not think that you will have seen anything so terrible.'

Reinhard said, 'The Luftwaffe has bombed enemy cities, but never on such a scale as this.'

'It's just the beginning. The RAF will be back by night, the Americans by day. Their aim will be to destroy all our great cities and leave us with nothing but ruins. People are fleeing and many believe that we should capitulate – give up and give in while we still can.'

'They're wrong.'

'I agree. The enemy may destroy our buildings but not our spirit.'

As he left, the police chief said, 'Don't give up hope about your father, Herr Kapitän-leutnant. He may have been away from home. Perhaps visiting friends or relatives?'

'Perhaps.'

But Father was a creature of habit and routine. The directorships that he held occupied his days satisfactorily and most of his old naval friends also lived in Hamburg. His only sister was many kilometres away in Munich and, so far as Reinhard knew, his father had not seen or visited her for years. Aunt Ursula had been widowed in the Great War and his childhood memories were of a thin and bitter woman.

He tried to contact Bruno at his fighter station, but there were no telephone lines working in Hamburg. There was no gas, lighting or water either. In the end, he went back to Lorient, hoping that there would eventually be some information for him there, but the only news from the city was of more Allied bombing raids that took place over the following nights.

The oil tanker blew up in a blaze of flame and white-hot metal and burning wood. A crimson glow and a pall of black smoke rose up out of the bowels of the ship as the eruptions continued in a spectacular firework display that must have been visible for kilometres. Neutral ships nearby had answered the tanker's SOS and Reinhard dived his U-boat to the sea bottom and left them to what rescue work was possible.

The tanker had been sailing unescorted, which was unusual in the North Atlantic, but those enemy ships who could make more than fifteen knots sometimes went alone, relying on speed. Reinhard had had dreams of catching the *Queen Mary*, or the *Queen Elizabeth*, their decks loaded with Allied troops, but they were virtually uncatchable. He might have had some regrets at sinking such fine and famous ships, but in the case of this tanker he had none. The inferno was payment on account for Hamburg, and there would be plenty more to come.

Until Hamburg, he had not hated the enemy – on the contrary he had respected him for his courage and determination. But now it was different.

They had been at sea for six weeks and orders now took them towards the Western Approaches where the Allied convoys drew closer to home and safety. It was a fruitful hunting ground; the U-boats could gather and wait expectantly for their arrival. Unfortunately, it was also very well defended. They made contact with a convoy during the night. The telegraphist rushed out of his cubby-hole with its position and Reinhard made rapid calculations on the chart. Two hours later they had come within three miles of the convoy – several large freighters, plus escorts, steaming steadily towards England.

The U-boat surfaced to a clear moonlit night with excellent visibility and only a moderate ocean swell. Good in some ways, bad in another. They would be able to sight the enemy ships from a greater distance, but their white bow wave and phosphorescent wake would be much easier to spot and they would be unable to get as near as he would like. Reinhard closed on the convoy on a parallel course, choosing his victim – the biggest freighter. A single well-aimed torpedo took care of all eight thousand tons of her. It hit her amidships and within ten minutes she was gone. As expected, the dark shape of an escorting destroyer had detached itself immediately from the convoy and was heading straight for them.

'Alarrrm! Dive! Dive! Dive!'

The klaxon shrieked, the main vents were opened and men tumbled down the conning-tower ladder, the last one spinning the hatch wheel tight as the sea closed over the U-boat. Reinhard ordered all hands forward at the double and those men not at action stations hurled themselves through the bulkhead hatch-ways towards the bows so that the boat's nose dipped sharply to help speed up their descent.

'Destroyer bearing twenty degrees to port.' The hydrophone operator turned his wheel a fraction. 'Getting louder.'

As usual, it was a guessing game. With luck, the enemy would cross their course astern, but then which way would he turn? Port or star-board? There was no crystal ball to peer into; no way of reading the British commander's mind. Unluckily, Reinhard guessed wrong. The des-troyer arrived dead overhead and circled slowly until it stopped for a while, its ASDIC groping for their hull like a blind man, fingertips pitter-pattering. He ordered the boat deeper, and then deeper still, down to 150 metres. The destroyer was on the move again, circling round, getting ready to drop depth charges. Luckily, it had to be done at full speed or the enemy would risk blowing themselves out of the water; if they'd been able to simply lob them over the side, their job would have been easy.

It was a cat and mouse game without many options for the mouse. He'd seen it played out in reality once – a tabby cat biding its time patiently, the mouse faking death until the moment when it made a frantic dash for life. There was no question of a U-boat dashing anywhere but it was possible to slip away silently by degrees. He'd done that successfully many times but the game was getting harder to play. The enemy had new and improved weapons and devices and gadgets; they had studied tactics and strategy and they had learned a lot about U-boats. They knew what they were doing. But, in the end, it came down to two men guessing – the commander of the escort ship and himself.

The destroyer's captain was guessing well. His depth charge explosions were too close for comfort – slamming blows that shook the U-boat from bow to stern, shattered glass, cracked metal and burst open valves. Even Engelhardt, with his nerves of steel, had flinched. Reinhard whispered the order to dive another 50 metres and then slow ahead with both electric motors. They began to creep away, holding a straight and steady course. The enemy commander would expect him to be up to the usual tricks and dodges – doubling back and doubling back again, constantly changing depths and direction – but the man could only take a stab at which way they'd turn and whether they'd go up or down. No tricks could be the best trick of all. Reinhard kept going and the explosions gradually faded away.

There had been reports of damage, some of it quite bad, but nothing that couldn't be repaired by a well-trained crew. Three hours later, Reinhard ordered the boat up to periscope depth and took a look round, a complete sweep of the horizon, before they surfaced from the deep, hull dripping, on to a deserted ocean under a starry sky.

Off the northern coast of Ireland, they came across another lone ship – not a coveted oil tanker as before, but an unarmed neutral Portuguese steamer chugging along, probably blissfully unaware that she was in the forbidden zone. She was too small to waste torpedoes on but big enough to be worth sinking with gun fire. Reinhard sent a warning shell across the steamer's bows and they watched from the bridge as her crew ran about the decks in panic and started lowering lifeboats. The lifeboat carrying her captain, a portly little man, pulled towards them and as they approached, he stood up in the bows and raised his arm in a stiff salute.

'Heil Hitler!'

A wave slapped against the lifeboat and he lost his balance and fell over backwards among his men, feet in the air. After a while he reappeared, replacing his cap, adjusting it carefully and dusting down his uniform. He saluted once more.

'Heil Hitler!'

It was apparently the only German he spoke. Reinhard called down from the bridge, in English, 'Where do you come from? What is your cargo?'

They had come from Iceland and they were carrying a load of fish to Oporto. The captain produced papers from a pocket to prove it and flourished them wildly in the air. The lifeboat was rocking about close to their hull and had to be fended off by the U-boat's crew. Not worth bothering with, Reinhard decided, or worth the risk of advertising their presence to the enemy by gunfire. After all, a U-boat cost four million marks – rather more than a hold of fish.

He waved a hand in curt dismissal. 'You may continue on your way, Captain.'

The captain tugged a cigar from another pocket like a bad conjuror and held it up.

'For you, kind sir.'

He shook his head impatiently.

A sack was produced from the bottom of the lifeboat and a scrawny chicken held up by its legs, wings flapping feebly.

'Please to take, sir. Very good to eat.'

'No, thank you.'

Finally, the captain understood that they were free to go. There were more shouts of 'Heil Hitler', servile thanks in bad English, bows and waves, as the Portuguese sailors rowed away back to their steamer. The whole encounter had been a lunatic farce.

Engelhardt chuckled. 'You should have

accepted, sir. You could have smoked the cigar and we could have eaten the chicken. Do you think they realize how lucky they were?'

He said grimly, 'No. I was in a charitable mood.'

The *Sunderland* appeared so unexpectedly from the solid ceiling of cloud that the lookouts on the bridge were late spotting it. Too late for the U-boat to dive deep enough to escape the effect of its bombs in the hammering attack that followed and, this time, the damage was too bad to be fixed in a matter of an hour or two. There were reports from all over the boat and Franz, his Chief Engineer, had a long list of problems which he read out as though he were going shopping. The U-boat was plainly unfit and unable to continue on active patrol with her two remaining torpedoes. She could barely limp along, dangerously vulnerable to attack.

Franz had finally come to the end of his list. 'I need a day – perhaps two – somewhere where we can surface after dark and work in peace.'

'That's asking a lot. We're in enemy waters.'

The Chief Engineer shrugged.

Reinhard went to the chart table and leaned over it, running a finger along the jagged coast line of western Scotland. 'As it happens,' he said slowly, 'I might know the very place.'

It would be twenty-seven years since his father had come to Islay in his U-boat, and seven years since they had sailed here in *Sturmwind*.

It was later in the year, of course – no longer summer, but autumn – and the seas off Scotland were even more violent and treacherous than he remembered. He kept the boat submerged to escape the worst of it and only came to periscope depth when they had passed the Rhuvaal lighthouse and entered the narrow sound between Jura and Islay. The deep central channel was tailor-made for a submarine. To see and not be seen. He swivelled the periscope from one island to the other, noting things he remembered well – the seals lying on the rocks below the cliffs, the wild goats, the sheep, the long-horned Highland cattle, the flocks of sea birds. It was raining, which didn't surprise him. He remembered the constant rain – more like a mist bathing the islands. They went by the whisky distillery and its wooden pier, and passed the narrowest point of the sound where the ferry went back and forth from Feolin on Jura to Port Askaig on the Islay side. Smoke was curling up from cottage chimneys in the port – peat fire smoke, of course – and the old ferry-boat was moored by the slipway, a flock of sheep being loaded. He could see the animals being herded on board, a black and white dog weaving to and fro at their heels, the ferrymen prodding them with sticks and shouting. They'd get a hell of a shock if Reinhard were to surface suddenly – if a U-boat were to loom out of the water before their very eyes. He smiled. This was how his father must have felt when he was sneaking around all those years ago, playing

229

hide-and-seek, thumbing his nose at the enemy. There was a lot of satisfaction in it – as there had been satisfaction in sinking that tanker, though in a very different way.

He took the boat through the narrow entrance to Glas Uig and into the shelter of the cove. The view through the periscope showed him that nothing much had changed, except the season. The leaves on the trees were brown, the grass not as green as in summer, but the jetty was there with its rusty mooring rings, the lichen-encrusted granite boulders, the whale's jaw-bone wedged in the rocks, the track leading up to the house. All just as he remembered. He kept the U-boat sitting on the bottom of the cove until after dark and then surfaced along-side the jetty.

While the repair work on the boat was being done, he left Mohr in charge and walked up through the woods with Engelhardt. The half-moon gave light that he scarcely needed. His eyes had become very accustomed to darkness, to distinguishing shapes from shadows, the real from the imaginary.

'There's a house at the top,' he'd told Engel-hardt. 'I came here once before the war. I'd like to take a look.'

They came out of the trees and there was Craigmore, a hundred metres or so away, be-yond the rough grass and the reeds and the white blobs of grazing sheep. He could see its outline rising above the bank, squat chimney stacks against the night sky, slate roofs, the sharp points of its gables. The storm shutters were all closed with no single chink of light to be seen. No sign of human life. No sound, except for the rhythmic rush and retreat of the waves over the rocks in the inlet below.

'Seems deserted, sir,' Engelhardt said.

'Looks like it.'

They walked across the grass to the dry-stone wall and the iron gate. At the bottom of the bank Reinhard stopped for a moment, looking up. This was where the child had appeared at the top – the boy who had turned out to be a girl, plunging down the slope towards him in search of a lost ball.

Is this what you're looking for?

The croquet lawn was still there, but without the iron hoops, and the grass was uncut. It must be a long time since anyone had played a game.

They walked on up to the house and he tried the handle of the front door. It opened.

Engelhardt said, 'We were wrong, sir. Someone's at home.'

'Not necessarily. They never lock their doors on the island.'

'That's trusting.'

He pushed the door open further. Inside, the house was in darkness. They went in, closing the door behind them, and he switched on his torch and played the beam round the hallway. Flagstone floor, panelled walls, stags' heads staring down at him with their shining glass eyes. No elderly retainer smelling of whisky to show the way, but Reinhard remembered where the drawing room was. Dust sheets draped the furniture like an undertaker's shrouds and it felt as cold and damp as a tomb.

Engelhardt shivered. 'Rather grim, sir.'

'It wasn't like this before. It was different when the family was living here.'

'Well, they must have shut up the place and pushed off.' Engelhardt peered behind curtains. 'They've put blackout blinds over the windows, sir. We could turn a light on, if you like.'

'There's no light to turn on. No electricity. Only oil lamps. No running water either, as a matter of fact.'

'My God!' Engelhardt, who had been brought up in considerable comfort in Stuttgart, sounded appalled. 'A bit primitive, isn't it? Still, I could probably get one of the oil lamps working.'

Reinhard left him to it and went into the dining room where the long table and the chairs were also covered with sheets. He'd sat here, in this very chair, beside the grandmother who'd talked to him about his schooling and the Navy, and next to Stroma who hadn't wanted to talk to him at all.

He closed the door and moved on down a long passageway to the kitchens. The torch showed him an ancient cooking range, rows of cupboards, scrubbed wooden table, tarnished copper pans and an outsize kettle. In the scullery he found a zinc bath hanging on a peg and a shallow stone sink set on brick pillars with a tap above. The old sock she'd told him about was tied in place – the makeshift strainer that held back the wriggly things but had somehow failed to keep out a snake. He turned on the tap and brown water gushed out.

It comes straight from the burn – brown because of the peat.

He shone his torch into the larder. The shelves were bare except for a crock of flour, a drum of salt, bags of dried beans and glass jars of preserved fruit. Something scampered across his foot – either a big mouse or a small rat.

The main staircase led up from the hall and he climbed to the first floor, opening doors on to bedrooms, beaming his torch in. The first one had a heavily carved four-poster bed and was probably where the grandparents had slept; three more smaller rooms looked as though they were meant for guests and another room that must belong to the brother, Hamish. The mantelpiece and shelves were crowded with model ships, including, he was amused to see, a U-boat type UC III like his father had commanded in the last war. The books in a glass-fronted case were boys' adventure stories: *The Curse of the Pharaohs, The Treasure of the Deep, Enemy Below* – complete with U-boat on the cover but not very accurately drawn. On the bottom shelf was a pile of old comics – coloured cartoons of brave British and brutish Germans in uniform, of tanks and guns, fighters and bombers and several more U-boats. One sinister character wore civilian clothes, a long coat, a scarf and what was apparently meant to be a Tyrolean hat. *Hamish thought you were spies.*

He knew, as soon as he opened the door, that the bedroom at the far end of the corridor was Stroma's. It was a simple room without frills or flowery patterns. Plain wallpaper and curtains, a green silk cover on the bed, a chest of drawers with a white china ewer and basin on the top, beside them, a tortoiseshell hairbrush and comb, and a small bottle of scent. Lily of the valley. He tipped a little into his palm and smelled the fresh sweetness of it.

Her childhood books were very different from her brother's: *The Princess and the Goblins, Heidi, At the Back of the North Wind, Little Women, The Secret Garden...*

He opened the door of the wardrobe in the corner. Grown-up clothes on hangers – a tweed jacket, skirts, a blue wool dress, a Scottish kilt in the same tartan colours that he remembered her wearing at the dinner. Country brogues and one pair of shoes with high heels.

She still came here to visit.

As he closed the wardrobe, the torch beam caught his reflection in the looking glass set in its door – shaggy-haired, unshaven and villainous. Just as well she couldn't see him now.

He went downstairs again and noticed a door that he had missed before at the back of the hallway. It led into what must be the grandfather's study. There was a large mahogany desk with a leather blotter, many books on shelves, a comfortable chair beside the open fireplace, a large-scale map on the wall. He shone the torch over all the details of the Craigmore Estate – the location of the house itself, fields, lochs, streams, farmhouses and crofters' cottages, shorelines and bays – including Glas Uig – were all clearly marked.

Where had the family gone? Why had they left? Surely not because of the war? This was as safe a place as anyone could find. No German bomber was going to waste its bombs here, no invading force going to attempt a landing on its treacherous rocky shores. He went over to the desk and pulled open the top drawer: a fountain pen, pencils, a bottle of ink, a horn letter opener, paper clips, a box of drawing pins. Another drawer contained writing paper and envelopes and postcards, another a cheque book and a sheaf of receipts, pinned neatly together. The grandfather was an orderly man.

In a bottom drawer, he found his diary for 1943 and flicked through some of the early entries. He was prying unforgivably but the diary wasn't a personal account; there were no private inner thoughts committed to paper. The entries were very brief, mainly concerned with the running of the estate. Meetings, reminders, appointments – which included three appointments in February and March with a Dr Mackenzie. The entries finished abruptly on 5th April. All the following pages were blank.

He replaced the diary and saw a bundle of letters at the back of the same drawer. The top one he pulled from its envelope was from

Hamish and dated 17th February, 1943. He skimmed through it.

I wish to God that I was serving in a destroyer, instead of a corvette. They're hellish ships to sail in, though we do our best. The destroyers have a much better chance of destroying the U-boats, which is what it's all about, of course. If we don't finish the swine, they'll finish us. In the end, we will. We'll go on sinking them until there are no more left.

I'm sorry I haven't been able to get up to Craigmore to see you for so long ... Things have been pretty hectic, as you can imagine. I haven't seen Stroma for months. She's done her WRNS training – I expect she told you all about that – and she's got roped into some very hush-hush work in Liverpool which she can't talk about. I'm sure she'll come to Craigmore as soon as she can.

He recognized the writing on the next envelope at once; the letter was dated a week later in February.

Dearest Grandfather,
Guess what! I'm a proper Wren at last. And I've been posted to Liverpool – so I'm much nearer to you and Craigmore.
The German bombers made a terrible mess of this poor city and hundreds of people were killed. Apparently, the Luftwaffe came over for eight nights in a row and dropped more than a

236

thousand firebombs as well as tons of high explosives and parachute mines. Everything went up in flames.

I can't tell you anything about my work here, but it's pretty tiring. We're on watch for hours on end and almost fall asleep sometimes, but we have to carry on somehow.

I had a letter from Hamish the other day – the first for ages. He still wishes he was in destroyers, not corvettes – especially a corvette called *Buttercup*! I must say it's rather a funny name for a warship.

I promise I'll come up to Craigmore as soon as I get some leave.

I know you'll be missing Grandmother very much. We all are.

With love from,
Stroma.

He put the letters back in the drawer. He had learned something. The grandmother must have died – probably during last year – and in April, the grandfather had followed her. Stroma and her brother were both serving in the British Royal Navy. He knew of the British WRNS – there was a women's branch in the German Navy, too. Secret naval work in Liverpool could only mean the Atlantic convoys and tracking down U-boats. By another ironic coincidence, Hamish's HMS *Buttercup* was the very corvette that he had so magnanimously spared.

On his way back to the drawing room, he

passed a row of coats hanging on hooks in the hallway, among them a raincoat with a scarf trailing from a pocket. A woman's silk scarf of red and blue with a pattern of curled feathers. When he buried his face in its soft folds, it smelled of lily of the valley. He knotted it carefully round his neck.

Engelhardt had made himself at home. An oil lamp had been lit and he was sitting at the grand piano, dust cover tweaked back, testing out the keys.

'Needs a bit of tuning but it's not too bad, sir – considering the damp. Bechstein know what they're doing. Oh, and I found some malt whisky in the decanter over there, sir. Glasses, too.'

Reinhard poured two shots and handed one over to his First Officer.

'*Zum wohl*!'

'*Zum wohl*! I like the scarf, sir.'

'Spoils of war.'

'Of course, sir.'

'I didn't know you were a pianist, Number One.'

'Nothing to boast about.' Engelhardt had unearthed some sheet music from the piano stool and was turning pages. 'They seem to have rather gone for Chopin.'

He began to play; the piece was the same one that Stroma had played so reluctantly. As Reinhard listened, he admired the family photographs arranged on the piano lid. Bewhiskered gentlemen in kilts, bustled ladies, shooting parties, outings in traps and carriages, the Italian grandmother veiled as a beautiful young bride, the brother and sister, Hamish and Stroma, posed side-by-side on a stool, at about seven and five years old. Stroma was all dressed up in a frilly white party frock with a big satin bow in her hair and he could tell from her expression that it had been done under protest. Exploring further beneath the dust sheet, he discovered a silver-framed studio portrait of Hamish in his Royal Navy uniform. Very serious and not dissimilar to his own Naval Academy version. Next to it was a portrait of Stroma in her WRNS uniform, but she was smiling – straight at him. He picked it up and studied it for a long moment before removing the photograph from its frame.

'More spoils, sir?'

'More spoils, Number One. And we haven't finished yet.'

They stole a sheep before they left Glas Uig, just as his father had done. Killed it, skinned it, dismembered it. The edible parts were carried triumphantly aboard the U-boat, the rest buried in the woods.

He put the photograph of Stroma away in his cabin, slotting it between two books on the shelf.

She looked as he had always imagined she would look when she was grown-up: the same bird wing eyebrows, smoky eyes, wide mouth, pointed chin ... Only the hair was different. No more ragged clumps. Instead, it was neatly combed and curled under the demure HMS cap which she wore at a slight angle. He wondered how tall she was – whether she still only reached below his shoulder and whether she would be as easy to carry as she had been before.

One thing was certain: her smile would fade in an instant if she knew that she was being taken unwittingly to war with him – on the wrong side, in a U-boat.

There was a letter from the Hamburg police waiting for Reinhard on his return to Lorient. His father's body had been found buried in the ruins of the apartment block and a formal identification had been made. Instructions for his burial were awaited.

It was a small consolation for himself and Bruno that at least they were able to bury their father beside their mother at the cemetery, instead of in one of the city's mass graves.

1944

The Commanding Officers' Tactical Course, an intensive course for escort ships' captains, was held at Western Approaches. Lectures took place in the morning, followed by a practice session in the afternoon when a pretend convoy game was played on the chalk-marked wooden floor of a large room.

Stroma had been promoted to Leading Wren and was sent to stand with a circle of other Wrens round the chalk marks, ready to move the model ships across the boards with long rakes. The weather was invented, urgent signals made-up, ships menaced day and night by imaginary U-boats. The point of the game was to work out how best to protect the convoy against all possible difficulties and dangers that might face a commander, and how to sink the U-boats.

There were new weapons, new tactics, new strategies to learn and new perils to think about. Some of the commanding officers sat confidently in their chairs and pointed with their sticks, giving the correct directives without hesitation, but others – usually the older men – found it harder.

The Wrens learned a lot themselves by

listening and watching – and quite often they'd worked out the next move quicker than the senior officers on the course, though, naturally, they kept quiet about it. One commander had three U-boats threatening his convoy of seventy ships and his mind seemed to have frozen. Minutes went by and still he said nothing, while everybody waited. Stroma was standing beside him, near enough to whisper quietly in his ear.

'There's a gap on the port side where the U-boats are located, sir. You need to close up the escorts.'

He gave her a grateful look.

Incredibly, the U-boats were starting to lose the battle in the Atlantic. In the beginning, they'd been the easy winners, sinking ship after ship – sometimes nearly a whole convoy – but the tide had been slowly and inexorably turning against them. Now, they were the ones being sent to the bottom by the escorts and the aircraft, and many more convoy ships – including the fast-constructed American Liberty ships – were being built and getting through. The atmosphere in the Ops Room at Western Approaches was no longer so grim, though nobody was counting any chickens.

Stroma met an officer from a Royal Navy submarine at a party. He'd just come back from a patrol and his boat had called in at Merseyside. They'd claimed a U-boat but, unlike Hamish, he didn't seem particularly jubilant about it – rather sombre, in fact.

'We caught them on the surface and sunk them with gunfire. They went straight down. None of them got out. Jolly bad luck.'

No, not a bit like Hamish.

'Bad luck?'

'Well, you can't help sympathizing ... when you're in the same boat, so to speak. You see, we know exactly what it's like for them, serving in a sub, and it's no picnic, believe me. Not that any of us would swop places with the chaps on the surface. We're in subs because we want to be, and, of course, everyone thinks we're marvellous and terribly, terribly brave. Rather a joke. We're the valiant heroes and the German U-boat crews are the dastardly villains. But actually, we're both just the same. And we sink their ships, too. I think they've got a terrific lot of guts. They took on the whole Royal Navy and now they've got the Yanks to cope with as well. Their odds on surviving are pretty bad already and they're getting worse. I rather admire them, to tell the truth.'

'It's not very admirable to be fighting for Hitler.'

'From what we've heard, U-boat crews don't have a lot of time for the Nazis, and Dönitz won't let Party activists serve on his boats if he can help it. He keeps the political thugs away. He's no fool. In a submarine you've got to have crews that can trust each other completely. They can't have some Nazi spying on them and telling tales as soon as they get into port if they forgot their Heil Hitlers.' He smiled at her.

'Submariners are quite a tough breed, you know, whichever side they're on. Nobody pushes us around.'

Towards the end of January, the Allies landed in Italy at Anzio and it seemed, at first, that the war might be coming to an end. Except that now there were rumours of new German secret weapons – weapons so deadly that there was no defence against them.

There had always been rumours, ever since the war had begun – some frighteningly believable, others plain absurd. Rumours that Mr Churchill was close to death, that spies in England were passing on titbits direct to Lord Haw Haw for use in his broadcasts, that enemy bombers never hit the same house twice, that one of their bombs could go round corners, that German troops were being parachuted into Wales disguised as miners, that hundreds of drowned German soldiers had been washed up on the south-east coast of England in another invasion attempt. Rumour upon rumour upon rumour.

Stroma went home on a forty-eight-hour leave, which meant that she spent most of the precious hours waiting on platforms or standing in train corridors. London was full of American servicemen, prowling the streets, crowding the bars and restaurants, commandeering the taxis. She shared one from King's Cross with some Eighth Air Force airmen who had only just arrived in England. They had seen the bomb damage in Liverpool when their ship had docked and now they were seeing London for the first time. They were shocked. One of them, a gunner from Kansas, said to her kindly, 'Don't you worry. Now we're over here, we'll see they don't do it to you no more.'

She smiled at him because he meant well and decided not to mention that it would have been nice if they'd come sooner.

She spent a lot of her leave sleeping. Her father was working until very late at the hospital and her mother was busy with the WVS. Delilah kept her company, curled up on the end of her bed.

She went for a walk in the park but it was bitterly cold. The trees were dark and stark, the grass dull and muddy. The barrage balloon was tethered at ground level, docile, the allotments displayed row after regimented row of winter cabbages, turnips, swedes, onions and Brussels sprouts.

She walked over to the lake and sat down on a bench, pulling from her pocket the stale crust of bread that she had brought for the ducks. They gathered at once, paddling furiously towards her, quacking and quarrelling. She distributed the pieces as fairly as she could.

'You shouldn't be doing that. You could be prosecuted and fined.'

A woman had stopped on the path behind the bench – an elderly busybody who was glaring at her.

She said politely, 'I'm sorry ... is there something wrong?'

'I ought to report you. It's against the law to waste bread by feeding it to birds and animals. It's meant for human consumption only.'

She looked down at the remaining piece of coarse, dark Government wartime bread, already speckled with green mould.

'Then perhaps you'd like to eat it yourself.'

She stood up and placed it firmly in the woman's hands. As she walked away, the ducks were emerging boldly from the lake and quacking round the woman's feet, pecking at her shoes.

There were no vacant seats on the return journey to Liverpool, and she had to sit on her kitbag in the train corridor. A Canadian pilot parked his luggage next to her and started a friendly conversation. He was from Vancouver, he told her, and this was his first time over in the Old Country. He thought England was a great place, even in winter. He was hoping he'd still be around when the spring and summer came because he'd heard that was really something to see. He produced photographs of his family to show her and she struggled to make them out in the blue electric light – the mother, the father, the elder sister, the two kid brothers. As he was in the middle of telling her a whole lot more about Vancouver, she fell sound asleep.

There were to be no more packs of wolves roaming the North Atlantic, by order of the Grossadmiral. The Allies had become too good at the game, the losses too great. In the first three months of the year more than fifty U-boats had been sunk. As well as destroyers and corvettes, the enemy now used frigates, built and designed for one purpose only – to sink U-boats.

From time to time, news of Reinhard's former Academy classmates percolated. Werner, Max, Gunther, Paul, Hans and Klaus were all dead. Only Harald and Rolf had so far survived. And, one after the other, commanders serving at Lorient failed to return with their crews. More empty pens in the bunker, more vacant places at mess tables, fewer high spirits and drunken celebrations. There wasn't a lot to celebrate. The wolf packs were no longer the hunters but the hunted.

Even so, each time Reinhard returned from a patrol, another stack of fan letters was waiting for him. The writers didn't seem to have heard that the 'Happy Time' was over, probably because the National Socialist propaganda machine had neglected to tell them so. They had quite forgotten to mention that the chances of a U-boat coming back safely from a patrol were getting smaller and smaller and smaller.

Of course, boats had advanced. New and larger types were being built, torpedoes improved, and there was a new invention which had been fitted to Reinhard's boat. It was no longer necessary to surface to recharge the batteries because an air intake called a Schnorchel could be raised above the surface and a U-boat could now use its diesel engines under water. They could stay submerged until they ran out of fuel, and the tip of the Snort was very hard for the enemy to pick up on radar. But, as Reinhard soon discovered, there were disadvantages. The diesels made too much noise for the hydrophones to be used, which meant that the periscope had to be raised as well to keep watch if they were not to be blind as well as deaf to the enemy's approach. Worse, the Schnorchel mast tip might be invisible on radar but it left a tell-tale trail in the water, as well as a plume of steam, which could be spotted by a sharp-eyed lookout on a passing enemy warship. Even worse, in rough weather, a valve in the head of the Snort would close, keeping out the sea, and the diesels would take air from the boat's interior instead. An easy way to asphyxiate the crew. And, worst of all, the Snort had taken away their freedom to chase and attack enemy ships. Their speed was now too slow for cunning manoeuvres; a target had to come conveniently within range of the torpedo tubes. The lean and hungry wolves had been reduced to plodding hounds.

Reinhard met Bruno by arrangement in Paris when their leaves happened to coincide. They had dinner at a restaurant where it was hard to believe that a war was going on at all. Chic women, fine food and wine, polished silver and sparkling crystal, obsequious waiters ... What a bitter irony, Reinhard thought, that an occupied city should somehow have escaped the ravages of war suffered by the cities of its occupiers. Hamburg, Cologne, Kassel, Frankfurt, Augsburg, Berlin ... all bombed into ruins, thousands of their inhabitants dead, maimed, homeless and destitute.

He listened to his brother extolling the virtues of his Messerschmitt 109. About the ease with which his squadron could pick off the American bombers lumbering along so slowly in their daylight box formations.

'We fly straight through the middle of them and they can't do a damn thing about it. They don't know where we'll be coming from next.'

He'd pulled the same sort of trick himself with the convoys and it could be very effective. 'But be careful, Bruno. They'll work it out in the end.'

'They haven't so far. When their fighter escorts have to turn back, they're left waddling along like ducks. That's when we arrive on the scene, of course. We make sure we time it just right.'

It reminded Reinhard of the good old 'Happy Time' when U-boats had pounced on the convoys in the mid-Atlantic once they were out of the protective reach of Allied aircraft. The Americans had finally come up with a long-range plane to bridge that fatal gap, and they'd probably do the same again for their bombers.

Sooner or later, and probably sooner, a brand new plane would appear that would be able to escort the American bombers all the way to their target and back again.

But his brother was the eternal optimist. The happy-go-lucky fighter boy with his head in the clouds and with a good deal less experience of fighting the war.

There was no point in spoiling a good dinner by pointing out some grim facts. Among them, that the North Atlantic convoy ships were now loaded to the gunnels with troops and weapons, as well as food and materials. It was obvious that the Allies were planning another landing, not in Italy this time, but in France, to be launched from somewhere in England. And what's more, their supply ships were getting through.

On a personal level, another troubling fact had occurred to him. Apart from the thin and bitter Aunt Ursula in Munich, he and Bruno had no other close relatives still alive. If – or rather *when* – he failed to return from a patrol, Bruno would be left completely alone. If the war was lost, he knew that Bruno would not take easily to defeat and humiliation and a long captivity – any more than Reinhard would himself.

'Christ, take a look at her!' Bruno's head had swivelled towards the restaurant entrance and the girl who was standing there alone – fur jacket, half-veiled hat, blonde curls, full lips painted a glistening scarlet.

The head waiter had hurried over to her and a

conversation was ensuing between them – much shrugging of his shoulders, hands outspread on each side to demonstrate the full tables, the girl pouting, the head waiter ushering her towards the door.

Bruno was on his feet. 'We can't let that happen, can we?'

Reinhard sighed. 'No, of course not.'

He would far sooner have spent the evening talking alone with his brother; it could be their last chance.

'Perhaps she has a friend.'

'I'm quite sure that she does.'

He watched his brother make his way over to the girl and bow and click his heels. The scarlet lips curved in a dazzling smile and she accompanied Bruno back to their table. He rose to his feet politely.

Her name was Claudette and she did indeed have a friend, who arrived five minutes later. The friend, Suzanne, was altogether quieter. She spoke in a low voice, wore little make-up and he noticed that though her clothes were stylish, they had been made-over from older and less fashionable garments. Her dress had been given a lower neckline, a tighter bodice, a shorter hem; her hat a new ribbon, and her stockings had been carefully darned. His French wasn't as good as his English but it was reasonable – which was fortunate, since she spoke no German.

He learned almost nothing about Suzanne during the meal, other than that she lived in some suburb of Paris, and though she asked a few questions of him, she seemed uninterested in the answers. Compared with Claudette, she was an amateur at the game and he wondered how she had become involved in the first place. He would have found her very dull but once or twice, when she had glanced at him, he had seen a flash of hatred in her eyes, which was intriguing.

At the end of the food and the wine, the cigarettes and the final brandies, Bruno went off with Claudette to some apartment. He was drunk, of course, but not so drunk that he would be incapable of enjoying the French girl or, Reinhard hoped, of guarding his wallet. He said goodbye to his brother, thumped him on the back and watched him go. He was not to know then that he would never see him again. That within a month Bruno would be shot down over the North Sea by American bombers and killed.

The other girl said, 'I can see that you are very fond of your brother.'

He didn't answer. He was not prepared to discuss his feelings with her. They were none of her business, or her concern. He took her back to his hotel room. She was fair game, after all. The dinner had cost a small fortune and both girls had eaten and drunk plenty. He had noticed this one, Suzanne, dropping petits fours surreptitiously into her handbag – sugar-coated grapes and cherries, miniature fruits made of coloured marzipan, little biscuits. Claudette had eaten one after the other, feeding them into her luscious mouth, but this one had squirreled them away.

He was neither kind nor considerate with her; in fact, he was brutal and, afterwards, he apologized.

'It's all right,' she said. 'I'm used to it. Do you have a cigarette, please?'

He lit one for her and another for himself.

'Lucky Strikes,' she said. 'What a treat! Where did you get them?'

'On the street. I believe they originally belonged to American airmen, now our prisoners-of-war.' He lay back on the pillow, drew on his cigarette, 'Why do this? You're not the type.'

'For food. For money, too. I have a four-year-old daughter; she must eat and have clothes to keep her warm, somewhere to live.'

'Parisians don't seem to be exactly starving or in rags.'

'You only see what we want you to see and pay through the nose for – black-market food, expensive wine, beautiful women, cigarettes ... Paris, as you Germans always imagine it to be. But it's not like that any more – not since you came. Now, we survive as best we can and make as much use of our conquerors as possible.'

He frowned. He could believe most of it.

'The petits fours that you hid in your handbag – were they for your daughter?'

'Yes. I take treats for her whenever it's possible.'

'Where is your husband?'

'He was a soldier. You killed him when you invaded France.'

'Then I can understand why you hate us so much.'

'How do you know that I do?'

'It shows in your eyes.'

She blew smoke towards the ceiling. 'I don't hate all Germans. Just most of them.'

'What about your friend, Claudette?'

'She quite likes them. So long as they pay well.' She turned her head towards him. 'I could stay for longer, if you like.'

When she left, he gave her a very generous sum of French francs, and handed her the rest of the Lucky Strikes. She stowed both neatly in her handbag and snapped the clasp shut.

At the door, she paused for a moment, looking at him over her shoulder. 'You know, I would have done it for nothing with you.'

In April, Stroma was sent on an officers' course. She emerged from it with the rank of Third Officer, as well as the infinitely nicer officer's uniform of fine cloth, a double row of brass buttons on the jacket, a ring round each sleeve and, most desirable of all, a tricorne hat.

She was posted back to Western Approaches and the Ops Room – this time as Plotting Officer in charge of a watch of four Wren ratings. She was responsible not only for the table plots, but also for the gigantic wall map which showed the position of any ship or convoy or reported U-boat in the whole of the North

Atlantic. The ship markers were moved across the wall according to the speed of the slowest ship in the convoy. Convoys carrying troops and special cargoes went fast; fastest of all were the Monsters – the converted luxury liners which sailed alone: the *Queen Mary*, the *Queen Elizabeth*, the *Mauretania* and the *Acquitania*. No U-boat had ever caught them and fewer and fewer U-boats remained to prey on the convoys.

As the ships unloaded at Liverpool, the men and weapons that they had carried across the ocean were sent on by lorry, train and plane. Rumours that the Allies would soon be landing in France spread.

Hamish had been given command of a new Flower-class corvette – HMS *Foxglove*, which he admitted was a slight improvement on *Buttercup*. Stroma had only seen him once during the past eight months, when they had met briefly at the same gloomy hotel bar as before, with the same bomb-damaged ceiling and the same broken windows. He was a lieutenant commander now, with more gold on his sleeve; he looked much older than twenty-two and frighteningly responsible.

'Whatever you lot have been doing down in that bunker of yours,' he said, 'it's been working. We've finally got those bloody U-boats beaten hollow. There are hardly any of the buggers left.'

'I know.'

He looked at her with uncustomary respect.

'Yes, I suppose you do. You'll have seen it all happening. You've come a long way since the days when you used to feel sorry for the fish we caught.'

'I think I'd still want them to get away.'

He shook his head in mock despair. 'Hopeless. By the way, I've got some good news. I'm engaged.'

'Engaged?'

'To be married, you idiot. She's a Wren – a coder in Plymouth. We met a few months ago, by chance. Her name's Alice.'

He went on talking about Alice, and how marvellous she was.

'I'm so glad for you, Hamish,' she said. 'When will you get married?'

'Not till after the war, obviously, so it won't be for a while. In Dorset, I suppose. That's where her home is, near Sherborne. She rather wants us to get married in the abbey.'

'You could take her to Craigmore for the honeymoon.'

He frowned. 'Not sure she'd care for it that much. Any more than Mother. You know how wet and cold it can be up there. We're used to it, of course – practically born to it. But Craigmore's pretty uncivilized. It's not everybody's idea of bliss, let's face it.'

It's mine, she thought, *and I always thought it was his too. All those wonderful times we had – fishing and sailing and swimming, the wild ponies, the otters and the seals and the birds, beachcombing and the rock pools at low tide ...*

all of it.

'What about you?' Hamish said. 'I bet you've been fielding a few marriage proposals.'

'Oh, nothing serious.'

There had been three and one of them had been Tom Lewis.

'Well, don't rush into anything.'

'I won't.'

Easy to say that, but turning them down had been awful. Especially awful with Tom. She should have realized much sooner how he felt – before he asked her to marry him.

'Will you think about it?' he'd said. 'Give it some time.'

'There's honestly no point, Tom,' she'd answered. 'I'm so sorry. I like you very much, but that's not enough, is it?'

He'd tried to make a joke out of it, to hide his disappointment. 'You never know, the scales could fall from your eyes one day, and you'll suddenly realize what an absolutely wonderful chap I am.'

'I know that already.'

'Well, then...'

'But I can't marry you, Tom. I'm not in love with you.'

'Is there someone else?' he'd asked. 'None of my business, of course, but just for the record.'

'No. There's nobody else,' she'd told him. 'Nobody.'

Hamish was signalling to the waiter now.

She said, 'Hamish, about Craigmore...'

'We'll talk about that another time. No need

to make any decisions yet. Let's have another drink.'

On the sixth of June, the Allies landed in Normandy but the German forces fought back ferociously and, in the same month, their rumoured secret weapon fell on England. A pilotless plane, launched like a rocket from France – the V1, a flying bomb, a buzz bomb, a doodlebug. Whatever the name, an endless procession of them came over, day and night. When their fuel ran out, the engine stopped and they crashed to earth and exploded. Stroma saw one go over when she was at home on leave – a small, dark shape with a fiery tail, its engine spluttering like a faulty motor bike. The engine cut out a few streets away and, after a sinister silence, there was a deafening roar, a flash and a great plume of black smoke.

By the end of June, the port of Cherbourg had been taken by the Americans. In July the British finally entered the town of Caen and towards the end of August Paris was liberated. Fifty-four U-boats had been sunk by the enemy during the first three months of the year. The total number lost was now more than four hundred. Fewer than a hundred U-boats were left.

But the war was not over yet. Yet another new German weapon had been unleashed on England. The V2 rocket was faster and more destructive than the old buzz bombs. It made no sound and gave no warning, no chance.

* * *

In the officers' mess at Lorient, Gerhard Metzler was doing his imitation of Winston Churchill, sporting a top hat that he'd fished out of the North Atlantic and frequently wore instead of his white commander's cap. He puffed on a cigar and slurred his English words, made V signs the wrong way round. It helped that he was drunk himself, Reinhard thought, amused. They all were. Drunk on wine and brandy and schnapps in order to blot out, for a few hours, the unpleasant reality of their situation. Most of them were going to die, and probably very soon. The odds were stacked high against survival. One in five boats never returned from patrol.

He watched Metzler switch from Churchill, to Field Marshall Goering, swaggering around and swishing about with his swagger stick, then another switch to the Führer himself, standing on a chair, wild-eyed and dishevelled, ranting and raving, one arm extended in the Nazi salute.

Metzler's clowning had got him into trouble with authority more than once – saved only by the intervention of the Grossadmiral himself. Coming into the base, on return from a long patrol, Metzler had called out from the bridge to the dignitaries assembled on the quayside.

'Are those damned Nazis still in power?'

On hearing the affirmative, he'd ordered 'Full astern' and the boat had backed away rapidly from the quay. There had been plenty of laughter all round, but Metzler had been sent for and given a serious dressing-down.

He finished the Führer sketch with a stiff-armed salute, went back to his place at the table beside Reinhard and picked up his glass again.

'Well, my friend, how long do you think before we have to slink out of Lorient, with our tails between our legs?'

'About a week. Not longer.'

'That's my reckoning, too. Brest will soon be lost to the Yanks. Our turn next. A pity. I'll be sorry to say *adieu* to France. It's been a pleasure. Especially the women. I hope to God we're not banished to Norway with all those ice-cold maidens.'

Metzler slouched down in his chair and twirled the stem of his glass, slopping its contents over the rim. 'Of course, we're dead men anyway. So, we don't really need to worry ourselves about such minor things any more, do we?'

'Not too much.'

'How old are you, Reinhard?'

'Twenty-five.'

'I'm twenty-seven. An older Old Man. But not quite ready to die. Not yet. Not yet.'

Within three days the U-boats in Lorient were ordered to sail from their pens, leaving behind two boats too badly damaged to move. No bands, no crowds, no waves or cheers, and certainly no tears. No Yvettes, or Solanges or Lulus to wave a sodden handkerchief; they'd be getting ready to welcome the Yanks and the Tommies. Instead, a sullen group of French dockhands had gathered on the quayside and spat into the inner harbour water as they passed by. Their departure would be no secret. The French had long ago scented liberation and every one of them would be eager to spy for the Allies.

They followed their minesweeper escort down the channel to the open Atlantic and headed out to sea. Metzler's boat drew alongside and its commander doffed his top hat before he turned away. Reinhard replied with a salute.

The English Channel had to be given a wide berth since the Allies' invasion – it was far too well guarded and thickly mined. The U-boats who had been sent on suicidal missions to stop the enemy fleet had almost all been lost. Even equipped with the Schnorchel to allow them to stay below the surface, the constant parade of enemy destroyers and escorts crossing and re-crossing the Channel gave little chance of getting near any of their troop ships, and U-boats who had been sent into the fray early on had almost all been destroyed. Instead, Reinhard was ordered to patrol north-west of Ireland. It was no longer possible to form into the wolf packs of old; now they hunted alone.

The sea had moderated after some grey and stormy days. The sun came out and the U-boat cut through the swell, her bow rising with a glittering shower of spray before sinking back into the dark green water. They lay in wait off the Irish coast before sighting a convoy approaching from the west, masts emerging gradually above the horizon. At least fifty ships, but heavily escorted. All Reinhard could hope was that the enemy might have grown a little slack with so much success, that they might find it hard to credit that a single U-boat, a lone wolf, would have the balls to attack them in the face of such odds.

He waited for darkness before circling astern of the convoy, picking on a large steamer who had fallen a little behind the rest.

'Stand by to attack.'

His Chief Engineer kept the boat trimmed at periscope depth – not easy in a strong swell. In the control tower, Reinhard crouched at the lens of the attack periscope. The tubes had been flooded, the bow doors open, the settings for speed, course and depth adjusted. Now Reinhard could see the whole ship, even bigger than he'd hoped. He ordered a slight change of course.

'Stand by tube one. *Achtung! Los!*'

The bell shrilled and the torpedo left its tube with a hiss of compressed air.

'Torpedo running,' the hydrophone operator reported.

In the control room, vents had been opened to flood the trimming tank in the bow, compensating for the torpedo's weight.

They waited in silence.

'Torpedo still running.'

'Up periscope.'

The torpedo was streaking towards its target,

its propeller bearings and those of the steamer's about to converge and then, at the very last moment, they crossed. They'd missed. *Verdamnt! Verdamnt!*

Reinhard looked round at the disappointed faces. 'Better luck next time. We'll try again tonight.'

Under cover of darkness, they slunk after an oil tanker cocooned in the centre of the box convoy. Forget the miss; this one was worth twenty steamers. Very large and very modern, her cargo could be as much as sixteen thousand tons of crude oil. Reinhard played a patient game of dodge with the escorts, the U-boat's presence conveniently masked by the thrashing propellers of the convoy ships. He bided his time, lurking at periscope depth, watching the tanker, waiting for exactly the right moment.

He sank her with two torpedoes – aimed so precisely that this time there would be no mistake. She erupted in a towering pyre of orange flames and black smoke before sliding backwards, stern first, bows last, down into the darkness of the ocean.

Naturally, the escorts came after them: destroyers bearing down with murderous intent. They had dived to sixty metres when the first depth charge explosions began and a stream of water bursting into the bow compartment sent the U-boat nose-down to the bottom where she stuck. The bilge pumps could not be used for fear of giving away their position to the enemy; all that could be done was to disperse the water, bucketful by bucketful, evenly round the bilges to try to restore the trim. More thunderous explosions, more leaks – spurting as from a sieve. The lights went out, glass shattered, ducts and pipes split open. The bombardment went on for the rest of that night, for the following day and the U-boat bumped and groaned on the sea bed.

The air was thick and foul, only breathable in quick, shallow gasps, and the emergency lighting useless in the murk. Reinhard ordered those men not working to their bunks, to put on nose-clips and breathe through the tubes attached to potash cartridges which absorbed the carbon monoxide. Where there was no bunk space, the rest huddled on the bare steel plates, some of them in inches of water. He and Engelhardt leaned on the chart chest.

Every half hour or so, with his Number One following, Reinhard went round each compartment with a pocket torch, picking his way carefully over men, giving a word of encouragement here, a clasp on a shoulder there, checking that the rubber breathing nozzles had not slipped from mouths. A very young rating had fallen sound asleep in his hammock, his mouth-piece lying on his chest. Reinhard shook his arm gently and replaced the tube – like restoring a dummy to a child. An Old Man was a father to his crew, after all. He knew every one of them by name, knew where they came from in Germany and about their families. They were all good men. At least half had earned the U-boat badge and the Iron Cross, second class.

Another destroyer thrashed past overhead. Another load of bombs tore the ocean apart, hammered the boat mercilessly. New leaks in the hull; fresh damage. The enemy were taking it in turns. It would be hours before there would be any chance of surfacing. If they ever could.

In spite of the barrage, though, the boat was somehow taking it. So far the hull had held out instead of collapsing like a crushed sardine tin. Perhaps they were lying in a kindly fold of the sea bed? Perhaps they were just plain lucky?

By the next night, the destroyers finally gave up and the sound of their propellers gradually faded away. Inside the boat it was dark and dank and silent as a tomb. Reinhard let several more hours pass. There was always the possibility of an enemy ship still waiting quietly for them to surface – the cat watching the mouse-hole. The bilge pump was put to work and soon after midnight he gave the order to blow all tanks. The U-boat shuddered, shook herself and rose slowly off the bottom.

Cold air rushed into the boat as the conning tower hatch was flung open to a black and starless night. With no sign of any enemy warships, Reinhard let the men take turns to go up on to the bridge and breathe their fill.

Engelhardt took off his cap and wiped his brow. 'We were lucky, sir. For a while, I didn't think we were going to make it, did you?'

He smiled as he lied. 'I never doubted it for a moment, Number One.'

Leaks were plugged, the magnetic compass

restored to working order, cracked gauges mended, dials readjusted, all possible internal damage repaired. Orders had been received to sail to Bergen, Norway and so the U-boat limped on her way.

They celebrated Christmas Eve at sea. The engine room rigged up a Christmas tree made out of branches and pine needles of wood and coloured paper with cotton wool for snow and pocket-torch bulbs sheathed in white paper for candles. The cook produced a feast of ham and potatoes and sauerkraut, followed by tinned strawberries and tinned cream whipped up into mountain peaks, and a sponge Christmas cake made from still-fresh eggs and covered with icing. Reinhard poured a glass of brandy for each man. *Prost! Prost! Prost! Frohe Weihnachten! Frohes Fest!* By God, they deserved it!

On the American Forces station, Judy Garland was singing 'Have Yourself a Merry Little Christmas', which made a nice change from 'Stille Nacht'.

A coastguard vessel guided them through the tricky fjord waterways and into the port of Bergen where a handful of men watched their arrival on the quayside in silence. From their awed expressions, it was clear that they had been drawn by the unaccustomed and rare sight of a U-boat returning safely from a patrol.

The Commanding Officer appeared and came on board to offer his congratulations. The sinking of the large oil tanker had already been noted and Reinhard was awarded Oak Leaves to his Knight's Cross and promoted immediately to the rank of Korvettenkapitän.

The boat entered the shelter of the concrete bunker where the rest of the repair and maintenance work would be carried out, and where she would be re-painted, refuelled, re-armed and re-provisioned for the next patrol. Meanwhile, by way of celebration of still being alive, they were invited to cocktails and dinner. If the immaculately groomed Commanding Officer was dismayed by their appearance – their dirty hair, matted beards, grey-green faces and hollow cheeks – he was too polite to comment. Instead, he made a rousing speech promising that better times were to come and that soon they would have the very newest type of U-boats – bigger and better and more powerful than ever before. They would be able to cut off the enemy's continental supplies and stop him in his tracks. The men listened equally politely, and went on drinking.

Snow lay several feet thick on the ground, but the officers' accommodation was well-heated and pleasant enough. There was even a real Christmas tree in the mess, with real lights. It reminded Reinhard of past Christmases in Hamburg when his mother had still been alive. St Nikolaus, carols, presents, a big feast ... It was all so long, long ago.

A party was arranged, with drink and food, music and some obliging and buxom Norwegian girls to dance with.

Bergen was an interesting old city, built on a fjord and surrounded by hills. Narrow cobbled streets, wooden houses, trams, old wharves, cod fishing boats. In spite of the snow and the cold, Reinhard wandered around like a tourist in peace time. The Royal Air Force had made some visits to the harbour, of course, but as usual the concrete U-boat bunkers had stood the test of even their heaviest bombs. Otherwise, the war didn't seem to have made much impact. He remembered hearing the curious story of how the country's capital had been taken – not by a crushing military attack, but more by bluff. A mere three thousand German troops had landed in Oslo and their military band and two accordions had begun a series of jolly concerts and sing-songs in the main streets, including the English 'Roll Out the Barrel', while the German soldiers paraded up and down, singing as they marched and watched by crowds of mesmerized Norwegian citizens.

A week later, Reinhard heard the bad and sad news that Metzler's boat had been lost at sea with all hands. A thousand, thousand pities! He could have told the old clown that the Norwegian maidens weren't nearly as icy as he'd feared.

Christmas Day had been a day like any other at Western Approaches. Someone had draped hand-coloured paper chains around, but otherwise it was strictly business as usual in the Navy Map Room for the plotters. The girls in

Stroma's watch were old hands at the job, except for the newest who was also the youngest. She had made a mistake or two where mistakes weren't tolerated; any more errors and she would be removed from her duties.

Near the end of their final watch, when they were all very tired, Stroma saw the girl standing at the bottom of the tall ladder, tears running down her cheeks, her body shaking.

'I can't go up there ... I can't do it any more.'

It was no good telling her that she could, and that she must. The girl was obviously too terrified to move, let alone climb the dizzy heights of the wall map. Stroma had done it many times and even to her it was unnerving. From the top, the map table looked a very long way down.

She said, 'Go and sit down until you feel better. I'll take over.'

She went up, holding on to the iron rail with one hand and then reaching over to the wall map to alter the latest position of a convoy.

It was always tricky. Signals came in as the convoy progressed across the ocean and you had to know the speed of a convoy, its ships and their escorts, to make the changes accurately on the wall. Usually, there were U-boats around to deal with as well, but this time none had been reported in the area.

When she'd finished she started to climb down again, feeling for the rungs with her feet as she went. Later on, she thought the accident had probably happened because she was tired and not paying proper attention, or maybe because she was in too much of a hurry. Whatever the reason, halfway down she somehow missed a rung. Her foot trod on air instead of metal. At the same time, she lost her grip on the handrail and fell the rest of the way down on to the concrete floor.

1945

'You're an extremely fortunate young lady, you know.' The surgeon wagged a finger severely at her. 'You could easily be dead.'

The pain was so bad that Stroma wasn't sure that she wouldn't prefer to be. The surgeon went on talking – not to her this time, but to the attentive little group of junior doctors and students gathered round the end of her hospital bed, hanging on his every word. He was an iron-grey-haired man with the look of a head-master, accustomed to instant obedience from all. It would not have surprised her if he had carried a cane.

Her injury was being discussed as though she weren't present – or, at least, not conscious. A very nasty break of the femur – the large upper bone in the leg. A spiral fracture, apparently caused by the way she had landed so awkward-ly on the concrete. The surgeon seemed to blame her for that extra piece of carelessness, and he was probably quite right. Of course, if she had fallen straight backwards on to her head, he probably wouldn't have to concern himself with her at all. Instead, she had twisted round, grabbing frantically at the rungs as they went by.

'We'll keep her in traction for a few more days,' the surgeon was saying, waving his hand at her leg suspended in the air by ropes and pulleys. 'Wait for the swelling to go down before we put the leg in plaster for at least two months. It's going to take time, and we have to hope that the break mends evenly, otherwise the patient could be left with one leg shorter than the other and a permanent limp.'

The satellite group all nodded, one of them even smiled at her brightly. Then they moved on to the next bed in the ward, occupied by an old woman who had also fallen – but over her cat not down a steep ladder – and had broken a hip.

Stroma shut her eyes. Only morphine would stop the pain and it wasn't time for another dose yet, so there was nothing to do but put up with it. Nothing to do but lie there and think how stupid she'd been. If she had paid proper attention, not been in such a rush, it would never have happened. She would still be at Western Approaches, doing her job, not stuck in a hospital ward for weeks to come. No use to the war effort. No use to anyone. At first she'd wept and felt sorry for herself; now she still wept sometimes, but it was no longer from self-pity, but anger at her own stupidity.

The other Wrens came to visit her, bringing books and magazines, precious sweets from their rations, lavender-scented soap, talcum powder, hand cream. She was overwhelmed by their kindness and put on the cheeriest face that she could – laughing at their jokes and listening to the latest gossip. But it was hard to watch them walk away down the ward and not be able to walk with them.

Her parents came up from London and she put on a cheerful face for them, too. Her father, of course, would know all about how tricky spiral fractures could be, but he didn't mention it. Her mother was shocked by how deathly pale she looked and said her hair needed washing. After they had left, she borrowed a hand mirror from another patient and saw that both things were true.

The leg had been in plaster for three weeks by the time Hamish turned up. She got him to sign his name, alongside the Wrens and the naval chaps who'd also visited. Some of them had drawn pictures and written rude verses. He read them and laughed. She had expected him to tell her what an idiot she'd been, but for once he kept his thoughts to himself.

'I bet it hurts a bit.'

'Not too bad. They give me stuff.'

'Hmmm. Well, they seem to think it'll be quite a while before you'll be let out of here.'

'I know. One of the Wren admin officers came the other day. She said they'll probably send me home to practise walking around. I'll be on crutches at first. It's going to be a real bore.'

'Well, you'll just have to be patient.' He glanced at the next bed where old Mrs Campbell with the broken hip was clicking away with her needles at something long and khaki-coloured. 'Perhaps you could take up knitting? Comforts for the troops?'

'The troops wouldn't get much comfort from a scarf full of holes. I'm hopeless at it.'

'Well, the war may be over soon, anyway. The Yanks and us seem to be doing pretty well in Europe and the Russians are very busy slaughtering Germans. It's practically full steam ahead.'

She said slowly, 'How about the U-boats?'

'Not many of the buggers left, I'm glad to say. It's been a hell of a battle, as you know, but we beat them hands down in the end. They know they can't win now.'

Reinhard must certainly be dead, she thought. And probably long ago. She hoped it had been a quick and merciful end for him.

Hamish had moved on from U-boats. 'By the way, Alice is already planning our wedding. Maybe in September. She wanted to know if you might like to be a bridesmaid.'

'I'd love to be, if I can walk all right. The surgeon said something about a limp if the bone doesn't mend properly.'

'Oh, I shouldn't worry about that. It'll be fine.'

'Well, I'll do my best. Will you stay in the Navy – when the war's over?'

'I think so. I'd rather like to make a career of it.'

'Admiral Mackay?'

'Maybe one day. If I'm lucky.'

She had no doubt that he would be. 'I wanted to ask you something, Hamish.'

'Fire away.'

'Well, apart from reading, I don't have much to do except lie here and think. And I've been thinking about Craigmore.'

'Hmm. What about it, exactly?'

'Well, when the war's over – whenever that is – I don't want to stay in the Wrens – not sure they'd have me back now, anyway – and I don't want to go and live in London and work in some office there. What I'd really like to do is go and live up at Craigmore – that's if you've no objection. I wouldn't live in the house; maybe in one of the cottages. If you wouldn't mind.'

'Of course I wouldn't mind, you idiot! But I think you should live in the house. It needs somebody to look after it. We can't just leave it empty forever. Of course, I'll be up there whenever I can – bring a few chaps for a bit of shooting and fishing and what not – and maybe Alice will come too, sometimes. We ought to try and get a housekeeper and cook ... Perhaps Ellen would come back.'

'We could ask her.'

He frowned. 'But wouldn't you be a bit lonely up there, Stroma? It's pretty isolated. Not much fun for you on your own, I'd have thought. OK for a few weeks, but all the year round? What on earth would you do?'

'Actually,' she said, 'I've got an idea.'

'Not something damn stupid, I hope.'

'No. I think it's rather a good one.'

He sighed. 'I may as well hear it.'

'Well, I happened to be reading an article in a magazine that one of the Wrens brought me. It was all about tweed cloth and how it's made, and when I'd read it, I started thinking.'

'Thinking about what, for heaven's sake?'

'About starting a woollen mill.'

He looked at her blankly. 'A woollen mill? What on earth for?'

'Well, it would be a good thing for the island. Something to give people employment when the war's over.'

'The distilleries will do that.'

'Yes, I know. But the island needs something else. There's the sheep, of course, and Highland cattle and the fishing and the game, but that's about the lot. Now, if we had a working woollen mill, it would make good sense. A lot of the women can spin. Grace has a spinning wheel – I've often seen her using it, sitting outside the cottage. She keeps some of the sheep's wool, spins it on her wheel, and then she knits it up into jumpers for Angus.'

'I've seen them. They're awful.'

'But if our wool were made into a good enough quality tweed – something really distinctive – it could be sold in England, perhaps even all over the world – like our whisky.'

He shook his head. 'You've been dreaming, Stroma, not thinking. Spinning's not enough; you need looms for weaving and that's complicated and expensive machinery.'

'Remember old Kildale mill? You've fished in the stream that runs right by it. Grandfather didn't bother much with it but it's on the Craigmore estate so it belongs to us.'

'But it's a ruin.'

'No, actually, it isn't. I went and took a look inside once, just out of curiosity. The building's in quite good repair. And it's still got two looms.'

'Nobody's worked there for about fifty years or more. The looms would be useless now.'

'I don't think so. They're beautiful old Victorian things. Made to last forever. I bet we could get them to work again. And I'd like to try.'

He sighed. 'Well, that's up to you, old girl. I wouldn't have the time. Personally, I think it's a crazy idea, but if it amuses you...'

'It's not a question of it amusing me, Hamish. I'm serious.'

'It'd need a load of money to get it started, you realize that?'

'Maybe not so much, and not all at once. Next time I get up to Craigmore, I'll go and have another look at the mill. And I'll talk to Mr Pirbright and Mr Ross about it.'

'That's OK by me. So long as they're involved, they'll stop you doing anything too stupid.'

'Was that your boyfriend, dear?' Mrs Campbell asked Stroma when Hamish had gone.

'No, he's my brother.'

The old woman sighed. 'So handsome in that

lovely uniform. I've always fancied the Navy. All the nice girls love a sailor, don't they?'

It was not until the middle of February that Stroma was released from hospital. The break had taken its time, but it had healed evenly. As the surgeon kept reminding her sternly, she was a very lucky young lady.

Learning to use the crutches to walk with was more difficult than she had expected. She couldn't imagine how Long John Silver always seemed to get around so easily. The crutches rubbed painfully and got tangled up in things, including herself. When she'd finally got the hang of them, after walking what seemed like miles up and down the ward and round the hospital, they'd sent her home to London.

She went by ambulance, in company with another Wren who had broken her ankle in the blackout, an able seaman who had mangled his hand in a boat's chain, and a young rating who had been badly burned in a boiler explosion at sea. He was swathed in bandages and didn't speak at all.

The V2 rockets were still falling on London, but there were fewer, and people had become used to them and were going on with their daily lives. With no sound and no warning, there was no way of avoiding fate, and so no point in hiding. But, if London was taking it, German cities were being hit even harder. According to the news on the wireless and photographs in the papers, they were in ruins.

Rosanne, who was working as a doctor's secretary in Reigate, came to visit at the weekend, wearing a sparkly ring on her left hand. She sat on the sofa, showing it off, and produced a photograph of her fiancé – an army lieutenant called Christopher. They'd met at a dance in Reigate and were engaged two weeks later. Like Hamish and Alice, they were getting married as soon as the war was over.

'He looks super. Your parents must be awfully pleased.'

'Yes, they are. They've never got over losing Jeremy, of course, but I'm hoping this might help.'

'Specially if you have children.'

'We plan to do that, as soon as possible. We want at least four.'

Rosanne was looking so radiant and so happy that, just for a moment, Stroma wished she'd said 'yes' to Tom, then she, too, could be wearing a sparkly ring and planning a lovely wedding and children. Tom was such a nice person that it would probably have been easy to live contentedly with him. Except, of course, that she wasn't in love with him. Which made it quite wrong, and not at all fair on Tom.

Rosanne said, 'Thank heavens Christopher wasn't sent to France. At least, not yet. He's furious about that, of course, but I'm so thankful. If only the war would end, he'd never have to go.'

'Everyone seems to think it'll be over soon.'

'It's hard to imagine, Stroma, isn't it? We've

all got so used to it – the blackout, the rationing, the bombs and everything. Do you remember that dreadful time when we saw that fighter being shot down?'

'Yes, I remember.'

She'd never forget. It still made her shudder.

Rosanne was putting her photo away in her handbag. 'And do you remember that awfully good-looking German chap who used to write to you? He went into their Navy and sent you that photo of himself in his uniform and Miss Calder tore it up. I wonder what's happened to him. Didn't he go into U-boats, or something?'

'Yes, he did.'

'Then he's most probably dead. Nearly all of them are, aren't they? I've read about it in the newspapers.'

'I believe so.'

'Can I sign your plaster before I go?'

The plaster came off a week later and underneath her leg looked white and thin – like a stick of celery. Physiotherapy and exercises helped, but it took ages to get used to walking again and her leg still ached a lot.

In April, the WRNS wrote a letter to say that they had decided she should be officially invalided out. She stayed at home for a while, going for walks and visiting the local library where she read all she could about spinning and weaving and making tweed.

Reinhard had received orders to patrol the Pentland Firth, between the north coast of Scotland

and the Orkney Islands, close to the Royal Navy base at Scapa Flow.

He reckoned there couldn't be more than about seventy U-boats left operating by now. Perhaps fewer. And the news of the Allies' advance was growing rapidly worse. The Americans had marched into Cologne and crossed the Rhine at Remagen. The river's length from Holland to Koblenz was in Allied hands, while the Soviet armies were storming into Germany from the Baltic to Silesia. The home towns of many of his crew had been overrun by the enemy. Only God knew what had happened to their families, whether there was anything or anyone left for them to go back to, or whether the U-boat was the only home that remained to them.

Before they had left Bergen, one of the new type of U-boats, promised by the Commanding Officer, had arrived at the port. Reinhard had been given a tour by its commander. The boat was far superior in every way to a Type VII – nearly three times as large, with push-button hydraulic controls and roomy quarters that verged on luxurious, compared with their own cramped squalor. It carried many more torpedoes, which could be fired at a depth of 50 metres without seeing the targets, and it could go twice as deep and was faster below the surface than above. It was a wonder boat that could force the Allies back on to the defensive at sea – if only they could be built fast enough and in large enough numbers and if the east and west fronts could hold out. He knew all such hopes were just dreams.

The wonder boat's commander had wished him luck – luck that they would certainly be needing in their antiquated death-trap. The old type of boats, with all their deficiencies and defects, were being sent into battle like war-horses who should have been relegated to the knacker's yard years ago.

They patrolled the Firth for several days without sighting a single enemy ship until one evening, at sunset, a Royal Navy frigate came sailing merrily over the horizon. All alone. Red Riding Hood, skipping along through the woods on her way to visit dear Grandmama, blissfully unaware of the wolf lurking behind the trees.

'They're getting cocky, sir,' Engelhardt said. 'Too big for their boots.'

'Don't worry, we have the cure.'

They trailed the frigate at periscope depth. For once, there were no enemy planes about, nothing to force them to dive, nothing to interfere with their quiet and steady pursuit. The sea turned ink-dark as the last of the light faded.

'Standby to surface ... Surface!'

As soon as the hatch was opened, Reinhard shinned up the ladder on to the bridge. The visibility was good, with a helpful swell to hide their low-lying presence. The frigate herself was easy to see through the binoculars – still sticking to her westerly course. He used the trusty trick of closing stealthily on a parallel course, and at a range of 1000 metres, three torpedoes were sent on their way in a fan shot. They all found their target. Even so, the frigate was tough; she took a while to heel over and start on her way to the bottom. Plenty of time for an SOS to have been sent and lifeboats to be lowered.

'That'll teach them,' his Number One observed. 'We're not bloody well finished yet.'

Their moment of satisfaction was short-lived, however. One of the diesels broke down and they were forced to return to Bergen at a snail's pace. On the way, the wireless reports grew steadily worse. The Ruhr was surrounded by the Allies, the British were closing on Hamburg and the Russians had occupied Vienna and were encircling Berlin. A special bulletin announced that the American President, Franklin Delano Roosevelt, had died, with the assurance that providence had removed one of the fiercest enemies of the German people. The tide of the war would, apparently, now turn in their favour. The announcement ended in a rousing military march. In Reinhard's view, the death of the American president would make little difference to the outcome of the war. Someone else would simply step into his shoes and carry on as before.

Back in Bergen, while they were waiting for the diesel to be repaired, news came that Mussolini, the Italian leader, had been hanged by partisans and two days afterwards, another important announcement was made over the wireless in the evening. Solemn music preceded it and the announcer's voice was loud and harsh.

'Our Führer, Adolf Hitler, fighting to his last breath, fell for Germany in his headquarters in the Reich's Chancellery. On April the thirtieth, the Führer appointed Grossadmiral Dönitz to take his place. The Grossadmiral now speaks to the German people.'

Reinhard was lying on his bed in his quarters, smoking a cigarette, when the announcement came through. Dönitz followed with a speech urging that the military struggle must be carried on to save the lives of millions of refugees, and that Germans must continue to fight and defend their rights. The national anthem followed.

It was the end. He knew that. The end of the long struggle and the sacrifice and the suffering. All of it in vain. His country was effectively finished. Germany was already in ruins, and she would now be in chains. The Allies had shown little mercy in war and he very much doubted that they would show any in peace.

Perhaps it was as well that Father had not lived to see this shameful day, or Bruno either, with all his dreams of triumph and glory. How would his brother have resigned himself to the total humiliation and ignominy that now lay before them?

He stubbed out the cigarette, lay back again on the pillow. God, he was so tired! Tired in mind and tired in body. Tired through and through after years of war spent sealed up in a ready-made coffin. He couldn't remember when he had last slept properly – an untroubled, peaceful, deep, restoring sleep. Longer than he could imagine. He put one hand over his eyes.

Three days later, they sailed from Bergen to obey the Grossadmiral's order to continue the hopeless fight. Berlin had been captured by the Russians, the Americans were occupying the whole of the Ruhr, the British were in Kiel. German forces had surrendered in Italy, in the Netherlands, in Denmark, in the north-west of Germany itself. On the following day, the Grossadmiral sent a signal, instructing all U-boats to stop all hostile action against Allied shipping. On the sixth of May, Dönitz sent another signal.

'My U-boat men, six years of war lie behind you. You have fought like lions. An overwhelming material superiority has driven us into a tight corner from which it is no longer possible to continue the war. Unbeaten and unblemished, you lay down your arms after a heroic fight without parallel. We proudly remember our fallen comrades who gave their lives for the Führer and Fatherland. Comrades, preserve that spirit in which you have fought for so long and so gallantly for the sake of the future of the Fatherland. Long live Germany!'

The British went on attacking and sinking the U-boats still at sea, taking no chances. And who could blame them? Reinhard gathered his crew together and outlined a plan that had been forming in his mind since it had become very clear that the Allies would win the war. They had had the luck to be away from port when the order had been given to all U-boats to disarm and to hoist a black surrender flag. They were out of reach of the authorities ashore. Their boat had recently been re-stocked with provisions and enough fuel to carry them to the other side of the world. They had a choice: surface and surrender to the enemy, which would mean being taken prisoner and thrown in a barbed-wire cage for months, perhaps years, accused of whatever war crimes the Allies cared to throw at them. Or, thanks to the Snort, they could stay submerged and hidden. Disappear. Sail away to, say, the southern hemisphere, to the Argentine, for instance, where there would be the chance to start a new life in freedom.

He made no attempt to persuade his crew or to hurry their decision. The choice was theirs. Those who wished to stay behind would be put ashore in Norway. Sixteen – mostly older and married with families – and Mohr, his Second Officer who had rashly got engaged on his last leave – voted to remain. The remainder – including, thank God, Franz, his Chief Engineer – elected to risk the voyage to South America.

Engelhardt, footloose and fancy-free, his home city of Frankfurt reduced to rubble and his widowed mother fled to the country to live with a strait-laced sister, made a predictable choice.

'When you think about it, sir, we'll be the last

wolf left. That's quite an honour.'

Reinhard said grimly, 'Well, let's hope it won't be necessary to show our teeth.'

He had planned to put the men ashore that night on a lonely stretch of mountain coast, using two rubber dinghies. The Norwegian waters with their rocks and tides and winds were treacherous and to land them safely meant having to go in close. He took the U-boat in very slowly, using the electric motors, and the depth went from seven fathoms, to five, to four, then to two ... She heeled over as her keel grazed a rock and her bows rose up out of the water. He called instantly for full speed astern but too late; she was stuck. They launched the dinghies and the men rowed off to shore, while they tried to release the boat – pumping water out of the tanks, re-trimming her and working the engines at full speed, but all to no effect. The short Norwegian May night would soon be over, and, with it, their chance of escape. He reckoned that there was no more than half an hour of darkness left. As a last resort, they sent compressed air through the tanks and under the keel, engines roaring at full speed astern, the whole boat shuddering, needles flickering dangerously on red. Miraculously, she pulled free, her bows sliding back into the water, turning on her keel.

The men signalled Bon Voyage as they reached the shore. It had been agreed that if they were caught and interrogated, they would say that their U-boat had struck a mine and that they were the only survivors. He knew that they would keep to their word.

The coastline was already visible in the dawn as Reinhard gave the order to dive. The U-boat vanished from sight, the seas closing over where she had been.

On VE Day, 8th May, the day after Germany had surrendered unconditionally, Stroma went with friends to join the crowds in the Mall in front of Buckingham Palace. Union Jacks hung from every building. People were wearing red, white and blue rosettes and comic hats, including policemen's helmets. They were singing and dancing and waving flags, climbing lampposts, hugging and kissing. Many of them were crying, some were drunk, others were simply delirious with joy. The day faded, but the crowds stayed and as darkness fell, the lights went on again all over London – street lights, shop lights, restaurant lights, together with wartime searchlights flickering across the night sky – this time for fun.

Stroma was swept along the Mall by the crowds towards the Palace where a young man was playing a trumpet outside the gates, blasting out some Dixieland tune. Two other players joined him – a drummer and a trombonist. A handcart appeared from nowhere and the three musicians climbed aboard and set off in procession, with people cavorting in their wake. An American soldier seized hold of Stroma and spun her round in a crazy dance. The crowds blurred and all she could see clearly was the American's smiling black face and his gleaming white teeth. They followed the handcart and its band, dancing all the way back down the Mall, down St James's Street to Piccadilly Circus and then to Trafalgar Square and back to the Palace where the King and Queen and the two princesses appeared on the balcony to a great roar of appreciation from the crowds.

Later, at two in the morning, she stood at her open bedroom window, listening to the music and the singing that was still going strong, and watching the fireworks still exploding in the sky. Her leg ached furiously but she didn't care; it had been worth it.

We won, she thought. *We beat them in the end. No more Hitler and his evil Nazis. No more cruelty and unspeakable misery for those in their power*. The newspaper photographs of the wretches found in the concentration camps and the shocking piles of corpses had been so hideous, so sickening, that she couldn't get them out of her mind.

After a while, she went and lay down on her bed in the darkness, thinking instead about Craigmore. The best place on earth to be. Her leg had mended and there was no reason why she couldn't make the journey, open up the house, take a look at the old mill, make plans to start a new life. The sea, the wind, the pure air, the heather-covered hills, the gentle rain, the peace and the quiet ... the island would work its magic, as it had always done, and take away all the grim memories and the nightmares of the war.

The Royal Navy was patrolling the seas round Britain as thoroughly as ever and Reinhard was forced to keep the U-boat submerged as they headed away from Norway towards the north coast of Scotland. They cruised at twenty-five fathoms during the day and at Snort depth by night in order to recharge their batteries. Short-handed, there was much more work for every man. His crew had started out as war-weary and exhausted as himself and he soon saw from the dull look in their eyes that they were totally unfit for the ordeal ahead. The months spent below without fresh air or daylight had turned faces grey and cheeks hollow, and skin infections took hold and flourished.

The conditions on the boat were even more unpleasant than usual. Rubbish could not be jettisoned underwater, and so was piling up in decomposing and stinking mess. Morale was already low among his men. Good men whose lives were in his hands, who trusted in him.

Reinhard reached a decision. Their route round the coast of Scotland would bring them near the southern Hebrides – close enough to pay another visit to Glas Uig where they could rest and regain some strength. They would remain under water in the cove during the day and surface after dark, when the men could go up on deck, breathe fresh air, take exercise, swim – prepare themselves better, mentally and physically, for the long voyage which could take as much as three months. It was worth the risk of discovery in order to increase their chances of success.

Engelhardt was delighted at the idea.

'Another sheep, sir? And maybe some fishing, too?'

'We'll see. For all we know, the house has been reoccupied. We need to make sure it's still empty.'

'I'll check, sir.'

His Number One was obviously remembering the decanter – and probably the Bechstein piano.

As before, they passed submerged along the Sound of Islay and slipped into the hidden cove. As soon as night fell, they surfaced. He sent Engelhardt up to the house and his Number One returned to report that it was in darkness with no sign of life.

'How about the whisky? Still there?'

Engelhardt looked injured. 'You said not to go inside, sir. So I didn't.'

'Quite right.'

He let the men up on to the decks in small groups of five or so, gave them time to breathe the Scottish air, stretch their legs, work their cramped muscles, strip off and swim in the clear water of the cove. No splashing, no talking, as little sound as possible. *A day or two of this*, he thought, *and we'll be fit to go*.

Stroma took the night sleeper up to Glasgow,

sharing a compartment with a Wren officer who was going home on leave. The Third Officer had every intention of staying on in the WRNS even though the war was over.

'I wouldn't go back to Civvy Street for anything. Not now. Too boring for words. And there's still going to be plenty for us to do.'

There would be plenty to do at Craigmore, Stroma thought, as the train rattled north through the dark. The house would be damp and dusty, full of cobwebs and mice – probably rats, too – and all kinds of insects that would have to be routed out. She would need help. If not Ellen, then another woman, at least, and a gardener to replace Mack. Everything would have to be put in order with the house before she could turn her attention to the mill.

From Glasgow, she began the long trek by bus to Gourock where she took a fishing boat to Dunoon. A farmer gave her a lift in his cart up the glen and as far as Portavadie where she caught the ferry across to and stayed two nights at the old hotel at West Lock Tarbert, waiting for the paddle steamer *Lochiel* to come in to Kennacraig and take her over to Islay.

They'd not seen much of the war, the locals told her. The army had been stationed in the area for a while, but that had been in the early days when they'd thought the Germans might invade Scotland. Daft idea, if ever there was one. There'd been rumours of U-boats snooping round the coast and some folks claimed to have spotted them on the surface, but that might have been after a dram or two. The RAF Coastal Command had been overhead with their big flying boats, making a lot of noise and commotion and scaring the animals, but they mostly went far out into the Atlantic to look after the convoys.

She watched cows being loaded on to the steamer – swung aboard by crane in nets, bundled high in the air, hoofs askew. Undignified, but they didn't seem to mind too much. After that, it was crates of this and barrels of that, sacks of the other, then two cars and a van. It took most of the morning to load the ferry and begin the four-hour crossing. She sat at the captain's table for lunch, as the family had always done, eating with polished silver knives and forks and on starched linen, for all the world as though they were on a luxury passenger liner headed for the New World and not being tossed about in an old paddle steamer butting its way across to a small Hebridean island.

At Port Askaig she got a lift with the post bus. The postman, Archie Brown, took her to Bridgend and then as far as Bowmore. From there she rode to Port Ellen in the cab of the old milk lorry. The driver, Donald MacPhee, who had more Gaelic than English, was always hard to understand and the loud rattling of the churns didn't help. But he kept smiling his two-toothed smile at her and she kept nodding and smiling back. At Port Ellen she stopped to buy provisions – butter, sugar, potatoes, tinned food, cheese, eggs – and, as she came out of the store, Dr Mackenzie happened to come by in his green Morris and he drove her the rest of the way, bumping and jolting down the long track to Craigmore. From him, she learned that Angus was ill – so ill that he had taken to his bed the week before and was still there, which meant it must be bad, though the doctor didn't actually say so.

'Will you be all right, Stroma? All on your own here?'

'Yes, of course.'

'Well, let me know if you need me for anything.'

'Thanks.'

She waved as he drove away, and then went into the house.

As she had expected, it was chillingly damp and fusty as a sealed tomb. She went from room to room, pulling off the dust sheets and piling them in corners and opening the windows and the storm shutters to let in the fresh air and the fitful sunlight. The spiders had been busy spinning huge webs and big beetles scuttled out of her path. In the kitchen, the copper pans – once Ellen's pride and joy – had turned black, the scrubbed table was spattered with mouse droppings and something with very sharp teeth had been gnawing at one of the chair legs. The dried food left in the larder had been nibbled through and there was an abandoned nest of chewed-up cloth and paper in a dark corner under the bottom shelf.

It would take weeks to get the place clean and habitable again, but otherwise everything was in its place – furniture, paintings, mirrors, rugs, oil lamps, ornaments, the stags' heads guarding the hallway. Or almost everything. Her Wren photograph had gone from its frame on the piano. Odd, but she assumed Grandfather had probably put it somewhere else.

She left the house and walked the mile to Angus's thatched cottage. The door and windows were shut, the hens scratching about outside, the usually flourishing potato patch overgrown. When Grace opened the door, Stroma saw by her face that things were just as bad as she had feared.

Angus was lying on the brass bed with his eyes closed. His face was like wax, his fiery hair and whiskers faded, his frame shrunken to a shadow of the giant of a man she had known and loved.

When she spoke to him, he opened his eyes slowly and they were faded, too. His voice was no longer a sonorous boom but a faint and hoarse whisper.

'Ye've come back, then, lassie?'

'Yes,' she said quietly. 'I've come back.'

'Ye'll be stayin' noo?'

'Yes. I'll be staying.'

He nodded. 'That's guid ... that's guid.'

She sat by the bed but his eyes had closed again.

'Can I bring some food for you?' she asked Grace.

'He'll no touch it – only a wee bit of broth sometimes, that's all.'

'What about you, though?'

'Och, there's the eggs, an' I've a sackful of potatoes and some vegetables. And I can always take a hen, if need be.'

'What about a rabbit? Would you like one?'

'Aye ... they make a good stew. Angus was always fond of rabbit. It might tempt him.'

'I'll be over tomorrow, first thing.'

Grace's spinning wheel was standing on the hearth and, as she left, she passed Angus's deerstalker and knobbled crook hanging by the door.

Dusk was the best time for shooting rabbits, when they came out to feed. She fetched a .22 from the gun room, loaded it and set off towards the large warren above the woods encircling Glas Uig. The rabbits were already out, hopping about, nibbling at the grass. They were easy enough to catch and, if she hadn't lost the knack, it would be a clean kill. She aimed carefully and bagged two of them in quick succession.

She decided to walk on down through the woods to the promontory where the trees thinned so that she would be able to see the cove below and satisfy herself that nothing had changed at Glas Uig.

In the evening light, the water was the colour of green glass, the rocks a dark necklace round the edge. Everything was very still and very quiet.

The sudden rippling on the surface could have been caused by a large fish, or by a freak gust of wind. She watched, puzzled, as the ripples spread wider and wider and became a boiling and bubbling whirlpool. A dark monster burst up from below, cascading water from its flanks. A monster as big as the whale that had once been trapped in the cove.

A U-boat.

The hatch was flung open in the control tower and men came out on to the decks and began securing lines to the jetty rings. Then another man appeared on the bridge – a tall figure wearing a white cap. The commander. She watched him leaning on the bridge railing, looking about him at the cove.

U-boat commanders had been feted like royalty, worshipped like film stars. They had been awarded medals, presented with flowers and champagne on their triumphant returns to port. Bands played for them, girls smiled at them, crowds waved and cheered. Someone at Western Approaches had shown her German newspaper photos of U-boats returning to port. Propaganda pictures to thrill the *volk* and alarm the enemy.

She dropped the rabbits and lay down flat on her stomach, the gun butt pressed into her shoulder, her elbow resting on the ground, the commander's white cap fixed in the rifle's sight. The .22 held five bullets and it was possible to kill a man even at that distance. Hamish, who had learned all about it from his war comics, had once explained to her that you had to go for the head or the heart if you wanted to be sure. But Hamish was a far better shot, and the light was poor and her hands were shaking. And even if, by some miracle, she managed to hit the U-boat commander, there would be a crew of at least forty others to be reckoned with.

She began to slither backwards on her stomach towards the cover of the trees, and had almost reached them when the commander turned and looked up the hillside, straight in her direction.

He must have spotted her because he jumped on to the jetty and began walking up the hill towards her. She turned and fled in panic up through the woods. A hidden rock brought her crashing painfully to her knees but she scrambled up and limped on.

The key to the front door of the house had been lost years ago and the bolts were too rusty to move. She ran into the drawing room and crouched behind the sofa.

The front door opened and she could hear footsteps on the flagstones in the hall. She shut her eyes and held her breath.

He came into the room and paused for a moment. When she opened her eyes she could see his sea boots through the space under the sofa. As they started to come towards her, she stood up, waving the rifle.

'Don't come any closer, or I'll shoot.'

He stopped.

'I warn you,' she said. 'I'll shoot.'

'Yes, I can see that you will.'

She waved the gun fiercely again. 'Put your hands up.'

'If you wish.'

He raised his hands slowly.

She stared at him, shocked. He looked as if he had been incarcerated in a dungeon for a long time. The haggard face, the beard, the matted hair, the oil-stained overalls, the battered white cap ... none of it resembled the immaculate German naval officer in the photograph that Miss Calder had torn into small pieces and tossed so disdainfully in the waste paper basket. The blue eyes, alone, were the same. If it hadn't been for them she would never have known him.

He said, 'You don't recognize me, do you, Stroma?'

'Yes, actually I do. But you've changed rather a lot, Reinhard.'

'Submarines are not very good for the health or looks. Tell me, is that gun loaded?'

'Of course it is. I've been shooting rabbits.'

'Don't you think I'd better have it now, before you kill me too?'

He moved forward, took the gun from her grasp, emptied out the remaining bullets and dropped them into his pocket. He laid the empty rifle down on the sofa between them and looked at her for a moment in silence. 'I have always dreamed of meeting you again.'

She said coldly, 'Have you really? What on earth are you doing here anyway?'

'The last time nobody was living here.'

'The last time?'

'Two years ago when we needed to make repairs to our boat, I came here. My father did the same with his U-boat in the first war, you see. We knew all about your secret cove before we came with *Sturmwind* that summer. This time, I sailed my boat into the cove and I came up here to the house with my first officer. We found that the door was not locked. I regret that we entered and we drank some of your whisky. Also, my officer played the piano. I hope you don't mind.'

'What a cheek! And that's my scarf you're wearing.'

'Yes, I took it from your coat pocket in the hall.'

'Did you take my photograph from the piano as well?'

'Yes, I stealed that also.'

'Stole.'

'I forget my English. I stole it. I'm sorry.'

'I suppose you went all over the house?'

'I am afraid so.'

'Upstairs?'

'Yes.'

She pictured him going from room to room, opening and shutting doors – prying in her bedroom, too. Looking at her books, her clothes, touching things.

He said, 'I saw the photograph of your brother, Hamish, on the piano. He is also in the Royal Navy, isn't he? He has served in the corvette,

300

HMS *Buttercup.*'

'How on earth did you know that?'

'You told me.'

'I told you? That's impossible.'

'I found a letter that you had written to your grandfather in his desk and you spoke of your brother and his ship. It was very interesting to me because I had come across HMS *Buttercup* in the North Atlantic. She had stopped to rescue survivors from a sinking ship. I was very sporting, as it happens. Instead of torpedoing her, we went quietly away. Your brother was very lucky.'

She said angrily, 'I must say I think you've got an awful nerve, Reinhard. Coming into this house, stealing things, playing the piano, drinking whisky, reading private letters.'

'I was curious to know what had happened to all of you – especially you. Why the house was empty.'

'That's no excuse. What else did you steal?'

'Nothing – unless you count a sheep. We killed one and took it for food.'

'That's stealing too.'

'Yes, of course, but we had nothing much to eat on our boat.'

She looked away from him.

'My grandparents are both dead now. I expect you found that out as well.'

'Yes, and I am so sorry. I pay them my respects.'

'Grandfather willed Craigmore to Hamish and me when he died. Do you know that too?'

'No. You once told me that this was your favourite place in the world, so you must be very happy that it is now yours. Your brother also.'

'Actually, Hamish doesn't want to live here. He's getting married to a girl from the south who doesn't much like the idea of living in Scotland.'

'But perhaps when you have left your women's Navy you will live here?'

'I've already left it.'

'Already? The war is only just finished.'

'They invalided me out.'

He frowned. 'You have been ill?'

'Not exactly. I broke a leg.'

'How did you do that?'

'I fell off a ladder.'

'What were you doing on the ladder?'

'That's none of your business.'

'Let me guess. You have been in Liverpool – I know that also from the letter to your grandfather – and that you were doing something very secret. It must have been to do with your Atlantic convoys. To do with U-boats and maps. And so to do with me. Am I correct?'

She didn't answer.

After a moment, he went on. 'I wrote you a letter after the war had started. I gave it to someone to send from Ireland. Did you ever receive it?'

'I burned it.'

'But you read it first?'

'I might have done.'

'If you did, you will know that I have never forgotten you. Have you ever thought of me? Have you wondered if I was dead or alive?'

She said flatly, 'I thought you must be dead. So many U-boats have been sunk.'

'Yes. There are not many of us left.'

'Why have you come here, Reinhard? Your Admiral Dönitz ordered you to surrender to the Allies.'

'Do you know what is going to happen to us U-boat men when we are taken prisoner?'

'No. Not exactly.'

'I do. It happened to my father at the end of the last war. He told me all about it. We will be treated as evil criminals, and we will be kept as prisoners for as long as it suits the Allies. For years, perhaps. I have already lost almost everything. My father died when Hamburg was bombed; my brother, Bruno, was not as lucky as yours. He was killed flying a Messerschmitt against American bombers. Many comrades are dead. My city is in ruins, also much of my country. I have only one thing left – my freedom, and that is very dear to me. So ... no, I am not going to surrender.'

She was silent. *Why should I care what has happened to him, or what will? He must have killed hundreds of people, thousands. He could still sink more ships, he could still kill more people; he's still the enemy.* And she thought of the hideous photographs she had seen in the newspapers.

She said quietly, 'I'm very sorry indeed about

303

your father and Bruno. But if you're treated badly, it will be because of the wicked things the Nazis have done. We've seen photographs in our newspapers of the concentration camps where they sent Jewish people. They gassed them in ovens – men, women and children. There were piles of corpses ... you must have known about it.'

'No,' he said. 'I heard that some Jews had been put in work camps but nothing of the rest, though I do not expect you to believe me. My war was at sea. Nazis were not welcome in U-boats and I never belonged to their Party. If what you say is true, my whole country is to be blamed.'

'You must have killed many men yourself, when you sunk their ships.'

'It was my duty. The British have killed many, too.'

She was silent again.

'If you do not surrender, where would you go?'

'Somewhere.'

'Do you think I'd betray you if you tell me?'

'Of course. You must.'

'They'll find you wherever you are. And they'll bomb your boat to bits.'

'They have not succeeded yet.'

'But they will.'

All the time, while they had been talking, she'd been thinking what to do. If she could get out of the room, she could make a dash for the barn where the old bike was kept. She could ride to Port Ellen and telephone RAF Coastal Command HQ at Bowmore. Their aircraft would locate and destroy the U-boat before it had a chance to get away. Before it could do any more harm.

She was quick but he was quicker. He reached the door first, slammed it and leaned his back against it. She retreated.

'Your knee is bleeding, Stroma – just like when I first met you.'

She glanced down at the trickle of blood. It must have happened when she'd tripped over the rock on the hillside. 'So it is. I ought to go and wash it.'

But he stayed where he was, barring the door.

'When you were twelve, you didn't wash a little cut. You thought it not necessary.'

'Well, I've changed.'

'Not so much, I think.' He looked her over. 'And you are still not very tall, are you? I do not think that you even reach my shoulder. Let's see.' He held out his hand. *'Kommen Sie bitte hier ... zu mir.'*

She must play along with him. Lure him away from the door so that she could get out of the room. Then through the kitchen and scullery, across the yard to the barn and the bike.

She took a step forward.

He shook his head. 'That's not enough. I cannot tell from so far away.'

She took another step.

It was a bad mistake because it brought her within his reach.

* * *

RAF Coastal Command had taken over the town's distillery but there was no guard at the entrance when Stroma rode the bike at breakneck speed into Bowmore. The only person to be seen was an RAF officer who was pinning something up on a noticeboard in the hallway. He turned round, startled.

'Can I help you?'

She was gasping, out of breath from the ride. 'I'd like to speak to someone, please. It's very important. Very urgent.'

'May I ask what it's about?'

'A U-boat.'

From his expression, she could see that he took her for some deranged creature: a mad woman that he would have to deal with very tactfully.

'You'd better come into my office and sit down.' He opened a nearby door. 'I'm Squadron Leader Bell. Do you mind telling me your name?'

'Stroma Mackay. I'm from Craigmore on the other side of the island. Sir Archibald and Lady Mackay were my grandparents.'

She could see him revising his first opinion to hysterical, but not totally mad.

'Yes, of course. I met your grandparents when we first came here. They were kind enough to invite some of us to dinner over at Craigmore. You must be very sad to have lost them both.'

He was a rather tubby middle-aged man and he smiled as a kindly uncle might smile, pulling

306

a chair forward for her before going to sit behind his desk. He rubbed his hands together.

'Now, Miss Mackay, what's all this about a U-boat?'

'I've seen one. In Glas Uig.'

'Glas Uig?'

'That's the Gaelic name of a cove not far from Craigmore house. The Green Cove. It's hidden by rocks and the water's deep. Deep enough for a submarine to go in submerged.'

'Really? It sounds a very mysterious place.'

'It is. You can't see it from the seaward side because of the rocks, or from the land side either because of the thick woods growing up the hill. There's an old track where they used to herd animals down to a jetty and ferry them over to Jura and the mainland, but nobody uses it now.'

The Squadron Leader cleared his throat. 'And you say you saw a U-boat there?'

He made it sound as though she had spotted a flying saucer.

'Yes. I saw it come to the surface.'

'That must have been quite a shock. When did that happen exactly?'

'Yesterday evening, as it was getting dark. I'd arrived from London the day before. There's nobody living at the house at the moment – not since my grandfather died. It's been shut up for the duration.'

He fingered his moustache – not the usual dashing RAF kind, but thick and close-clipped like the overhang of a thatched roof.

'Wasn't it getting rather late to be wandering about?'

'Not for me. I know the way down to the cove very well. I've known it since I was a child. My brother and I used to play there.'

More throat-clearing. 'So you went for an evening walk.'

'Not a walk. I went out to shoot rabbits. Dusk is the best time.'

'Really? And you saw a U-boat surfacing in the cove? Remarkable.'

'I'm not making this up, Squadron Leader. I've served in the WRNS as a Third Officer and I was stationed in the Map Room at Western Approaches. I do know what a U-boat looks like.'

'I'm sure you do. Are you on leave from the WRNS at the moment?'

'Actually, I've left the service.'

'Oh?'

'I had a fall and broke my leg rather badly. I was in hospital for several months. They decided to invalid me out.'

'I see.'

She saw what he saw. The fall had somehow unhinged her, or perhaps she was one of those people who invent fantastic stories to get attention.

She said slowly and clearly, 'There was a U-boat in Glas Uig. I'm telling you the truth.'

He said jovially, 'Well, I gather they've been popping up all over the place, waving their black surrender flags.'

308

'This one had no black flag. And it wasn't surrendering. I thought you'd want to know about it.'

He cleared his throat again. 'Quite. I'll be making a full report, Miss Mackay. You probably don't realize, but we no longer have Sunderland flying boats moored at Bowmore. The weather up here's rather against us, unfortunately. We nearly lost the lot when there was a big storm in March 'Forty-Three. They've been moved elsewhere, together with most of our coastal chaps.' He smiled wryly. 'They've left me like Alfred watching the cakes, so to speak. Or rather, the stills. I can't grumble about it, I must say – though, of course, they're not in use at the moment, more's the pity.' He looked at her uncertainly for a moment, not sure if she appreciated his little joke. 'Tell me, you said this happened yesterday evening. Why didn't you let us know about it before now?'

'There's no telephone at Craigmore. I cycled over this morning, as soon as it was daylight. The phone at Port Ellen was out of order so I came on here as fast as I could.'

'Very commendable.'

She wondered what he would say if she told him that her behaviour had been anything but commendable. Far from commendable, it had been treasonable. Supposing she told him that the commander of the U-boat had come up to the house and that she had gone to bed with him – or, to be strictly accurate, he had taken her there. Picked her up and carried her upstairs. In her defence, there hadn't been a lot of choice in the matter.

But the worst of it was that she was neither ashamed nor sorry. Not a bit. On the contrary, she was glad. Insanely glad. Insanely happy. Insanely in love with the enemy. That she had, in fact, been in love with him since she was twelve years old. What would he have to say to that?

And what would the squadron leader have to say if she'd told him that, furthermore, if it hadn't been for her sacred, sworn duty to her country she would never have breathed a word to anyone about this particular U-boat? That, in her heart, she wanted it to get away.

In her distress, she started to weep. The squadron leader leaned forward and patted her arm kindly.

'There, there, my dear. There's nothing to be upset about. If your U-boat's out there, our chaps'll clobber it, all right.'

He stood up, chair legs screeching. 'Would you like a cup of tea before you leave, Miss Mackay? I'm sure we can manage that.'

She found a handkerchief in her pocket and wiped her eyes. 'No, thank you.'

He saw her to the door, pumped her hand vigorously. 'I'll let you know, of course, if there's any news.'

Back at Craigmore, she went upstairs to her room, sat down on the bed where she had been with him.

When she'd woken up at dawn, Reinhard had

gone. She'd run down to the cove but it had been empty, the surface glassy smooth, no dark shadow lurking beneath, no movement.

After a while, she got up and went over to the open window. She stood staring at the grey-green sea and the white-flecked waves, and listening to the harsh and mocking mews of the gulls.

They had spent sixty days submerged. Sixty days without breathing fresh air or seeing daylight. No other way was possible if they wanted to avoid detection by the Allies. They looked like corpses, green and mouldy as the boat itself. The already-dead. When they were on watch, they moved stiff-jointedly about like robots, and when they were off-watch they collapsed on their bunks in a mindless stupor. Black fumes from over-pressured diesel exhaust valves rolled like fog through the boat, vital machinery parts kept failing and had somehow to be repaired, rubbish piled up in a stinking, maggoty heap, men lost their appetite, fell ill, came out in rashes and boils, were very close to breaking down. If Reinhard's crew had relied on him before to preserve their lives, they did so now for the will to live.

British warships were everywhere and at Gibraltar they were clustered in clumps like flies. Even using the Snort at night to recharge the batteries risked discovery and whenever it was raised, they picked up the radar of enemy ships or planes in their area. There were times when Reinhard doubted that they would manage to sneak by and when one of the diesels stopped and took two days to repair, it seemed impossible that their luck would hold out.

They were off the west coast of Africa before he finally gave the order to surface. Compressed air hissed into the tanks and the depth gauge in the conning tower acted like a heartbeat gathering sudden strength. When Reinhard wrenched at the wheel in the control tower and flung wide the hatch he saw a million stars shining above his head.

He hauled himself slowly and stiffly up the ladder on to the bridge and breathed in the balmy air of the southern seas. A phosphorescent trail shimmered in their wake and a bright moon, riding high, illuminated an empty ocean. No enemy ships in sight. No ships at all. Only the U-boat.

His first officer joined him. 'Rather a welcome sight, sir.'

'Yes,' he said. 'Very welcome.'

The rest of the crew climbed up in turn and stood, taking deep lungfuls of air and gazing round in awe, like men who had emerged from a tomb.

Fuel was running short. If they were to reach Argentina, Reinhard decided that they could only dive deep in a desperate emergency and could not use the Snort again. Both were too wasteful. They stayed on the surface, travelling at a slow speed for ten hours on one diesel. For the remaining fourteen hours they used the electric motors. If the worst came to the worst they could head for Brazil, or even make a sail for the boat.

Dolphins turned up to escort them, playing alongside and diving under the boat. At night they passed passenger ships and, once, a large liner, lights blazing, overtook them, close enough for them to see people walking up and down the promenade decks in evening dress and to hear the ship's dance band playing.

Surfaced, they could listen to music again – to sambas and rumbas and tangos, American swing and jazz – and to the news, which it might have been better not to hear. Occupation had followed Germany's crushing defeat. The Americans, the British, the French and, worst of all, the Soviets had parcelled up the whole country between them. Berlin, isolated in the Russian sector of the country, was cut up in shares, like a cake. Survivors were somehow existing in ruins and queuing for soup and a crust of bread. Those crew with families left behind suffered for them; some of them regretted their flight.

Stroma was Reinhard's only regret, and it was a bitter one. God help him, he'd behaved with her exactly as she would have expected a Nazi to behave. Five years of savage war had turned him into nothing less than a brute. What else could she think? He had given her no chance.

They approached the Cape Verde islands one night and watched the sun rising over the high cliffs. At periscope depth they passed close to an island where fishermen were at work and headed for another that was deserted, where the water was a clear blue and the sand pure white. They anchored off-shore and swam and lay in the sun. The men were all in good spirits now and in far better health. The skin troubles had cleared up; their faces and bodies were browned by the sun; their muscles became stronger by the day. Clothes were washed attached to a line and towed behind the boat, then dried on deck under the tropical sun. They slept out at night and ate their meals under makeshift awnings slung between the guns. To vary their diet, they caught fish with harpoons or hand grenades. More dolphins came to play and an enormous whale swam round the boat and followed them for several hours.

When they crossed the equator they acted out the old ceremony, rigged out in improvised fancy dress, with Reinhard as Neptune, a broom for a trident. Nobody would have taken them for a battle-hardened U-boat crew.

It grew cooler as they went further south, and without charts of the area, their course had to be by dead reckoning. They steered well clear of the rocks and reefs of the coast of Brazil and, as they came closer to Argentina, the men began to pack up their belongings in knapsacks.

'We have two options,' Reinhard told them. 'Either we take the boat into port, give our-selves up to the Argentinian authorities and hope that they don't hand us straight over to the Allies, or we scuttle our boat, use the dinghies

314

to get ashore and go our separate ways. It's for you to decide.'

They talked it over. Few of the crew knew any Spanish or looked in the least South American, but they had a ready assortment of civilian clothing. Finding jobs as skilled fitters should not be a problem for some, while others were prepared to do any kind of labour. When a vote was taken, it was unanimously agreed to seize their chance of freedom and a new life.

Scuttling the boat was painful for Reinhard. Easy to do, but difficult to witness. He and the boat had been through hell together and a part of him went down with her.

Engelhardt said quietly, 'An honourable end, sir. Putting her to rest. Much better than being sunk by the enemy, don't you think?'

There was some truth in that. Apart from clothes, he had saved three things from the boat – his binoculars, the photograph of Stroma, and her scarf.

On a deserted beach, he shook hands with his Number One before they went their separate ways. Engelhardt held some useful cards: he was short enough and dark-haired enough to pass unnoticed among Latins and he spoke some Spanish, as well as English. His trump card, of course, was his boundless optimism.

Reinhard's own height and blond hair drew attention and he decided to stay away from cities and the curious eyes. He jumped a freight train and got a job in a slaughter house where no questions were asked of any hired hand so long as he did the job. It was gruelling and gruesome. The stench of blood and guts, the pitiful terror of the animals and the callous indifference of the handlers were more harrowing than anything he had experienced in war. After several months he left, jumped another train and found work on a large and remote *estancia* west of Buenos Aires. By then his Spanish was good and he had invented a plausible past with a half-German mother to account for the height and the blond hair. The *estancia* owners were much more interested in the fact that he could ride a horse well and that he had no objection to long days spent herding cattle out on the pampas. He slept in a bunk-house with the gauchos, or else out under the stars. The hard life suited him fine: there was no time to think or remember or regret.

From time to time, listening to visitors to the *estancia*, he learned news of Europe. His country was still occupied and starving, men still kept behind barbed wire. The Kriegsmarine had been disbanded by the Allies. But, apparently, the city ruins were being cleared away, brick by brick by brick.

Unfortunately, the *estancia* owner's wife took too much of a liking for him and it became wiser to move on. He worked on another *estancia* for more than a year before he found a job as a clerk in a shipping office in Buenos Aires where his knowledge of languages came in useful. People accepted him and his re-invented past. They were no longer very interested in fleeing Nazis, or former U-boat commanders. The city was vibrant, the sun hot, the food good, the women beautiful. What more could one want?

By chance, he met Engelhardt, who had married an Argentinian girl and settled down in Argentina very happily. It was not impossible to imagine doing the same himself one day.

And yet he knew that he never would.

Hamish's ship had been sent to the Far East to continue the war against Japan, and he was still away when Angus died in late July. Stroma had made all the necessary arrangements for the funeral. Their old friend was buried in the ruined kirk where their grandparents lay and everyone on the estate attended the ceremony. Mr Pirbright, Grandfather's solicitor, travelled from Glasgow with Mr Ross, the younger partner. Afterwards they came to the house to take a dram and to discuss Craigmore.

A replacement for Angus would have to be found and, now that the war was over, more workers should be taken on, order restored, improvements made, plans drawn up for the future of the estate.

'I'll stay in the house for the time being, at any rate,' she said in answer to their question. 'And Hamish will come here whenever he can. As you know, he's to be married in September.'

Mr Ross said, 'You'll be needing some staff, of course: a housekeeper and cook, cleaners, someone to see to the gardens. Would you like me to help you to find them, Miss Mackay? We could advertise in the mainland newspapers, perhaps in *The Lady*?'

'No,' she said. 'I'd want them to be *ilich*.'

'Ilich?'

'Island folk. Born here on Islay.'

He nodded. 'Of course. That would be best.'

She refilled their glasses once more.

'I wanted to talk about something else as well, if you don't mind. An idea I've had.'

Mr Pirbright, lulled by the whisky, smiled at her indulgently. 'By all means, my dear. What exactly was that?'

Hamish came up to Craigmore in the middle of September to do some fishing, and to escape the preparations for his wedding to Alice.

'I suggest you elope, Stroma,' he told her. 'Much simpler. You wouldn't believe the amount of nonsense that goes on. Lists a mile long, invitations, seating arrangements, hymns, readings, flowers ... Christ knows what else. It's endless. Thank God, I don't have much of a say in any of it. All I really have to do is turn up on the day.'

But he seemed perfectly happy about it all and, having met Alice in London and seen them together, she could see why. Her sister-in-law-to-be was beautiful and kind and as much in love with Hamish as he was with her.

For old times' sake, Hamish took her out on the loch in the dinghy one day.

She sat in the stern, trailing her fingers in the

dark and ice-cold water while he rowed to the windward end and shipped the oars. She watched him going through the familiar ritual with the cane rod – choosing the fly from the box and attaching it carefully to the hook before he stood athwart the boat and cast the line out into the water. He cast several times before there was the swirling movement that meant a take. Even now, she felt sorry for the fish and its desperate struggle, but she was ready with the net to help land it and passed her brother the priest to finish it off quickly and decently.

After he'd caught three more trout he offered her a turn with the rod.

'No, thanks.'

'Not still squeamish, are you?'

'Four's enough for supper.'

Instinctively, she looked for Angus as Hamish rowed back, half-expecting to see his giant figure waiting for them on the shore.

The new gamekeeper came from one of the other estates on the island and the new cook was a widow from Killinallan. She was nothing like as fussy as Ellen about things and there would be no minute scrutiny of the four trout. An ex-POW had been employed to restore order to the gardens, helped by a lad who had just left Bowmore school. A daily woman with weight-lifter's arms walked from her cottage five miles away to see to the rough jobs. Craigmore was slowly coming back to life again.

After the trout dinner, she told Hamish about the plan for the mill.

'Mr Pirbright and Mr Ross think it's basically a good idea. I took them over to see the mill and Mr Ross is going to do some sums. I'm finding out exactly what it would cost to repair the building with local labour and put the looms back in working order. And I've talked to Grace. She says that lots of women on the island can spin and she thinks they'd be willing to help.'

Hamish, like Mr Pirbright and Mr Ross, was in a mellow mood after several whiskies. 'Well, good luck to you.'

'You don't mind?'

'Mind? Why should I?'

'Well, it'd be half your money. And you'll have a wife to consider. Alice might not be quite so keen.'

He waved his glass around. 'Craigmore belongs to us both, Stroma. It's our responsibility. Alice won't interfere. And besides, if Ross's sums don't add up, he'll put the brakes on the whole idea. I'm not worried, either way.' He reached for the decanter again. 'By the way, I've been meaning to ask you, why have you cried off from being a bridesmaid at the wedding? Alice wanted you as the head girl, or whatever it's called.'

'I'm awfully sorry to let her down, Hamish, but I can't be.'

'Can't be? Why on earth not?'

'Because I'm pregnant.'

The decanter stopped in mid-air. 'What?'

'I'm having a baby. Not till sometime in

February, but it already shows. Haven't you noticed?'

'Christ almighty, Stroma! Who's the bloody father?'

'He's almost certainly dead.'

'The war?'

'Yes.'

'The Navy?'

'Yes.'

'Well, we can bloody soon find out if he's dead or alive. There are lists, you know.'

'No, we can't.'

'Why not?'

'I can't tell you, Hamish. I can't tell you anything more about him.'

He splashed whisky into his glass. 'Have you gone raving mad, Stroma? You can't just have a baby with no father, let alone no husband.'

'I'll say he died in the war. The islanders won't be shocked. In fact, they'll probably be very nice about it.'

'So, you'll stay here?'

'Yes. I've already seen Dr Mackenzie. He's going to look after me and the baby. Besides, I want it to be born here at Craigmore. To be an *ileach*. To belong to the island.'

'That's all very well, but have you thought about what life will be like for him, or her? Being illegitimate? A bastard?'

'Yes, I've thought about that, but there's nothing I can do to change things.'

'You could get it adopted.'

'I'd never do that, Hamish. You know I

321

wouldn't.'

He gulped at the whisky. 'Tell me, have I ever met this chap?'

'You came across him.'

'Came across him? What's that supposed to mean?'

'It's all I can tell you. Can I have some of that whisky, please?'

'Do you think you should?'

'Yes, I do.' She held out a glass. 'I hope Alice won't mind about it too much.'

'Good lord, no. She's not like that. In fact, the whole white wedding thing's a bit of a farce, to tell the truth. It's been the war ... Never knowing if you'd be dead tomorrow ... Different rules. We've all been in the same boat.' Hamish smiled wryly. 'But somehow I have a feeling that my future mother-in-law might continue to take the old-fashioned view.'

1949

At the shipping offices in Buenos Aires, Reinhard was promoted from a humble stool in a dark corner to a chair and a desk with clients of his own. People seldom asked questions about his past and, if they did, he was ready with his answers. From time to time, he came across other Germans who were equally anxious to stay out of the limelight, but, if possible, he avoided them.

He had followed the news reports of the trials which had begun in Nuremberg soon after the end of the war: the Allies' long process of deciding which Nazis were guilty of war crimes and which were not so guilty. The Grossadmiral, who had been so idealized and respected by all his U-boat crews as a fair and human man, had been given a shockingly harsh sentence of ten years' imprisonment. The rest, it seemed, had entirely deserved their punishments.

As Reinhard had expected, the U-boat crews had generally been badly treated – perceived as hardened Nazis and kept captive long after their fellow naval men had been released.

Two years later, Reinhard had read about the

blockading of the western sectors of Berlin by the Soviets and about British and American planes flying in food and supplies and coal to keep the citizens alive and stop the Russians from seizing the whole city. A round-the-clock Allied operation. Night and day, fair weather or foul, one plane arriving every few minutes – not to kill people this time, ironically, but to keep them alive. The Russians had finally given up and the railways and highways and canals had been reopened, trains and trucks and barges allowed to pass to and from Berlin once more.

It had dawned on him at last that the Allies were now busy hauling Germany to her feet, not crushing her under their victorious boots. He had also realized that it was time for him to go home. The call was too strong. A life of relative ease in the Argentine was not enough. Freedom, after all, was not enough. He could no longer turn his back on his country, whatever the consequences.

The shipping office was handling a cargo of frozen meat bound for Hamburg – one of many consignments heading towards starving Europe. It was easy enough to sign on as an extra deckhand and work his way across the South and North Atlantic.

The ruins of his home city shocked him anew, but rubble had been cleared away, buildings repaired, others begun, and the port was crowded with Allied shipping.

He slipped ashore, avoiding officials and checkpoints, and walked the streets, passing people who looked emaciated and exhausted and, yet, who seemed to have some hope in their faces.

He came to the bank that his father had used and where he and Bruno had also kept accounts. The old building had been damaged in the bombing raids, but stood intact. And the same manager was there.

Reinhard had known Herr Bekker for many years. Loyalty to his U-boat crew made it out of the question to tell him his true story, but Reinhard had no need to invent a new one. The manager was the soul of discretion and only too glad to see him alive. They had been officially notified of Bruno's death, he said, but unable to establish any precise news of his own fate.

'You were reported as missing, presumed dead. That's all we knew. With the world still in turmoil, no one can be certain of these things. We waited in hope.'

The bank, it seemed, had kept the money in his account safe, together with the inheritance from his father.

'A not inconsiderable sum, all told,' the manager said. 'Your father was very astute in his investments, as you know. You will have no worries on that score.'

It was a minor worry at the moment, he thought wryly – the major one being that he had no official discharge papers. Nothing to show that he was not some dangerous war criminal on the run from justice in post-war Europe.

'I may be able to help you,' Herr Bekker

assured him. 'On the whole, the British are very reasonable and we're fortunate to be in their zone. I have some useful contacts and I'd be happy to vouch for you personally, of course.'

The British naval officer who interviewed him was an older man, grey-haired and with a tobacco pipe on the desk before him. A commander, with three gold rings to his sleeve. He looked affable, almost jolly, but Reinhard was not deceived.

'What was your position in the Germany Navy?'

'U-boat Commander.'

'Hum. I thought we'd dealt with all you chaps. You seem to be the last one left.' He leaned back in his chair, fingering the pipe. 'How did you manage to turn up here?'

His boat, Reinhard said, had been attacked and sunk by British aircraft off Norway just before the end of the war. He had been on the bridge and had been the only survivor. He had managed to reach the shore and had taken refuge in the mountains. Subsequently, he had been held prisoner in various temporary Allied camps and eventually escaped to Sweden where he had stayed in hiding until he had thought it feasible to return to Germany. It was perfectly possible, and as hard to disprove as it was to prove.

'Were you a member of the Nazi Party?'

'No, I was not.'

'A member of the Hitler Youth?'

'No.'

326

'All you Germans always deny it. How did you become an officer in the German Navy – much less a U-boat commander – if you were not a Hitler Youth or a member of some other Nazi organization?'

'You have been misinformed, sir. Our Navy did not recruit officers from the Hitler Youth and Party membership was not required in any form. As you are probably aware, Admiral Dönitz himself was never a member of the Nazi Party.'

'We've captured all the Party records, you know. It's very easy for us to check.'

'Do so, by all means. You will not find my name among them.'

'Any false statement on your part will incur a severe penalty.'

'I understand.'

'So, you take full responsibility for your actions as a submarine commander?'

'Certainly. I did my duty.'

'To your Führer and to the Nazi Party?'

'To my country.'

The commander moved some papers around on his desk.

He said, 'Actually, I was in submarines myself during the First World War. We had a fine crew and an excellent captain. A band of brothers, you might say. Very close. The fate of one was the fate of all. I've always considered submariners to be a breed apart. No doubt you agree?'

'Totally, sir.'

The commander took his time consulting a long list of names of people apparently still wanted by the Allies, turning page after page and running his finger slowly down them. Finally, he put the list aside.

'Well you don't appear to be among any of those.'

He stamped the discharge papers and handed them over. He even smiled.

'Good luck, Korvettenkapitän.'

With the Kriegsmarine no longer in existence, and no uniform to wear, Reinhard was, of course, no longer entitled to be addressed by any rank. He understood that it was a mark of respect from the other man, and it was a moment before he could speak.

'Thank you, Commander.'

He paid a visit to his father's grave, where he placed a bunch of flowers that he had managed to buy from a street stall. Bruno had no grave. His Me 109 had gone down over the North Sea and they might easily have both shared the same resting place. Though he had always anticipated his own death, he had clung to the hope that his brother would somehow survive.

He thumbed a lift from a British army lorry heading out of the city towards Kiel, and sat up in the cab beside the driver. The corporal was friendly and curious. His English was difficult to understand but Reinhard got the gist.

'You were in U-boats, mate! Blimey, I wouldn't have changed places with you for all the tea in China. You'd never get me into one of them things. Worst thing I can think of. Shut up in a perishin' tin can like bloomin' sardines. What did you do – fire the ruddy torpedoes?'

'I was the captain.'

'Bloody 'ell!' The corporal glanced at him with awe. 'I wouldn't have wanted the job.'

'Not for all the tea in China?'

'You can say that again, mate!'

'Oh, it wasn't so bad.'

They went a few more miles across the flat and open country. The corporal tried a new tack.

'Ever come across Rommel? Your bloke in the desert?'

'I'm sorry, no.'

'Was out there meself for a time. Us Tommies thought a lot of 'im. Better'n some of our wankers, we reckoned, sir – if you'll pardon my French.'

It certainly wasn't a French word but he understood its meaning. The British never ceased to amaze him. Apparently they had no compunction in praising their enemy, if they thought he deserved it.

At Kiel he said goodbye to the corporal who drove off with a grin and a thumbs-up. Then he walked the rest of the way to Schleswig.

Old Hans, who had run the boatyard there, had died during the war – old age rather than a bomb for once – but his son Peter had taken over. It was much the same as it had always been, and *Sturmwind* was still in her place out on the shingle and covered with tarpaulin.

'She'll need a good clean-up,' Peter said. 'And some work on the engine, but otherwise she should be all right. I'll give you a hand, if you like.'

He spent several days working on the boat and sleeping in the main cabin at night. In the evening he ate at a wooden café built on a pier over the water, ate fresh-caught shrimps with mounds of potatoes and drank rough schnapps.

It took some time to restore *Sturmwind* to anything approaching her former glory, and he doubted that his father would have been satisfied with the result. But more important than chalk white ropes and gleaming brasswork were the changes that he needed – changes that would make her easier to sail single-handed. Peter helped him and they had the boat ready and provisioned by the end of July.

He took the route he had taken before with Father and Bruno, crossing the North Sea, blown along by the south-westerlies. That was the easy part. He passed south of the Orkneys and into the rip tides of the Pentland Firth – a sea passage he had last taken in the protection of a U-boat. When he turned the north-west corner of Scotland the fierce headwinds and the mighty Atlantic swell seized hold of *Sturmwind* and did their best to dash her on to the rocks.

He sailed on by the Inner Hebrides down to Mull, by the Strait of Corryvreckan and its treacherous currents and back-eddies, the hungry whirlpools. He and *Sturmwind* battled

330

through alone.

A minke whale turned up off the coast of Jura and kept him company for a while before some dolphins arrived to show off their paces. He went by Rhuvaal lighthouse at the north-east end of Islay and entered the sound between the two islands, past the colonies of seals on the rocks, the wild goats on the cliffs, the deer and the cattle and the sheep grazing the seaweed on the beaches. The mauve Paps of Jura rose to port, the whisky distillery lay on his starboard, and, further on, the slipway and stone cottages of Port Askaig came into view. Under the impassive but curious gaze of some locals, he tied up at the far end of the jetty and walked along to the inn.

It took a moment for his eyes to adjust to the dim light inside the hostelry and to make out the woman behind the bar. A middle-aged woman in a print dress, and a knitted dishcloth in her hand that she was using to swab the counter. When she spoke, he could barely understand a word.

'A beer, please,' he said, smiling politely, hoping he had answered what she had asked.

'A pint?'

'Yes, please.'

'What sort wuid ye like?' She rattled off names, none of which meant anything to him.

'The one you think best.'

She nodded and he watched as she pulled the pint into a glass, letting the foam rise to the exact top of the rim, and not a millimetre below or above. For dead-on, pin-point accuracy, he would have recruited her in his U-boat any day.

He paid with one of the Scottish notes thoughtfully provided by the Hamburg bank and she gave him a pile of coins heavy enough to make holes in his pockets. The beer wasn't to his German taste, but it was drinkable.

He looked round. There was nobody else in the bar and so he had her complete attention. All her eyes and all her ears.

She polished some glasses before she spoke again. From the two or three words he understood, he gathered she was asking where he had come from.

'I'm sailing,' he said. 'Round the islands.'

'Is that so? Most furriners wouldna' take the risk.'

By 'foreigners', he thought, she probably meant anyone not bred to the islands.

'I've sailed here before,' he said.

'When wuid that be?'

'About thirteen years ago.' He wisely didn't mention the other, later, visits. 'With my father and brother. We didn't come in to Port Askaig, though; we sailed along the coast instead to Craigmore house. Perhaps you know it?'

'Aye, I know Craigmore, of course.'

'We met the owners: Sir Archibald and Lady Mackay.'

'Och, they've passed on, God rest their souls. The grandson and granddaughter have it now. Hamish and Stroma. Did you meet them, perhaps? Hamish doesna' spend much time here –

not now he's married to an English girl – but Stroma lives here. She's opened Kildare Mill again.'

'That is interesting.'

'Yes. They say she's got all sorts of ideas for it.'

'Is it for making cloth?'

'Aye. 'Twas a ruin for years but she got the old looms workin' again. The sheep's wool's spun in the cottages an' then woven at the mill. Very fine tweed, it is. Special to the island. 'Tis even sellin' in London now, so I'm told.'

'I expect Miss Mackay is married now?'

'Stroma? No, she's not.' The woman leaned closer across the counter. 'Mind you, she's got a bairn, just the same.'

'A bairn?' He didn't know the word.

'A child. A boy. Three or four years old. Still, it's not fer us te judge, is it? The father was kill-ed in the war, so we heard. A naval gentleman. Puir wee lad. Tragic to lose his father.'

A couple of hundred metres from the entrance to Glas Uig, Reinhard lowered the sails and used the engine to bring *Sturmwind* gently through the gap in the rocks and into the shelter of the cove. He tied up at the old jetty and walked up the track through the woods. When he reached the top he stood looking at Craig-more through his binoculars for a while – the gabled slate roofs, the great chimney stacks rising above them, the whitewashed walls, the black painted shutters, standing firm against

333

the Atlantic.

He lowered the binoculars and walked on across the rough grass towards the stone wall and the iron five-barred gate that led to the bottom of the slope, rising to the croquet lawn. As he swung himself over the gate, he could hear a child laughing and a ball came whizzing over the top and bounced down towards him. It rolled to a stop in the long grass at his feet and he picked it up: not a hard painted croquet ball but a soft tennis ball, worn smooth and faded to grey.

A small boy appeared at the top. He was barefoot, wearing shorts and a blue shirt and he had very blond hair – so blond it was almost white – and there were fresh grazes on both knees. He plunged down the slope, searching in the grass.

'Is this what you're hunting for?'

The boy raised his head, startled. He came closer and took the ball, staring up at him. Reinhard found that he was gazing down into his own eyes.

'Archie! Where are you? Archie!'

Stroma was standing at the top of the slope.

'The man found my ball, Mamma. He's given it back to me.'

'That's very kind of him. I hope you said thank you.'

'I forgot.'

She came down to where he was standing with the boy.

In a moment, she said, 'This is Archie. I

334

named him after his great-grandfather.'

He nodded. 'A good name from a good man.'

'We're forgetting our manners, Archie. Would you ask the gentleman if he would like to come up to the house?'

The boy smiled up at him. 'We could go on with the game. And you can join in, if you want.'

'That would be very nice, thank you.'

The child scrambled back up the slope.

She said, 'So you didn't die after all, Reinhard. Why didn't you come back?'

'Because I thought you would never wish to see me again.'

'You were wrong about that.'

They looked at each other without speaking.

The boy had reached the top of the slope and waved his hands to attract his attention. 'It's up here. Come on, I'll show you.'

'Don't worry, Archie,' his mother called. 'He knows the way.'